REALITY ISN'T ALWAYS AS IT SEEMS…

Jake circled his arms around Lily, and in seconds, they were standing in a flurry of snow. "What the blazes!" he said, whirling away from her. "Did you see that?"

"See what?"

"The snow! Don't tell me you didn't see it."

Lily laughed a nervous laugh. "Snow? Here, inside the cabin? Well, now, that's quite impossible, isn't it?" Her wings continued to tingle, and she fought to keep them still.

"I must not have closed the door all the way when I came in with the tree," Jake said as he hurried to secure the cabin door. But then he looked about at all the snow that was already melting on the floor and at the sparkle that was everywhere—in the air, on the floor, but mostly all over his arms. "What's going on here?" he asked. "Where did all this glitter come from?"

Lily caught her lip in her teeth. She'd used far too much fairy dust. "I guess I got carried away making these," she said as she batted aside one of the hanging snowflakes.

"I don't get it," Jake said, still looking at his arms. "That's twice we've been in the middle of a conversation, then all of a sudden, I'm covered in glitter." He looked at Lily's arms. "But you have none on you."

Lily held out her arms and pretended to look for glitter she already knew wasn't there. If things continued this way, she feared the evening would end in disaster. What she needed to do was rewind time so that she and Jake could spend a few moments together enjoying the tree they'd decorated. It was the only solution, she reasoned, the only way to salvage the evening.

PRAISE FOR ALEXA DARIN

LOVE TRIP

"Want fun in the sun? Read this book. It's laugh-out-loud funny."—**Sheila Roberts**, national best-selling author of *On Strike For Christmas* and *Three Christmas Wishes*

"This book is a fun escape from reality and perfect for a beach vacation."—**Rachel Van Dyken**, *Books by the Glass*

KISS ME TWICE

"This one is a buried book treasure."—**Stephanie Queen**, *USA Today* best-selling author

"Ms. Darin has given her readers a sweet, yet tender, amusing, love story…"—**Robin Leigh Morgan**, author of *I Kissed a Ghost*

KISSES DON'T LIE

"A zippy romance that will leave you smiling."—**Susanna Carr**, author of *Pink Ice*

"*Kisses Don't Lie* is a hunka hunka burnin' fun!"
—**Geralyn Dawson**, *USA Today* best-selling author

"Thanks to Alexa Darin, Elvis lives!"—**Vicki Lewis Thompson**, *New York Times* best-selling author

"Fantastic! Full of mischief, mayhem, romance, and happily ever afters… one of my favorite books of the year… immensely engaging from the very first sentence."—**Amanda Haffery**, *Romance Junkies*

"Humorous… delightfully quirky."—*RT Book Reviews*

GOOD WITH HIS HANDS

"Sharp, witty writing."—**Meryl Sawyer**, *New York Times* bestselling author

"A promising debut."—*Seattle Post-Intelligencer*

ALSO BY ALEXA DARIN

GOOD WITH HIS HANDS

KISSES DON'T LIE

KISS ME TWICE

LOVE TRIP

SNOW HAPPENS

Snow Happens

ALEXA DARIN

Top Down Publishing, LLC
www.topdownpub.com

Top Down Publishing, LLC
PO Box 13181
Mill Creek, WA 98082

SNOW HAPPENS
Copyright © 2021 by Alexa Darin
All rights reserved.

Print ISBN: 978-0-9966306-0-3
eBook ISBN: 978-0-9966306-1-0

Cover design by Ashley Lopez

Image copyright: *iStock.com/CoffeeAndMilk*

Logo designs by Lemoncraft

Print formatting by Dana Delamar
ByYourSideSelfPub.com

For Lily...

You are the light in every day!

Chapter One

It wasn't much, just a tickle in her stomach, yet it was enough that Lily knew something was amiss. She stepped out onto the cabin's porch and gazed past a snow-covered clearing to the edge of a great expanse of forest, where she saw nothing. No reason for the bothersome tickle. Even her companion, Cinder, hadn't so much as raised her antlered head to indicate there might be cause for concern.

It was just the isolation, Lily decided. She wasn't accustomed to spending so much time alone. This time of year, she was usually busy preparing for the big day, with all the hustle and bustle and tree lighting and gift buying and cookies to bake. Too, she'd expected to be spending the holiday somewhere more festive. Like New York City, where she could enjoy shows on Broadway, treats from the best bakeries in Manhattan, and, of course, the Yuletide Carolers. Plus, what about twinkle lights? The only twinkling she'd seen since arriving at this location was what winked down at her from the star-lit sky.

With a resigned huff, Lily turned her focus to her reindeer companion who was foraging for bits of grass hidden beneath the snow. To be sure, this was a new experience for both of them.

Especially Cinder. Being a member of Santa's back-up sleigh team, she'd never had to forage for anything. This close to Christmas, she was well-fed so she could participate in the rigorous training sessions that would ensure her readiness to step in and take the place of any member of the regular sleigh team should one of them become grounded due to illness or injury. It didn't happen often, maybe once every couple of decades, but when it did, every reindeer at the North Pole needed to be fit and ready to fly on the big eve. Which Lily thought made it all the more curious that Santa had insisted she bring Cinder along on this particular assignment. He'd never done so before, and she had never needed or wanted a travel companion, preferring instead to work alone with humans who were in need of her services. Not only that, but she was surprised at her assignment location. Northern Idaho, judging by the scent riding on the air. Not that Idaho wasn't a perfectly lovely place to visit, but a rustic cabin in the middle of a forest? With not one human in sight?

No. Just no.

Lily pressed her lips together. She had to stop thinking like that. It was not her place to question Santa's motives *or* the assignment location he'd chosen. And if he'd deemed she needed Cinder as a travel companion, he must have had good reason. Though a few more details about the subject of her assignment would have been nice.

He will come to you. That's all Santa had provided. Not even a name or age of the person who'd been approved to receive the services of a Christmas fairy. Nor had Santa mentioned the nature of the problem. Was *he* a human who had lost his enjoyment for life? Was *he* in need of a miracle? Or was this assignment just a simple case of helping some poor soul rekindle his Christmas spirit? Because if that's all it was, Lily could think of several sister fairies who would have been thrilled with this assignment location, away from all the noise and hectic goings-on of the season. Even fairies sometimes needed a break from the *fa la la la la.*

Some fairies, but not her.

Lily let out another huff, still trying to push aside all thoughts of having a New York City holiday. She looked once more to the tall firs bordering the forest and was intrigued by how they appeared to be standing like sentry guards keeping out intruders. Though she suspected what lay *beyond* the trees might be even more intriguing. And certainly more interesting than sitting by the window watching snow accumulate. As much as she loved a snow-filled sky, she was more than ready to get out and explore her surroundings. The cabin had become so stuffy she could barely breathe. And perhaps the tickle she'd been experiencing had something to do with her assignment. What if he was out there in the dark wood somewhere and needed her help?

But, no, Santa had said *he* would come to her. So, *he* was not out there, waiting to be found. Still, Lily thought, it couldn't hurt to take a walk and have a look-see. A short outing would surely put her in the proper frame of mind for her assignment. Though leaving the cabin meant she would need to prepare herself for a possible encounter with humans. Being a Christmas fairy, she wasn't bothered by the cold, but humans, whose winter attire bordered on amusing, would likely not understand seeing a person out in such brisk weather wearing only a green silk sheath that was more appropriate for a summer day. Nor would they be able to comprehend her ability to venture out into the snow barefoot. She did so love the feel of icy snow squishing between her toes.

Looking down at her feet, she gave some thought to her attire. A pair of boots would be best, but they were so very ugly, not to mention difficult to walk in, so slippers would do just fine. Plus, she could wear a shawl made of thick wool about her shoulders, and perhaps a Christmas hat on her head, such as what Santa wore when delivering toys.

An easy task, Lily closed her eyes to imagine the change in her apparel, and in a flash, it was done. Then she stepped down off the porch and made her way over to Cinder, who had moved on from foraging in the snow to stripping lichen from one of the trees near the entrance to the forest. Standing quietly at Cinder's side, Lily breathed in the scent of pine needles and dampness. She was already feeling better, and couldn't wait to be on her way. But as eager as she was for a change of scenery, this was an unknown location and she didn't dare enter the dark wood without first taking a moment to listen for anything that might warn of peril. It wasn't for herself that she was concerned, but rather for Cinder, who could be seen as prey by some large beast looking for an easy meal.

Finally, after waiting several moments, and becoming satisfied it was safe to proceed, Lily took a parting glance over her shoulder at the cabin and imagined the fireplace filled with burning embers in case her assignment should arrive while she was away. Then she nudged Cinder along, saying, "Walk with me," and she and Cinder were quickly swallowed into the shadows.

Lily felt completely at ease. She strolled along a dim path, touching icicles that had formed on tree limbs, and shook branches, laughing when the snow drifted off into her face. Though not so different from the wintry landscape of the North Pole, the frozen forest was still such a miracle of nature that it was easy to forget about attending shows on Broadway. And who needed treats to sample when it was treat enough to be in a place that held such beauty?

Then there it was again. The tickle. Daring to be ignored.

Lily paused. She pressed a hand to Cinder's back, causing the reindeer to also pause. Holding her breath, Lily's gaze darted from left to right and back again. But she saw nothing. Nor did she hear anything that gave her cause for alarm. Even so, Cinder's safety was more important than a day of exploring. She and Cinder would return to the cabin immediately.

"Let's go," she whispered to Cinder, giving the reindeer a pat-pat and a firm nudge.

Cinder ignored the nudge. She stood firm, with her gaze fixed on the other side of a stand of birch trees. And just beyond the trees was a small lake.

Lily looked to see what had Cinder's attention and was relieved when she saw it was another reindeer, a young bull, standing at the edge of the lake. In awe, she couldn't take her eyes off the youngster. She had never seen a reindeer in the wild, except for those at the North Pole, and none there had fur so unusual. A magnificent creature, the young reindeer's coloring was such that he was nearly invisible against the snowy landscape.

Cinder, too, stared at the male reindeer for a long minute, not moving or making a sound until, finally, she raised her muzzle to the sky and gave a loud grunt, which echoed off the trees and got the male's attention. Upon seeing Cinder, he returned her greeting with a grunt of his own.

In no hurry now, Lily allowed the two reindeer a moment to gaze at one another, but when neither seemed willing to take it any further, she gave Cinder another pat-pat to let her know it was time they leave the forest. They'd been away from the cabin long enough.

This time, Cinder paid attention to the signal, and with a bob of her head, she bid her new friend goodbye.

"Maybe we'll see him again while we're here," Lily told Cinder as they started back along the trail. But then a glint of something shiny caught Lily's eye. She stopped to look about, but saw nothing. Then she looked back to the male reindeer. He had his muzzle to the snow and seemed unconcerned for his safety. Cinder, too, showed no awareness of a possible threat. But Lily didn't feel their ease, and she wasn't about to make a move until she knew whether the threat was real or imagined. Looking again, she examined every bush and every tree and everything in-between until she found the source of the glint. It was the barrel of a rifle positioned against a man's shoulder. He was crouching in the brush, not far from the young reindeer, close to the lake's shoreline.

Chilled through, Lily looked back to the young reindeer. He was still searching the snow for treats. He had no awareness he was about to be shot.

But not if she could prevent it.

Lurching forward, she raised her arms high above her head

and swung them wildly while she screamed at the reindeer to run. But all he did was raise his head from the snow and stare at her.

Frantic, Lily looked about the ground for something she might throw in the reindeer's direction to scare him. She was too far away to make contact, but if she could somehow make him see her as a threat, he might react. Seeing only wet bushes and snow, she opted for snow. She scooped up a large handful, formed it into an icy ball, and threw it as hard as she could at a nearby tree. When the ice cracked against the bark of the tree, it was just loud enough to make the reindeer pay attention, and he bounded off into the trees.

Relieved, Lily returned her gaze to where she'd seen the hunter. But he was gone. Then she heard a splashing sound, and she looked to the lake, where she saw a big yellow dog standing at the shoreline, chuffing at a man—the hunter—who was now in the water and grabbing at chunks of ice.

Lily wanted to laugh. Almost did. But she managed to stifle herself. It wouldn't be right to laugh at another's misfortune... even if he was a hunter who'd been about to shoot a reindeer.

As she continued watching the man struggle, she became concerned he might need help. After another few moments, she decided he most definitely *did* need help. Moving quickly, she picked her way through the thick bramble, hoping to reach him before he injured himself. But by the time she was standing at the yellow dog's side, the man had already dragged himself onto the shore of the lake and was gulping in air. Lily's assessment of the man was *he would live,* and she and the dog stared at the man waiting for him to compose himself. When his gaze finally met hers, she asked, "Are you all right?"

The man's gaze hardened. "I just pulled myself out of an ice-cold lake, and now I'm sitting in mud. How do you think I am?"

Lily stepped back. She was familiar with such a tone. It was how humans communicated when they were fighting the temptation to say something profound and usually not very nice. She folded her arms across her chest, thinking of a few angry words of her own she wouldn't mind sharing with the hunter.

Though now wasn't the time to lecture a stranger on the evils of harming one of Santa's reindeer. Instead, she took a calming breath and said, "I just wanted to make sure you'll be okay if I leave you."

"Go ahead. Leave," the man said, his jaw tight. "If I can get myself on my horse, he'll get me home."

Lily looked about. She saw no horse, or any other kind of animal. Not even Cinder. And though Cinder's disappearance was disturbing, it was also a comfort, lest the man might want to continue his hunting using Cinder as his target. "What horse?" she asked.

"Over there," the man said, pointing over his shoulder at a tree. He turned and looked. "Great," he said as the color in his face deepened. "You scared my horse off with your screaming. Guess I'll be walking back home." He grabbed his hat from the mud and stuffed it on his head. "What were you screaming about, anyway?"

Lily lifted her chin. "You were about to shoot a reindeer. It was my duty to save him."

"Yes, I'm sure it was," the man grumbled. He looked the length of her, and it was like he was looking at her for the first time. "What are you wearing? A summer dress, out here in the cold?"

Lily pulled the shawl tight about her shoulders as she silently scolded herself for not being better prepared. "I was running out of firewood. I hadn't intended to be out here for more than a minute to collect enough for the night." She pulled the shawl tighter. "I hadn't realized the temperature had fallen so." As far as explanations went, she thought it pretty good.

"There's snow on the ground," the man said. "How could you not know it was too cold to be out here dressed like that?"

"I really must be going," Lily said. "If you're not hurt, I'll be on my way." Any further discussion about the weather seemed pointless.

"I'll manage," the man said. He moved his right leg and grimaced. Then he flexed his foot and grunted sharply. "Or maybe not."

Lily stared down at the man's foot. "Are you able to walk?"

"I guess I won't know until I try," the man said. "But do me a favor, the next time you think you see something, before you start screaming, make sure there's good reason. If you'd waited another minute, you'd have seen I meant the reindeer no harm."

"No *harm?* You were going to *shoot* the poor animal!"

"I wasn't, but it makes no difference now because he's gone," the man said. He flexed his foot again and winced.

Seeing the man in obvious pain, Lily was torn. She had no desire to help someone who was so disagreeable, but if he had truly injured himself, it was only right she offer him a place to recover. "I have a cabin nearby," she told the man, adding, "I can take you there, and you can sit by the fire and rest while I hang your clothes to dry. And if you're hungry, I can give you something to eat."

The man looked down at his shirt and pants, made a futile effort at rubbing the mud away, and quickly gave up. "I suppose it would be foolish of me to turn down an offer to get out of the cold." His gaze steadied on her "You say you have a cabin nearby? In these woods?"

"Yes. It's not far." Lily turned and pointed. "Just a short distance, in that direction."

The man stared into the trees. "I've been in this forest a good many times. I don't recall ever seeing a cabin."

Lily shrugged. "I'm sure it's not a product of my imagination." She knew for sure it wasn't. The cabin was already there when she arrived.

"No, likely not," the man said, looking her over once more. "If we're going to spend time together, we should probably exchange names. I'm Jake Longmire, and my dog's name is Sierra."

"Hello, Sierra," Lily said as she held out a hand to the yellow dog. "What a pretty girl you are. My name is Lily."

The dog licked Lily's hand, and Lily laughed at the feel of the dog's velvety tongue smoothing over her skin. Then she turned her attention back to the man—Jake. "Do you need my assistance getting to your feet?"

Jake looked up at her through a frown.

"I'll take that as a yes," Lily said. She angled herself beside him and stood firm as he got to his feet and rested an arm about her shoulders. He was heavier than expected, though she attributed part of his weight to his pants that were wet and still caked with mud. As they began walking, he remembered his rifle, and she cringed when he grabbed it. Though he'd denied wanting to harm the reindeer, she knew better. A man doesn't aim a weapon at something unless he intends to shoot it.

"How far did you say this cabin of yours is?" Jake asked, his entire body now vibrating from the cold.

"Beyond the trees," Lily answered. She pointed again, and as she and Jake made their way through the forest, she watched for Cinder, hoping that the reindeer had returned to the cabin and knew to stay out of sight.

Chapter Two

The hunter's teeth clacked the entire way back to the cabin, but he uttered not one word of complaint, just kept putting one foot in front of the other, trusting Lily to lead the way. When they finally made it out of the forest, Lily sensed Cinder's presence, and she knew Cinder had made it back safely and was in the barn. Lily made a mental note to check on her later.

By the time she and Jake entered the cabin, it was toasty warm and ready for human guests. Jake stopped just inside the door and looked around like he couldn't decide what to do, so Lily took a quilt from a wood chest at the end of the sofa and handed it to him, saying, "You should probably get out of your wet clothes." She nodded at the bedroom door. "You can wash up in there if you like. Leave your clothes, and I'll rinse them. They shouldn't take long to dry once I hang them by the fireplace. Then, after you've rested, you can be on your way." At least that's what she hoped for—an easy end to her time with such a disagreeable fellow. Though if he was truly injured, no telling how long she would need to provide him shelter. And that would only complicate things if he was still in her care when her assignment arrived.

"I appreciate your help," Jake said. His gaze went to the floor where his boots had left wet prints. "I'm afraid I've made a mess of your floor," he added, looking sheepish. "Guess I should have left my boots on the porch."

"Messes can be cleaned," Lily said. She nodded again at the bedroom door.

Jake removed his wet hat, and she took it and hung it on a hook next to the door. Then she watched him as he walked toward the bedroom, waiting until he'd shut the door before she went out to the porch, where she could get away from the heat of the cabin. How humans stood such warmth was a mystery. Though if Santa were to grant her wish, she supposed it was something she would learn to live with and, in time, maybe even learn to enjoy. Not as much as she enjoyed pushing her feet into cold, crisp snow, but then nothing was that enjoyable.

Standing in the cool winter air, Lily forgot about the man, Jake, and her thoughts turned to the conversation she'd had with Santa just before he gave her this assignment. They'd discussed this year's Christmas wish, and though no promises had been made, it was encouraging because Santa hadn't immediately dismissed the idea of providing her the opportunity to find love. She replayed the conversation in her mind.

Let's talk about this wish of yours, shall we? Santa had begun. *I wonder if you have a clear understanding of what will happen should I decide to grant your request.*

It means I will no longer be a Christmas fairy, she had responded.

And?

And I will lose my magic.

And?

Unable to come up with any further *ands*, she had gone quiet, and Santa had continued, reminding her that he would be announcing his choice for Head Christmas Fairy at this year's Christmas Eve Ball. Reminding her, too, that both she and Vivienne had been nominated to take over the position.

Lily pressed her lips tight. *Vivienne.* How Santa could consider putting the elder fairy in charge of all the other fairies for an entire year was beyond reason. He couldn't possibly be serious. But if he was, that was his choice, and it didn't change her mind about wanting to find everlasting love.

And that's what she'd told Santa.

Not one to easily give up, Santa had then made a detour in their conversation, telling her that if she were to become human, she would begin to age and would one day wake up and find herself to be elderly. She would develop wrinkles. Her hair may even turn gray. *How would you feel about that?* he had asked.

The idea of growing old had not given Lily reason for pause. Growing old was not to be feared. She'd already celebrated more than two hundred birthdays, and truth be told, she'd held up well. And though developing lines and crevasses in the skin would eventually be a concern, perhaps she would be one of those who aged well. After all, she'd seen many an elderly human who had somehow found a way to avoid getting wrinkles. Though, sometimes, their faces did have a stretched appearance.

Lily pinched the skin on one of her cheeks to see how far it would stretch.

Not far.

Just as she was about to test the other cheek, she heard Jake's call through the cabin door, and it was experiment over. She went back inside and found Jake wrapped in the quilt and looking much happier. His teeth had stopped clacking, his frown had disappeared, and he didn't look nearly as stern as when she'd first seen him. In fact, looking at him now, he seemed like a different man. Pleasant, like someone she might enjoy knowing. If he weren't a hunter.

"I won't be long," she said over her shoulder as she hurried to the other room to tend to his clothes.

The bathroom was rustic but functional, with a claw-foot bathtub, where Jake had discarded his pants and shirt. Beginning with his shirt, Lily took her time to rinse it clean. Then, not eager to go back into the other room, she took even more time rinsing his pants, and as she watched the last of the muddy water swirl down the drain, her thoughts turned to the young reindeer in the forest. If she hadn't been there to intervene, no telling where he'd be right now, but probably not anywhere good.

"Meant the reindeer no harm, my foot!" Lily scoffed, angry all over again at seeing Jake's rifle aimed at the young bull. And before she could stop it, her wings came to life and released a small flurry of snowflakes that quickly settled on the floor and melted. Frustrated, she looked down at the watery mess. She was just glad her guest in the other room hadn't witnessed the incident. It would have been impossible to explain.

As she wrung the water from Jake's clothes, she tried to think of what she could do to keep him from returning to the forest to continue his hunting. Accidentally helping his clothes fall into the fire seemed a good plan, though if she did that, she would be stuck with him. And, too, purposely causing the destruction of a man's clothing went against the Christmas Fairy Code of Conduct. It was something a fairy such as Vivienne might do. Vivienne lived loosely by The Code, revising it to her own liking as she saw fit, and she cared not one bit about consequences.

Putting that idea aside, Lily gave her problem with the hunter more consideration. Perhaps she could hide his rifle. Surely, there would be no wrong in relieving a man of his weapon if his intent was to use it in a way that went against the Christmas Fairy Pledge. After all, so it was written, Christmas fairies were obligated to do whatever they must to keep Santa's reindeer from harm. Even those not currently living at the North Pole. And to make sure, she silently recited the entire pledge.

As a Christmas fairy, I will be patient and eager to please, and I will be filled to the tips of my wings with the Christmas spirit. I may use my magic during an assignment, but never for the purpose of attaining a successful completion. Nor may I ever use magic for my own material benefit or to attain a Christmas wish. I will treat my sister fairies with respect and I will stand united with them at all times to preserve and protect our community at the North Pole, including Santa's reindeer, who must at all times be kept from harm.

Lily smiled. It was definitely her duty to prevent harm from coming to any reindeer, no matter where they made their home. But, again, her conscience got the better of her. Hiding a man's weapon was also not something a Christmas fairy would do… no matter how she reasoned it to be a solution.

Setting aside all thoughts to inconvenience the hunter, Lily finally returned to the other room, where she found her guest and his dog sleeping soundly. Mindful of a person's need for rest after a traumatic event, she quietly hung the hunter's clothes by the fire, taking care to secure them so that they *wouldn't* fall and burn. Then she sat across from him, giving him a long, appraising look. Now that his lips had color and his hair was no longer dripping with water, he looked peaceful, handsome even, with a strong albeit stubborn chin and kind eyes that she'd noticed were the color of rich cinnamon. And even with the lines on his forehead, which seemed to be a permanent feature, she suspected he was not a man who lacked attention. So far as she could see, his only apparent flaw was his desire to hunt reindeer. And as far as flaws went, that was huge.

With a quiet sigh, she got up and went to the kitchen to keep from doing something she shouldn't. She opened the cupboards and drawers, taking inventory, and was happy to find everything she needed for her nutritional needs. And after a morning such as she'd had in the forest, what she needed at that very moment was something sweet. So baking it was.

To set the mood, while assembling ingredients, Lily hummed a medley of Christmas carols. Then, once she had everything lined up on the kitchen counter, she got busy, and by the time she removed the last try of treats from the oven, she had three pies, four dozen cookies, and one fruitcake—enough sugar-filled goodies to last at least five days. Three, if she had to share.

Eager to have her energy restored, she sampled a cookie. And then another. Then she contemplated the flour and sugar and bits of candy cane that seemed to cover every surface in the kitchen. Cleaning was such a chore, it could wait. What she needed was more sugar. She looked to the counter, at the candy cane pie. It was her very first, from a recipe that Mrs. Claus had recently given her, and she couldn't wait to try a bite. Candy canes were a vital part of a fairy's diet, and though the pie came with a warning not to overindulge, lest one be overcome with the desire to fly themselves to the moon, she cut herself an extra-large slice, then sat at the table to enjoy every bite.

Before she'd even set her fork down, she was feeling much better, and with her energy soaring, she closed her eyes and imagined the kitchen returned to its original condition. Then, happy with what she'd accomplished, she twirled about the kitchen, humming another medley of Christmas carols, beginning with "Jingle Bells" and ending with "Christmas Waltz," which she hummed three times in a row, all the while wishing she had a dance partner.

Her gaze strayed to her guest who was still asleep on her sofa, and she wondered if he might be the type to enjoy a whirl about the kitchen. In her gaiety, she twirled up next to the sofa and was just about to wake him... until she noticed his foot dangling off to one side.

The human was in no condition to dance.

Lily blew out a small breath and sat across from Jake to watch him and his dog sleep. Though, almost immediately, Sierra stirred and, upon seeing Lily, got up and wandered over to relax next to Lily's chair.

After another minute, Jake also woke, and when he caught both Lily and his dog staring at him, he sat up. "How long have you and my dog been watching me?" he wanted to know.

"A while," Lily said. "Now that you're awake, you must be hungry." She gestured toward the kitchen. "While you were sleeping, I did a little baking. I have cookies and pie—pumpkin, apple, and candy cane. Candy canes are good for energy. You slept so long, I should think you could use a large slice."

"Thanks, but I'm not that fond of sweets," Jake said. His gaze ran the length of her. "You haven't changed your clothes."

Lily looked down at herself, at her dress. "Why would I change? The cabin is so warm, and I am no longer out in the cold."

"I guess I'm just used to seeing people all bundled up this time of year. But never mind. It's none of my business what you wear," Jake said.

"I should bundle up when indoors?" Lily asked.

Jake shrugged. "Maybe wear something a little warmer than a summer dress." He pressed his lips together. "Like I said, it's none of my business." He looked about the room for a moment, his eyes surveying, then his gaze came back to her. "If you don't mind my asking, what are you doing out here all by yourself?"

"I'm here to spend Christmas," Lily said.

"Alone?"

Lily clasped her hands around her knees and smiled. "I thought it would be a nice change from the usual. I find such peace here in the forest." She didn't think any further elaboration was needed with someone who wouldn't be her guest much longer.

"I can understand that," Jake said. "I'm not much for the holidays, either."

Ah, this man has lost his Christmas spirit, Lily mused. And then, once more remembering Santa's words, *He will come to you*, she gasped and nearly fell off her chair.

"Something wrong?" Jake asked.

Lily stared at him. Surely, Santa had made a mistake. He would never expect her to help a hunter of reindeer. Yet, here the man was, and though, technically, he hadn't *come* to her, he was the only human she'd seen since arriving at the cabin. And with the snow that was already on the ground and more likely to come, she couldn't see anyone else happening upon the cabin unless they drove a sleigh or operated one of those snow machines. Still. It was too impossible to believe, and even thinking it had her feeling light-headed. She needed fresh air. Lots of fresh air. She put a hand to her forehead and made her way to the door. But when she opened it and saw the sky was full of tiny snowflakes, she let out another gasp and had to grasp the doorframe.

"Are you okay?" Jake asked. "Do you need to sit down?"

Lily shook her head. "I'm fine." But she wasn't fine. She needed another dose of sugar, so she could think. She hurried to the kitchen, to where the pies and platters of cookies were lined up along the back of the counter. "I just need something to eat… a piece of pie," she said. "Are you sure you won't join me? I have plenty, and I don't mind sharing."

Jake laughed lightly. "Glad to hear it, but I'm more a meat and potatoes kind of guy. So, if it's no trouble, I could use something warm to fill my belly. I had a thermos of coffee and a couple of sandwiches in my saddlebags, but since my horse has run off, well, they won't be doing me much good now."

"I don't cook meat," Lily said, her nose wrinkling, "and I haven't any potatoes at the moment. But if it's something warm you require, I'd be happy to make a pot of hot chocolate. A good dose of chocolate cures just about any ailment, and I wouldn't mind having a cup myself. I also have a nice fruitcake that might still be warm. I'm aware most people don't care for fruitcake, but mine is different. It's edible and healthy, full of nutrition. Would you like to try a piece?" She held it up for him to see.

Jake's face bore a scowl. "No. No fruitcake for me."

"Are you sure? You said you were hungry."

"Not for fruitcake," Jake said. "Hot chocolate will be fine."

Lily's shoulders slumped. Fruitcake was so misunderstood. She placed the cake back on the counter, then turned to the cupboard to gather ingredients for making hot chocolate. She'd prepared it from scratch so many times, it was easy. The secret to great hot chocolate was in the stirring, and stirring didn't take long at all. Just a few minutes.

"I hope you like it," she said when she handed Jake a mug full to the brim.

He took a small sip. "It's good. Thank you."

Lily peered at him over the rim of her mug, still finding it hard to believe he could be her assignment. Though if he was, it meant their time together had just begun. It also meant she had to set aside her distaste at his being a hunter and go about helping him just as she would any other human. The hard part would be keeping him there at the cabin. She looked to the window and saw that the tiny snowflakes were now huge, the size of quarters.

"How's your ankle?" she asked, determined that if he *was* her assignment, she would do her best to see it through to a successful completion.

"It's been better. I'm sure it's just a minor sprain," Jake said, then added, "Don't worry. I won't be here imposing on you much longer."

"Perhaps you should spend the night," Lily said. "Your ankle will have more time to recover, and if you wait for morning, you'll have better light to see your way through the forest."

Jake looked down at his foot, tried to flex it, and frowned. "I hate to say it, but you might be right. I just hope it doesn't snow all night. It'd be a long walk home on a sore foot unless I were to get lucky and find my horse."

"Maybe you will," Lily said, but not wanting it to be so.

"Maybe," Jake agreed. "Odds are, though, he's already headed home."

Lily set her empty mug down and put a hand to her mouth as she yawned. "Goodness, I got up so early, I feel like I'm in need of a nap. If you don't mind me leaving you alone, I'd like to go to my room for a while." She was already on her way, needing the solitude so she could clear her mind.

"Don't worry about me," Jake said. "My dog will keep me company."

Lily shut herself in her room. Once behind the closed door, she commenced pacing. Pacing went along with thinking. And her thinking was that snow might be the only thing that would keep the hunter there at the cabin for more than just one night.

Lots and lots of snow.

Chapter Three

Jake was relieved when the woman left him and went into the other room. As he drank his hot chocolate, he found himself listening intently to the crackle of burning wood and wondering if he might've been thrown from his horse and hit his head and was now in some kind of delusional state. But it wasn't his head that hurt.

Satisfied his mental state was still fully intact, he perused the room. His mom would have liked this place. She'd always wanted somewhere she could go whenever she needed time alone. Which they'd all needed after... Well, no need to go there. Not when he had plenty of physical pain to keep his mind occupied.

He swung his gaze to the window and was disappointed to see the sky was thick with snow. He looked down at his foot. His ankle had swollen up some, but he still didn't think his injury was serious enough that he couldn't get himself back home. And maybe if he headed out right now, instead of waiting for morning, he'd find his horse hanging around out there somewhere.

He glanced at his clothes hanging next to the fireplace. They had to be dry by now. He stood and put some weight on his foot to check the level of pain. It was pleasant, but it was bearable. He grabbed his shirt and pants, pulling them free from where they hung, and got them on easy enough. But when he tried putting on his boots, all he got for his effort was a forehead covered in sweat. He'd underestimated the swelling in his ankle.

Frustrated, he tossed the boot aside so that it landed with a thud next to the fireplace. A moment later, the bedroom door opened, and Lily peered out. When she saw his boot lying next to the fireplace, she came up beside him.

"You're not thinking of leaving, are you? I thought we agreed you were going to stay the night."

"I changed my mind," Jake grumbled. "I thought I'd try to get out of here before the snow gets any deeper." He looked down at his swollen foot. "Problem is, I was only able to get one boot on."

Lily knelt and examined his ankle. "You really are damaged, aren't you?"

"It would appear so," Jake agreed.

"What you need to do is elevate your leg," Lily advised. She stood and gave him a gentle push back so that he was prone. Then she tucked a pillow under his head and two more under his leg. "There, that should help," she told him, "but I'm afraid you may be here a while. Maybe even beyond tomorrow morning."

"I don't think so," Jake said, sitting back up. "I'll stay the night, but I'll be leaving first thing."

"If you say so," Lily said. "But you should at least try to stay off your foot as much as possible the rest of the day." She pushed him back down and tugged the boot off his good foot, then she picked up the other boot and moved them both far enough away that he couldn't easily reach them.

Unease settled in the pit of Jake's stomach as he watched the woman take charge of his boots. And though it was a stretch to think she could overpower him, he didn't know her well enough to trust she hadn't put something in his hot chocolate. He eyed the empty mug sitting on the coffee table. He didn't feel drugged or strange in any way, but her moving his boots out of his reach was highly unnerving, and so unnecessary. With his foot all swelled up, he had no choice but to stay the night. "If you don't mind," he said to Lily, "I'd feel better if you'd put my boots over here next to me."

Lily gave his boots a scant glance. "They're fine where they are."

Jake felt his adrenaline surge. "You can't keep me here. I need to get myself home. Even if it means I have to walk out of here wearing only one boot."

Lily stood next to the sofa, hands on hips. "Don't be silly. Who said anything about keeping you here? If the swelling in your foot has gone down by morning, you can leave. But if not, you'd be smart to stay. I mean you no harm if that's what you're thinking. You're perfectly safe here with me."

"Good to know," Jake mumbled, feeling like an idiot for letting his imagination run wild.

Lily continued. "This close to Christmas, I'm sure you have festivities you'd like to attend. Caroling, tree lighting—"

"I don't care about festivities. I just need to get myself home," Jake repeated.

"Oh. Well, okay. Though I imagine you probably still have shopping to do," Lily said. "Unless you're already finished, in which case, I commend you."

Jake felt another surge of adrenaline. "You're not listening! Christmas isn't my thing, and I have no shopping to do! In fact, I try to avoid the stores this time of year."

Lily smiled sweetly. "So there's really no reason for you to leave. At least not until the swelling in your ankle has gone down."

"Like I told you," Jake said, "I'll be leaving in the morning."

Lily raised her chin. "We'll see." She went over to where she'd placed his boots and picked them up, saying, "If you change your mind about wanting something to eat, please feel free to call me." Then she closed herself *and* his boots in the other room.

Jake listened for a click to indicate she'd locked the door, but none came, which told him she wasn't concerned for her safety.

He wished he could say the same for himself, but he couldn't, and he doubted he would get any sleep that night. He lay back with a heavy breath and gave some thought to what he'd gotten himself into. It wasn't good, and not likely to get any better until he could get his boots back.

Wrestling with that for a while, he finally got up and made it to the kitchen, where he looked to see if there was anything to eat other than cookies, pie, or fruitcake. Nada. And nothing in the cupboards, either, except for baking supplies. He didn't bother looking in the small refrigerator because the pain in his ankle was nagging at him to get prone on the sofa again.

Lily put Jake's boots away in the closet. If he was her assignment, Santa had a plan. He wouldn't have chosen this particular human to receive the help of a Christmas fairy without good reason. Though she doubted Santa knew Jake was a hunter of reindeer.

She tapped a finger to her bottom lip. Why anyone would want to harm a reindeer was beyond comprehension. They would have to be deranged. And if the hunter was deranged, this was going to be a most challenging assignment.

Opening the bedroom door, she peered out at her guest draped along the entire length of the sofa. A tall one he was, but at the moment, he didn't look all that scary. In fact, with the light of the emerging moon coming through the window and casting blue shadows over his face, he looked downright sickly, like he might be oxygen-deprived. She hoped he wasn't ill in addition to being injured.

"I agree. The human does look a little peaked," a voice said quietly in Lily's ear.

Lily swung around and came face-to-face with the fairy she least expected or hoped to see—her roommate from the North Pole. *"Vivienne!"* she said to the elder fairy in a fierce whisper.

"Liliana!" Vivienne said in reply, just as fierce.

"What are you doing here?"

"Santa sent me," Vivienne said, offering a sly smile. "He thought you might be lonely and in need of companionship."

Lily's eyes narrowed. "You and I both know that's not true."

"Which part?"

"All of it. Santa would never send *you* to keep me company. Plus, he knows I already have Cinder here with me." Lily moved over to the window and looked to make sure the barn hadn't been swallowed into the atmosphere. It hadn't. Which meant Cinder was still in residence—and probably in need of a reassuring visit, which would happen just as soon as she had a chance to sneak away. She turned to Vivienne. "What are you *really* doing here?"

Vivienne's lips tightened. "If you must know, I needed someone to talk to." She tossed her hands up. "You're never going to believe what Santa has tasked me with. He wants me to help him put the final touches on his Nice and Naughty Lists. Me! Can you imagine?" She paced across the room and back, then swung around and got in Lily's face. "I'm about to share a secret with you, and it had better remain a secret."

Lily eased herself onto the bed. "Perhaps if it's that important, you should keep it to yourself."

"Yes," Vivienne said, "that would seem the wise thing to do. But if I don't tell someone, I'm afraid my wings might combust. You wouldn't want that, would you?"

Lily gave Vivienne's question a moment's thought and decided she wouldn't want any fairy's wings to combust. Not even Vivienne's. "I suppose not," she said, though not very convincingly.

Vivienne's eyes narrowed. "Hmm. I'm not sure I believe you."

"What is it you wanted to tell me?" Lily asked. The sooner Vivienne shared her secret, the sooner she would leave.

"As I was saying, what I'm about to tell you must be kept between just you and me. *Comprendo?*"

Lily nodded yes.

"Very well," Vivienne said. She sniffed and took a small breath. "You may find this surprising—after all, you know me so well—but I have a problem with the little ones."

"You mean with children?" Lily asked.

"Yes, children."

"You don't like them?"

"I wouldn't go that far," Vivienne said. "I'm just what you might call child-challenged. I don't understand them, and they don't understand me."

"Hmm," Lily said. "Have you ever considered you might be in the wrong line of work?"

"Brilliant deduction, little Miss Goody Goodness. Problem is, being a Christmas fairy *is* my line of work, and I'm too old at this stage of my life to do anything else."

Lily didn't know if that was true. Vivienne was a senior fairy, but she wasn't old by any means. At least not by fairy standards. Santa was probably even older than Vivienne. Though rumor had it, he was *extremely* old, and she doubted Vivienne would want to hear that.

"Honestly," Vivienne continued, "I don't know what Santa was thinking. As if I don't already have enough to do at this time of year."

"If you're tired of being a Christmas fairy, I'm sure you could find something else you'd enjoy doing," Lily said. "You might even be able to help out in the Toy Room."

Vivienne's brow drew together. "The *Toy Room?* You think I would enjoy building *toys?*"

"It was just a suggestion."

"Well, save it! Anyway, I never said I was tired of being a Christmas fairy. And it's not that I don't want to give the old man a hand with his lists, but here's the thing… I have no idea how to tell the nice kids from the naughty kids. If you ask me, they're *all* naughty. And that's why I'm here. I need your advice."

"Mine?" Lily put a hand to her chest. "Oh, I don't think that's a good idea."

"Nonsense! It's a brilliant idea! You're so sickly sweet, you couldn't possibly steer me wrong. So, tell me," Vivienne said as she settled next to Lily on the bed, "how do you tell the difference between naughty kids and nice kids? What behavior defines them?"

Lily took a moment, still reluctant. If Vivienne made a mess of things when deciding which children belonged on which list, all blame would fall on her. Best to keep it as simple as possible. "Well," she began, "each child is different. But basically, nice kids are polite. They help others, and they do their chores, and they are always kind to animals." She smiled. "And, of course, naughty means just the opposite."

"Oh, *please*," Vivienne said. "Just because a child doesn't do his chores, doesn't mean he's naughty. And kids who do everything they're told aren't nice! They're boring! They're like you, goody good-doers who never cause a scene or get into any kind of trouble. I'll bet they never even talk back to their parents."

"Yes, but—"

"But nothing! Forget it! I'll just have to wing it!" Vivienne commenced pacing with her red velvet dress swishing after her. "Really, I should have known better than to come to you for advice. And honestly, Santa must be losing his edge asking for my assistance. Surely, he could have enlisted the help of one of those lazy elves who work in the Toy Room. I should think any one of them would enjoy a respite from building wooden trains."

"The trains are much more sophisticated these days, and the elves aren't lazy," Lily said. "They put in a lot of extra hours every year building toys to make sure no child goes without. And these last few weeks before Christmas, they happen to be extremely busy."

"Bah! The elves do nothing but goof off all day."

"You mean when they test the toys?"

"That's exactly what I mean!" Vivienne said. "Every time I go to the Toy Room, it's like they're having a party! All those planes flying around in circles, cars zooming from one end of the room to the other, dolls crying and wetting their diapers! It's complete chaos, and if I were Santa, I'd put a stop to it!"

"But testing the toys is part of their job," Lily reminded Vivienne. "They build the toys, and then they must test them to ensure they work properly. And after that, every toy must be wrapped and appropriately tagged before being loaded onto

Santa's sleigh. It's extremely time-consuming, and many of the elves must work long hours to get everything done on time."

Vivienne waved a hand. "Whatever. Back to our conversation about Santa asking me to help with his lists." Her eyes went squinty. "I'm just wondering if someone put him up to it. One of the younger fairies, I suppose. They're so jealous of me I wouldn't put it past *all* of them to be in on it."

Lily tucked her knees to her chest. She wasn't about to tell Vivienne that *she* was the guilty party. The smartest thing to do at the moment was change the subject. "Have you heard the news?" she asked Vivienne.

Vivienne's head snapped around. "What news?"

"This may be the year Santa grants my Christmas wish!"

"Oh, that," Vivienne said, yawning. "I suppose I did hear something about it through the North Pole grapevine. We'll see if it really happens."

"Oh, it will! I can feel it! This is the year I will find love!" Lily exclaimed. And in her delight, she came off the bed and twirled about, wings spreading and releasing snow until she and Vivienne were both surrounded by tiny snowflakes, several of which scored a direct hit to one of Vivienne's eyes.

"Gah!" Vivienne shrieked. "Will you never learn to control those things? I'm on my way to my own assignment, and the last thing I need is to show up with my mascara running!" She blinked repeatedly as she fended off more snowflakes.

Lily concentrated and managed to calm her wings. "Sorry. I'm just so excited that Santa has finally agreed to consider my wish for love."

"Yes, well, I wouldn't get your hopes up just yet. I'm sure you know Santa can't *force* a man to fall in love with you. He can only present you with the opportunity to *find* love. After that, the rest is on your shoulders. And don't forget, there's a time limit."

"Time limit? How can there be a time limit on love?" Lily asked.

Vivienne gave a dry laugh. "My dear, there's a time limit on everything. If you don't like it, that's something you'll have to take up with Santa. Now, as I was saying, finding love isn't just about what *you* want. It takes two to make a connection, which means that once you've identified a love interest, he must also proclaim his desire to be with you. And this so-called love connection must happen by midnight Christmas Eve, or it can't happen at all." She flipped over her wrist and tapped a silver band. "Oops! Looks like you're already running out of time."

The corners of Lily's mouth turned down. "That can't be true. I'm on assignment, and I will have no opportunity to meet anyone here." She raised her chin. "Besides, Santa told me he would give me his decision *after* Christmas."

"Hooey. You know the rule regarding the granting of wishes."

"It doesn't matter what the rule is," Lily said. "Santa makes the rules, he can change them anytime he wants." She wasn't about to let Vivienne dash her dreams of finding love.

"Hmm, I suppose you're right," Vivienne agreed. "But even if Santa grants you a late wish, you'll need to have the object of your desire already participating in the process. And since your options here are limited, perhaps you should look no further than Mr. Sleepy out there in the other room."

Lily sputtered, half laughing, half gasping. "Don't be silly. The man on my sofa may be my assignment, but he's certainly not my love interest."

"Look, Bimbette, try reading between the lines. This is the first time Santa has told you he would consider your wish, right?"

"Right," Lily cautiously agreed.

"So, why would he send you here on an assignment, with the only available man being Mr. Handsome Human out there?" Vivienne jammed a finger at the bedroom door. "I'll tell you why... Santa is overwhelmed. He's killing two birds with one stone. Have you seen how long the Nice List is this year? It's no wonder he asked for my help."

"I don't think so," Lily said. "Santa is never overwhelmed. Busy, yes, but I can assure you, he has everything under control."

"Really? What about the last-minute switch he made with your friend Calista? This dreary cabin is where *she* was supposed to be spending Christmas, so she could take the year off and enjoy the holidays somewhere quiet. But now here you are, while Calista has locked herself in some luxurious New York City apartment, taking bubble baths and eating box after box of See's Candies. Word is she's taken a particular liking to the Dark Chocolate Nuts & Chews." Vivienne's eyes were gleaming. "Jealous much?"

Jealous a lot, but Lily wasn't about to let Vivienne see that. "I'm sure Santa has his reasons for switching Calista's location with mine. But I still say you're wrong about the human. Santa would never expect me to fall in love with someone who hunts reindeer."

Vivienne drew back like she'd been slapped. "A *hunter?* Mr. Sleepy is a *hunter?* As in *Bang! Bang! You're dead?*"

Lily nodded. "When I first saw him, he was about to shoot a young reindeer."

"Not Cinder!" Vivienne said on a gasp. "Why, Santa would have a fit! A hunter going after one of his back-up reindeer would make the front page of *The North Pole News*."

"It wasn't Cinder," Lily said. "And what do you care? You've never liked her."

"True," Vivienne admitted. "She's spoiled, always getting more than her fair share of attention from the elves. I hear they even give her extra reindeer chow like she's some kind of royalty." She shook her head. "I really don't understand the interest the elves take in the reindeer, but I suppose it's a way to relieve boredom after building toys all day."

"Boredom has nothing to do with it. The reindeer need to be well-cared for," Lily said. "They can only fly when they have proper nourishment. Anyway, as far as me and the man on the sofa making a connection, it's not going to happen. He and I are completely incompatible. I'm all freshly fallen snow, Christmas carols, and twinkle lights, while he doesn't even *do* Christmas."

"Oh, he's one of those," Vivienne remarked. "Well, that's an easy enough fix. Simply show him the magic of the season, and how much fun it could be if he shared it with someone like you, and I guarantee, by the stroke of midnight on the big eve, he'll be more than ready to get down on one knee to propose marriage."

"I'm not sure," Lily said. "With him being a hunter—"

"Never mind that!" Vivienne said. "If you expect Santa to take your wish seriously, you need to prove you're willing to work at getting over your differences with the human. No one said having a relationship would be easy. Trust me," she continued as she tipped her head at the bedroom door, "Santa sent you here for a reason, and now it's up to you to make the most of it. And not to put a further damper on things, but I'm sure you've been told about the Unable to Grant Stamp."

Chapter Four

Lily's stomach churned with the feeling she was about to be let in on a secret she should have already known. She wrung her hands, trying to think if she'd ever heard of such a thing as an Unable to Grant Stamp. No, she was sure she hadn't.

"Please, what is this stamp you speak of?" she asked Vivienne.

"I'm sure Santa meant to tell you, but perhaps with things being so hectic this year, he forgot," Vivienne said. She paused, feigned concern. "You really mustn't worry. And, of course, you still have time to change your mind and ask for a new wish, something not so complicated as love. But if you decide to keep your wish, and it turns out to be unattainable, unfortunately, there are dire consequences."

Lily swallowed. "Such as?"

"You'll lose an entire century of Christmas wishes."

Lily's eyes widened. "A century? But that's a hundred years! Santa would never do such a thing!"

Vivienne did a palms-up. "It's not *Santa's* doing. It's a rule that was established the year after an evil fairy named Ailsa tried to ruin Christmas. Taking away the wishes from a fairy who makes an impossible request is a safety measure, to make those who would consider asking for something outrageous think twice."

Lily put a hand to her chest. "It seems so severe. I can't imagine Santa allowing something like that. He's far too kind for such drastic measures." She gave Vivienne a doubtful look. "Are you sure you're not just making this up? I've asked for the very same thing for the past two decades, and I've yet to lose my wishes."

"That's because Santa has always given you a flat-out rejection," Vivienne said. She raised her right hand. "I swear on my wings, what I'm telling you is true. And I should know. A few years back, I had my own misfortune of making an unattainable Christmas wish. Surely, you've noticed how I never request anything from Santa."

"I just assumed you didn't care about wishes," Lily said, "that maybe you didn't need, or want, anything."

"Oh, if only that were so," Vivienne lamented. "Would you like to hear my story?"

Lily nodded, genuinely curious.

Vivienne looked at her wristband again. "Since we're short on time, I'll give you the extremely edited version." She settled next to Lily on the bed and began. "Once upon a time, I, too, wanted a white picket fence and a human man to love. But I had no plan. Much like you, I was young and foolish, and I believed everything would all work out in my favor, that the man would love me no matter what. And he did… until I revealed I was a Christmas fairy. Then he walked away without even a single glance over his shoulder."

"Oh, my," Lily said quietly.

Vivienne folded her hands in her lap and continued. "As you can imagine, I was deeply disappointed. Not only was it the end of any dreams I had for lasting romance, but it was also the end of my Christmas wishes for the foreseeable future." She sniffed and produced a tissue out of thin air, then gave Lily a look. "And before you get all misty-eyed, no need to worry about me. I'm over it. I'm halfway through my punishment, and in another fifty years, I'll have plenty to wish for."

"I'm sure you will, but I am still sorry for your misfortune," Lily said. She now had a better understanding of why Vivienne, at times, could be so sour. Lost love and no wishes for an entire century? That would be enough to push any fairy into despair.

"Like I said, I'm over it." Vivienne tossed the tissue aside and took to examining her fingernails, which were always perfect—red and glossy and never chipped. "And, really, I'm better off for the loss because I won't be distracted thinking about what I might find in my stocking on Christmas morning. Which means I'll be able to fully concentrate on my position as Head Christmas Fairy."

"You're assuming an awful lot, aren't you? Santa has yet to announce who that will be. And what if he chooses someone unexpected?"

"Someone unexpected? I can't imagine who that would be. And, anyway, as of today, there are only two of us in the running, and one of us desperately wants to leave the North Pole. So, no," Vivienne said, "there will be no surprises. I think you and I both know who Santa is going to choose."

"I never said I was desperate to leave the North Pole."

Vivienne waved a hand. "Whatever. Just don't blow it with the human."

"Why do you care if I blow it?" Lily asked. "If I fail to get my wish, and Santa chooses you to lead the fairies, you'll have everything you want, including me under your command. Which I suppose means you'll expect a batch of fresh-baked cookies for breakfast every morning."

Vivienne's top lip curled. "Now, who's assuming? No, my dear, as much as I adore fresh-baked cookies, what I adore even more is the idea of you permanently leaving the North Pole. It gets so tiresome always having to hear how perfect you are."

"I doubt anyone thinks I'm perfect. I certainly don't."

"There you go again. Being perfectly sweet. But never mind. Back to the hunter. What you need is a plan to win him over. You don't want to make the same mistake I did."

Lily pressed her lips together. "I'm truly sorry for what happened to you. But I don't believe love needs to be planned. If it's meant to be, it will happen. And anyway, I don't know that I can achieve anything with Jake. Even if I were to take an interest in him, I think perhaps he would just like to go home and forget about me."

"Why is that?"

"I made him fall into an icy lake and hurt himself."

Vivienne laughed. "I wouldn't worry. Humans are a forgiving people. Your hunter will come around. But just in case, wouldn't it be nice to have a little insurance?"

"What kind of insurance?"

"This." Vivienne held out her hand and in it was a small, gold foil-wrapped box bound with a red velvet ribbon.

Lily eyed the box. "What is it?"

"A gift. From me to you."

Lily's eyes narrowed. "You don't give gifts."

"I'm making an exception," Vivienne said, her lips pulling tight into a forced smile.

"Hmm."

"Hmm, nothing. Can't I want to help a sister fairy in her quest to find love? Maybe I'm just an old softie when it comes to romance."

Lily cocked an eyebrow. "Soft? You?"

"Why *not* me?"

Lily could think of so many reasons why not Vivienne, but she felt it best she keep them to herself. And even though she questioned Vivienne's sincerity, she couldn't help but wonder what might be in the pretty box that would be of any help to her. She also wondered if the man in the other room could really be her Christmas wish. It didn't seem possible. But if he was, and she made no attempt at gaining his love, it would mean an entire century of lost wishes. A hundred years of nothing. The very idea had her feeling queasy.

Maybe she hadn't thought this through. Love was such a complicated wish. And Vivienne was right. She still had time to change her mind. She could ask for a new pair of skates, or a Josh Groban Christmas CD... or even a new roommate. A fairy not named Vivienne. That would be an easy wish for Santa to grant. He could simply put Vivienne out in the Reindeer Barn, which was such a fun idea she had to put her fingers to her lips to stifle a laugh.

"I'm glad you're able to see the humor in your situation," Vivienne said, "but tick tock, I don't have time to stand here all day. Do you want my gift or not?" She shoved the box at Lily.

Lily cautiously took the pretty package, reasoning there was no harm in accepting a gift that came in such a tiny box. "Thank you," she said. Then she put the box to her ear.

"Oh, for heaven's sake, it's not a bomb!"

"I know," Lily said. "It's not ticking. But if you don't mind, I'll open it later." She set the box on the bed.

Vivienne raised an eyebrow. "Why wait? Santa has finally agreed to consider your request. It's the opportunity you've been waiting for, ergo"—she gestured to the box— "why not make it a sure thing?"

Lily glanced at the box. "Do you really think it possible the hunter is my Christmas wish?"

"It seems reasonable, don't you agree?"

"Maybe. It's just that, well, I would have thought Santa might provide me more than one man to choose from."

Vivienne did an eye-roll. "This isn't *The Bachelorette*. Santa isn't about to send an entire string of men into the wilderness for you to have a look-see. Have you taken a peek outside? You're lucky to have even *one* man to choose from with all that snow out there." She let out a heavy breath. "Like I said, tick tock."

Lily made a move to pick up the box, but then a knock came at the bedroom door, and she shot Vivienne a look. "That's Jake!"

"I gathered!" Vivienne whispered.

"You need to go!" Lily said, and she did a shooing motion with her hands.

Vivienne laughed quietly. "Oh, Miss Goody Goodness, don't you know by now you can't *shoo* me away."

"Is everything okay in there?" Jake called through the door.

"*Please*, just go!" Lily pleaded with Vivienne. Her wings shot out, fluttering wildly and releasing so much snow that she and Vivienne found themselves standing in a complete white-out.

"Stop! You'll ruin my dress!" Vivienne screeched as she put up her hands to shield herself.

"I can't help it!" Lily cried.

And just like that, Vivienne was gone.

Chapter Five

Lily made a mental note. When wanting to rid herself of unwanted company, a sudden burst of snow was a very effective tool. She tucked the box away in the closet, between two folded sweaters, thinking she could open it later. Then her gaze came to rest on the floor where the snow had melted, leaving behind tiny puddles of water. She started to close her eyes to imagine them away, but Jake was persistent with his knocking, and she couldn't keep him waiting. She opened the door, hoping he wouldn't notice the watery mess at her feet.

"Jake! Hi!" she said. "Did you need something?"

Jake leaned and peered around her into the room. "I'd about fallen asleep, but then I thought I heard voices." His gaze went to the floor. "Did you spill something?"

"No," Lily said. She looked up at the ceiling. "Perhaps the roof is leaking."

Jake tilted his head back. "I don't see any water spots."

"I don't know what to tell you," Lily said, spreading her hands. "I'm not a plumber."

Jake grinned. "I take it you're not a roofer, either."

Lily held his gaze for a minute until it became uncomfortable, then she pressed her fingertips to his forehead by way of changing the subject. "You don't look well," she said. "Are you feeling okay?"

"I'm fine," Jake said. "It's the fire. I was getting overheated. But my ankle feels better, just a little residual pain. I think elevating it helped. I'm sure I'll be good to go by morning."

Lily's mind raced for something to say that might convince him to stay. Not only because she believed him to be her assignment, but if Vivienne was right, and he was also her chance for love, she couldn't possibly let him leave before they had a chance to get to know each other. She glanced toward the window. The snow was coming down so thick the trees surrounding the cabin were barely visible. "I know you're eager to leave," she said, "but it's still snowing, and I really think it might be best if you stay and wait for the swelling in your ankle to completely go down before you try to walk home."

Jake shook his head. "I appreciate your concern, but I can't wait that long. I might end up being stuck here 'til spring. I don't want to seem ungrateful, but I think I should leave at first light. So, if you'll just give me my boots, I'll try not to wake you when I go."

"Don't worry about me," Lily said. "I'm usually awake early." She slipped past him, ignoring his request to return his boots. "You must be starving by now. Let's get you something to eat," she said over her shoulder as she led the way to the kitchen.

"No thanks. I'm still not hungry for pie or cookies."

"I think I have something else you might like," Lily said. She closed her eyes briefly to imagine a pot on the woodstove, filled with a concoction that looked like a picture she'd once seen on the front of a magazine. The cover had read "Twenty Recipes To Try On A Cold Winter's Night," which seemed appropriate on a night such as they were having.

"I'm confused," Jake said. "A while ago, all you had was cookies and pie."

"That was then. This is now, and now, I have stew. Have a seat, and I'll dish you up a bowl." Lily gestured to a chair at a small table that sat adjacent to the kitchen, and then she went to the stove and lifted the lid on the pot, allowing a savory aroma to escape into the room.

"Smells good," Jake said as he sat at the table.

And looks good, too, Lily thought as she stirred the contents of the pot. She only hoped she'd gotten the recipe right. Sometimes, going by just a picture, things didn't turn out as planned. But with a little luck, her guest was so hungry he wouldn't notice if it wasn't perfect.

After filling three bowls, she set one on the floor for Sierra and the other two on the table, one for her and one for Jake. Then she sat and watched Jake stare into his bowl. He didn't make a move to try even one bite. "Is something wrong?" she asked.

"I'm still confused," Jake said. "I didn't see you cooking anything earlier. In fact, I got up a while ago to see if I could find something more substantial than pie or cookies."

"And?"

"I found nothing."

Lily shrugged. "I guess you didn't look close enough."

"I guess not," Jake said. He watched intently as his dog devoured her portion of stew.

"Don't worry," Lily said. "I would never give her something that isn't dog-friendly."

The lines on Jake's forehead softened. "I suppose I shouldn't be too concerned. Labradors will eat socks and be happy about it."

Sierra licked her bowl clean, and then stared up at Lily like she was still hungry.

"Should I give her more?" Lily asked.

Jake shook his head. "No. She'll eat as much as you're willing to feed her, even if her stomach is about to pop."

Lily nodded at Jake's bowl. He still hadn't taken a single bite. "Please, eat. Everything in your bowl is not only dog-friendly, but human-friendly, as well."

Jake pushed the contents of his bowl around some, and then he finally took a small bite, after which he looked at her, saying, "You mentioned before that you don't cook meat, so I'm guessing this is a vegetarian dish, and you're a vegetarian."

"I'm not against milking a cow and making butter or gathering eggs from a hen," Lily said. "I just don't understand the killing of an animal to fill one's belly when there are so many other options." She took a small bite of her stew and then pushed her bowl aside.

"You're not going to eat?" Jake asked.

"I think I'll just have a snack." Lily got up and grabbed a couple cookies from one of the plates on the counter. "These are enough for me."

"You've been nibbling cookies and pie since I got here. Pardon my saying so, but I don't think I've ever seen anyone eat so much sugar."

"Sugar happens to be my favorite food."

Jake raised an eyebrow. "Are you serious?"

Lily hesitated before answering. She was serious, but she was also aware that most adult humans were concerned with their sugar intake. Which baffled her. Where did they get their energy? "I also enjoy green bean casserole and stuffing and mashed potatoes," she said at last. Which was completely true, though she did prefer the dessert that usually came after.

"That sounds like a holiday meal, without the turkey or ham," Jake said.

"It's still a meal, is it not?" Lily said as she finished the second cookie. "And as far as nutrition goes, pumpkin pie is rich in beta carotene, which is good for eye sight." She wanted to add *which would better enable you to see the animals you intend to shoot*, but that seemed counterproductive if she expected to get to know him better. "Please eat," she urged again, hoping he would. Continuing a conversation about her eating habits was pointless and could only lead to more frustration.

Jake took a few small bites of his stew and then paused, looking like he might be waiting to see if there were going to be consequences. After a minute, he finally relaxed and emptied his bowl. "That was good," he said. "Was that tofu I detected?"

"It's a secret," Lily said, though she had no idea. She was just glad the meal had been a success. With dinner over, she had Jake stay seated while she cleared the table. He needn't help with the dishes, and it was best he keep off his sore ankle as much as possible. But as she stood at the sink and became aware of him watching her, her nerves got the better of her and she let a bowl slip from her hands and fall to the floor, shattering. She quickly knelt to pick up the broken pieces, then as she stood, she felt something warm trickle down her knee.

Jake jumped to his feet. "You've cut yourself. Sit here, so I can take a look," he said, gesturing to a chair.

Lily did as she was told and waited while Jake grabbed a towel. She wanted to tell him not to bother, that it didn't hurt, but his concern was nice and it had her stomach feeling all fluttery.

As Jake wiped the blood away, his brow pulled tight. "I don't get it. There's nothing here." He wiped again, and looked closely at her knee.

"Maybe it wasn't that bad," Lily offered.

"Bad or not, you were cut, and now there's nothing. Not even a scratch."

"I don't know what to say. I must be a fast healer."

"No one heals that fast," Jake said.

"Obviously, *I* do," Lily said. She stood and went to finish the dishes, and by the time she was done, Jake had moved over to the sofa and looked to be asleep. Wanting to make sure, she watched him for a long minute, and then she left the cabin to go check on Cinder.

"I have something to tell you. It's about the man we saw at the lake," Lily said to Cinder. "I had to bring him back to the cabin with me, and I think he may be my assignment. Which means no wandering around outside and, especially, no going back into the dark wood. You need to stay hidden here in the barn until I let you know it's okay to come out." She took Cinder's antlers in her hands and forced Cinder to look at her. "Do you understand what

I'm telling you?"

Cinder grunted, her big brown eyes holding Lily's gaze. Lily took this to mean the reindeer understood. "Good girl," she told Cinder. Then, letting go of Cinder's antlers, she ran a hand over the reindeer's back, noting how her fur, usually shimmery and soft, needed a good brushing. But with Head Grooming Elf, Gormar, back at the North Pole taking care of the other reindeer, the task of grooming fell to her. Which Lily didn't mind at all. She looked about the stall, found a bucket of supplies, and chose a mix-bristle body brush that in no time had Cinder back to being her lovely reindeer self.

"There," Lily said, dropping the brush back into the bucket. "I dare say, even Gormar would be proud of how beautiful you look right now."

Cinder tucked her head into Lily's chest, and Lily held her there. "I have something else to tell you," she said to Cinder. "It's about the man. I think he might be more than just my assignment. I think he could be someone special that Santa sent here to me."

Cinder nudged Lily's hand. She wasn't interested in Lily's love life.

Lily smiled. She knew what Cinder wanted. Closing her eyes, she imagined a handful of reindeer delicacies—mushrooms, apple pieces, leafy greens—and when Cinder was finished eating, Lily hugged Cinder's neck firmly and ended their visit.

Hurrying back to the cabin, Lily snuck inside and went straight to her room, ready for sleep after such a long and eventful day. When morning arrived, she was happy to see that Mother Nature had delivered another round of snow, and she watched out the window for several minutes as it came down… until she remembered Jake's plan to leave at daybreak.

Rushing to the bedroom door, she flung it open, expecting to see her guest had gone. But, of course, he couldn't leave because she still had his boots. And he was still asleep on the sofa.

With a relieved breath, Lily stole into the kitchen and cut herself a large slice of pumpkin pie. After that, she chose a cookie—chocolate chip—from one of the plates, and while she ate it, she got an idea. One thing she'd learned from prior assignments was that humans enjoyed warm beverages in the morning, and more often than not, coffee seemed to be the beverage of choice. She glanced at Jake. He seemed to be a more-often-than-not kind of human. If she provided him a cup of coffee to start his day, he might not be upset over waking up to another snow-filled sky. He might even decide to stay.

Wishful thinking, perhaps, but it was all she had.

Pondering what ingredients might be needed to brew a pot of coffee, she tried to remember if she'd ever seen any of her sister fairies or elves brew one. She hadn't. Mornings at the North Pole were usually spent sharing stories over mugs of hot chocolate. No one she knew drank coffee. But with it being so similar in color to hot chocolate, how hard could it be to prepare the perfect cup?

The look on Jake's face said it all. He didn't like the coffee. After barely taking a sip, he set the steaming mug down on the coffee table.

"It does not please you," Lily said, not needing his confirmation.

"I don't think I've ever had coffee that strong," Jake said, clearing his throat. "Maybe I'll just have a big glass of water."

"You need more than water," Lily argued. "I'd be happy to make a pot of hot chocolate if you enjoyed the last I made." She turned and went to the kitchen without waiting for his answer. Of course, he enjoyed the hot chocolate. She'd never known anyone who didn't.

While she stirred a pot on the woodstove, she kept an eye on Jake as he flexed his foot back and forth. He didn't seem to be in pain, though being able to flex his foot without pain and walking through deep snow for a considerable distance were two entirely different things. She couldn't see him attempting to walk out of there for at least one more day.

"Your ankle feels better this morning," she said as she set his hot chocolate before him. She'd even added homemade marshmallows as a special treat.

"It does," Jake said. "The swelling has pretty much gone down, too." He grinned, looking at the white puffs floating around the top of his mug. "Are these homemade marshmallows?"

"They are," Lily admitted, happy to keep the conversation from turning to the weather. She watched Jake take one of the soft white puffs into his mouth and couldn't help but stare at his lips that looked like they were meant for kissing. She wondered how it would feel to kiss a mouth like his. Heavenly was her guess. She sighed.

"Something wrong?" Jake asked.

"No, why?"

"You sighed."

Lily's cheeks grew warm. "I was just thinking… of something." She couldn't possibly tell him what that something was.

After taking several sips of his hot chocolate, Jake wrapped his hands around the warm mug and he looked to the window, where the morning light revealed a haze of white flakes. "It's snowing again," he said, a frown replacing his smile.

Lily reluctantly followed his gaze. "Yes. Are you still planning on leaving?"

Jake watched the snow come down for a minute as he enjoyed the last of his hot chocolate. Finally, he said, "As much as I'd like to think I could walk out of here, even with a sprained ankle, I'm afraid I might end up needing to be rescued again." He paused. "I noticed a barn at the back of the cabin. I don't suppose there are any snowshoes or anything else in there I might use."

Lily shook her head. "No. Nothing. It's just an old, empty barn." She immediately felt awful for the deception. She wasn't skilled at it, and nothing good ever came from telling lies. Not even tiny ones. Once a lie began, it usually led to another, and then another, until a person had told so many, they needed a journal to keep them all straight. Though, sometimes an untruth was necessary.

"I'm sorry to be here intruding on your solitude," Jake said. "I know what it's like to need time alone."

"I don't mind your company," Lily said. "You seem harmless."

Jake laughed lightly. "Some might argue with you on that point." He looked to the fireplace. "I may not be able to get myself back home, but I think I can at least go out and see if I can find more firewood. And who knows? Maybe while I'm out there, I'll come across my horse. So, if you don't mind bringing me my boots…."

"I'll get them," Lily said, knowing it would do no good to try and prevent his leaving. If she'd only noticed they were getting low on firewood, she could have replenished it while he was sleeping. Now, all she could hope for was that his horse was long gone.

Chapter Six

Jake was relieved to get his boots back. So, maybe he didn't need to be concerned about the young woman trying to keep him there against his will. She might walk a little on the odd side, but she probably didn't pose any kind of threat to him. All he had to worry about now was the snow.

Once outside, he looked about at his surroundings. There wasn't a lot to see except for a few small animal tracks. His gaze went to the tree line that was a good fifty yards out. With the additional snow they'd gotten during the night, it would be a hike just reaching the tall firs. But that was little deterrent. He needed to try and make it back to the lake to see if he could find his horse.

Beginning his trek, he put his head down, determined. The frosty air curled along the back of his neck, sending a chill through him, but that, too, was no deterrent. He was used to Idaho winters, and didn't mind the cold.

By the time he reached the trees, his ankle was throbbing, and by the time he stood at the shore of the lake, he was done, ready to go back to the cabin. As much as he wanted to get back home, he was in no shape for a long walk in the snow. It looked like he was going to be a guest at the young woman's cabin for at least another day. Two, at the most. Then, if he had to, he'd crawl back home.

Feeling miserable, he looked about for any sign that his horse might still be in the vicinity. He saw more small animal tracks, but that was about it. He'd kept his eye out for firewood along the way, but it was as he'd expected, everything was too damp for burning. Taking one last look along the lake's shoreline, he spotted tracks that ran in a tidy single-file pattern. They looked to be canine, though not dog. They belonged to a wolf. Probably the same one he'd seen before.

He did a quick scan of the surrounding area, and didn't see any eyes staring back at him. That didn't make him feel any better. Though wolves weren't typically a danger to humans, he saw no reason to hang around and find out if this particular wolf was going to be a problem.

Lily stood at the door long after Jake made his way into the forest, and she continued watching for several minutes after he disappeared, hoping he'd change his mind and come back. When he didn't, she turned from the door and, once again, came face-to-face with Vivienne.

"What are we waiting for?" Vivienne asked.

Lily put a hand to her chest. "Why do you do that? Why can't you announce yourself before barging in on a fairy?"

Vivienne frowned. "That *is* how I announce myself. Would you rather I send you a notice by mail?"

Pushing the door shut, Lily asked, "Why are you here? Don't you have somewhere else to be? Someone else to torture?"

"I'll ignore that," Vivienne said. "And as far as me having somewhere else to be, do you mean my Christmas assignment? The one involving the man in a coma who has recently awakened? *Pfft*," she said, waving a hand. "Can you say lost cause?"

Lily drew back. "I would never say that. *Lost cause* is not in a fairy's vocabulary. I'm sure Santa wouldn't have sent you on that assignment if there were no chance for a happy ending."

"Santa doesn't know what I know," Vivienne said. "Coma man may be awake, but he's still in a deep sleep where his fiancée is concerned. She's gone and married someone else. Ergo, lost cause."

"No. It just means it will be a challenge to provide your assignment a bit of Christmas cheer. That's your job, is it not? You can't possibly be thinking of giving up so easily."

"Hmm," Vivienne said. "I suppose you're right." She put a finger to her chin. "There is this nurse who's been caring for my assignment for the past year, and she does seem the devoted type. Perhaps I could set things in motion for the two of them to get together."

"That's the right attitude," Lily said, happy she was able to help Vivienne see there was always another way to a successful outcome.

"We'll see," Vivienne said, giving Lily a sidelong glance. "But never mind that… have you opened the gift I gave you?"

"I have not. I've had other things on my mind, and I've decided to wait and open it Christmas morning."

"No, no, *no!*" Vivienne said, shaking her head. "That will be too late. You need to open it now!"

"Why?"

"Didn't we already talk about this? I'm sure we did. But I'm ever so happy to go over it again with you. Here's the deal… I'm looking to be named Head Christmas Fairy, and you want to fall in love. It's a win for you, and it's a win for *moi*. Any more questions?"

Plenty, Lily thought, but she didn't have time to ask them. Jake could return at any moment. "I still don't know why it can't wait," she grumbled. "But if opening your gift will get you to leave me in peace, then that's what I'll do." She rushed to retrieve Vivienne's gift from the bedroom closet, and when she returned, she set the tiny box on the table and stared at it.

"What are you doing?" Vivienne asked.

"The wrapping is so pretty, it seems a shame not to enjoy it for a minute," Lily said. She waited another few seconds before she finally picked up the box and removed the wrapping. Then she pinched her eyes shut while she removed the lid. When nothing happened, she opened her eyes and was surprised to see a sprig of fresh greenery. She looked at Vivienne. "Mistletoe?"

"Well, of course, mistletoe. To help things along between you and the hunter. As you know, mistletoe is the gold standard for a budding relationship to move beyond the friendship phase. And Christmas will be here before you can say *dashing through the snow*, so you don't want to dally. I suggest you hang the twig ASAP!"

Lily's brow pulled tight. "I already told you, if love is meant to be, it will happen. Falling in love should be organic, not something that happens because of any outside influence."

"Hmph," Vivienne scoffed. "You don't seem to mind using mistletoe's influence when you're on assignment and trying to kindle a romance between two humans."

"That's different."

"How?"

"Humans sometimes need a nudge in the right direction."

"Exactly," Vivienne agreed. "Like I said, mistletoe is the gold standard."

Lily narrowed her eyes. "Why are you being so pushy?" She examined the mistletoe, skeptical of Vivienne's feigned helpfulness. "I'm sure you know there's a rule against fairies using magic for personal gain."

"What magic? This mistletoe is as organic as it gets. I picked it myself from the North Pole garden. Trust me. With this twig and a smidgen of luck, you'll be hearing wedding bells before the new year."

Lily caught her lip in her teeth, suddenly nervous about the whole becoming-a-bride thing. She didn't even know Jake's favorite color, or whether or not he enjoyed watching old movies, or… or anything. It was just too soon to be thinking about wedding bells. "The new year is only a short time away," she told Vivienne. "It wouldn't give me much time to plan a wedding, or even say goodbye to everyone at the North Pole."

"Weddings are over-rated," Vivienne remarked. "And I wouldn't worry about saying goodbye. You won't remember your pals at the North Pole once you join the human world."

Lily inhaled sharply. "Why would you say such a thing? Why wouldn't I remember?"

"Oh, dear," Vivienne said, "I thought you knew."

Lily tossed up her hands. "Please stop doing that!"

"Doing what?"

"Telling me things!"

"You'd rather be kept in the dark?"

"No, but you seem to get such great satisfaction from giving me bad news."

"I never said it was *bad* news. But if you'd rather not know," Vivienne said, shrugging.

Lily tipped her head back, groaning. "If it's important, just tell me." She held her breath, waiting.

"It's not a secret," Vivienne continued. "And, frankly, I'm surprised no one else has mentioned it. But, then, maybe they were all afraid. You seem to be so touchy these days."

"*Please!* Just get on with it!"

Vivienne raised an eyebrow. "Now, who's being pushy? But since you insist… as I was saying, once you become human, things change. You will no longer have any memory of your time at the North Pole. Nor will you believe in fairies or elves or even Santa Claus. Most adult humans don't. They consider everything that goes on at the North Pole to be nothing more than a fairy tale. If you ask them, they're the ones who create Christmas magic for their children—with the help of department stores, of course. Really, we fairies get no credit at all."

Lily was mouth-open aghast. "That can't be! I would never stop believing in Santa or the magic of Christmas." She put a hand to her chest, where her heart throbbed with unfamiliar pain. She looked at Vivienne, whose lips were turned up like she was having a moment of great pleasure. "You said it wasn't bad news."

"Well," Vivienne said, still smiling, "I suppose it depends on whose perspective it is. Poor thing. Have you a sudden case of heartburn?"

"Yes, my heart does hurt so terribly," Lily said, nodding. "It is most unpleasant."

"Not to worry," Vivienne said, waving off Lily's distress. "You'll survive. And if you're determined to become human, heartache is something you might want to get used to. It seems to be a common theme among them. Of course, if you're having second thoughts, you could return to the North Pole and become Enar's *princess*. That's as sure a bet as I'm standing here in front of you."

Lily frowned. "Enar and I are friends. That's all."

"Well, then, by all means, go for it with the hunter. But do yourself a favor and hang the twig. At the very least, it might get you your first kiss. As far as I've heard, the only thing your lips have ever come into contact with are all those baked goods you seem to be so fond of."

Lily lifted her chin. "There's nothing wrong with being chaste."

Vivienne squeezed Lily's shoulder. "You keep telling yourself that, my dear. Just don't forget about the Unable to Grant Stamp." And with a flip of her hand, she was gone.

Still holding her hand to her chest, Lily took a long breath, then she turned her focus once again to the mistletoe, lying all fresh and green in the tiny box. She took the mistletoe into her hand and put it to her nose. It had no scent. Certainly none that would suggest a magical quality. Still, where Vivienne was concerned, a fairy could never be too careful. Lily tucked the sprig back in the box and returned the box to the closet. Which is where it would stay. She was nowhere near ready to nudge things along with Jake. Not yet, anyway.

Happy to be rid of Vivienne, she went to the kitchen and ate a cookie. Then another, and as the minutes passed and Jake still hadn't returned, she once more scolded herself for allowing him to go in search of firewood when she could have so easily replenished the woodpile herself.

After eating two more cookies and waiting another fifteen minutes, she became worried. What if Jake had fallen again and needed her help? Or what if he'd wandered too far in search of wood and couldn't find his way back to the cabin?

Worse yet, what if he'd gone to the barn and found Cinder!

Chapter Seven

Going back without so much as a few sticks of firewood for his effort was disappointing, but as Jake emerged from the forest, a block of blue color—a tarp—at the back corner of the cabin caught his eye. He made his way over and pulled it aside, where he found a large stack of weathered wood.

But why hadn't Lily mentioned it?

He ran a hand over his jaw, wondering what else she hadn't mentioned. He turned and faced the barn. Lily had told him it was empty, but he knew better. Nobody built a barn and left it empty.

He made his way over to the barn door and was about to open it when he heard a voice calling to him. Turning, he was surprised to see Lily rushing toward him wearing big clunky boots and a puffy coat that nearly swallowed her in its bulkiness. She looked downright comical. "Nice coat. Purple suits you," he said when she reached him, adding, "I'm glad to see you've finally dressed for the weather."

"I was hoping to avoid another lecture. And the coat is lavender, not purple," Lily said. She held out her hands. "Where have you been?"

"I went back to the lake to see if I could find my horse.

Unfortunately, he was nowhere around. I didn't find any wood, either. Then, when I came back here, I saw that tarp over there." Jake nodded at the exposed stack of wood. "Why didn't you tell me you already had a good supply out here?"

Lily looked. "How was I to know there might be firewood under a sheet of blue plastic?" She waded through the snow a few steps closer to him. "I was worried about you."

Jake smiled at her concern. "Worried? That I might not come back?"

"No… maybe," Lily said. "But I was also concerned about you being out in the snow with your injured ankle."

"I'm a little sore, but I'll live. And you didn't really think I'd leave here without my dog, did you?" Sierra had joined them, and she sat at Jake's side while he scratched the top of her head.

"No, I suppose not," Lily said. She gave Jake a small smile. "You must be hungry. I've got a big pot of vegetable chowder simmering on the stove if you'd like to come in and eat." A few snowflakes fell from the sky and landed on her cheek. She looked up, her eyes lighting. "Looks like we're in for more snow."

"Looks like it," Jake agreed, though none too happily. "You go ahead. I'll grab a couple pieces of wood and be right in."

"Please don't be long," Lily said softly as she turned to go back to the cabin.

Jake watched Lily make her way through the snow for a minute, then he glanced over his shoulder at the barn. As much as he wanted to have a look inside, it could wait. He was famished, and whatever was in the barn wasn't going anywhere.

Thank goodness, Lily thought when Jake came through the door after her. If she hadn't caught him before he went into the barn and found Cinder, she could only imagine the conversation they might be having right now. As it was, he wasn't happy about going in search of firewood when there'd been a ready supply at the back of the cabin. But maybe he'd forget all about that when his belly was full of good food. She'd imagined another recipe from the same magazine as before, and now all she had to do was serve it up. She raised the lid from the pot and was happy to find a bubbling concoction looking just as it had in its picture.

As she stirred the contents of the pot, Jake came up beside her and stood so close it gave her a strange sensation in the pit of her stomach that, in turn, caused her wings to vibrate. Afraid she might lose control, she commanded herself to think about something that would calm them. An image of Vivienne came to mind, and that was all it took.

"I think it's ready," she told Jake, needing to put some distance between them.

Jake settled in his usual chair, and Lily set a bowl before him. Then she quickly filled a bowl for Sierra and placed it on the floor. Half of it was gone in an instant. "Goodness, your dog was really hungry," she said to Jake.

"She's a Lab. She's always hungry," Jake said.

Lily looked about the table. One more item was all they needed. She quickly imagined a small loaf of bread warmed to perfection in the oven. And while she was at it, she imagined a special spread made with butter and honey, because no meal would be complete without *some* sugar. "Excuse me while I get the bread," she said, going back to the kitchen.

Jake's eyebrows rose when she returned and set the small loaf, already sliced, on the table. "I don't know how you're preparing all this food," he said, "but I guess I should just be grateful." He glanced down at Sierra, who was still licking her bowl. "You're spoiling my dog. She'll expect homemade meals from here on out."

Lily watched as Jake rubbed the top of Sierra's head. She'd never had a dog; there were none at the North Pole. But from what she'd witnessed among humans, she knew the bond between dog and master could be as strong as any shared between parent and child. "She seems devoted to you. Have you had her long?" she asked Jake.

"Eight years," Jake said. "I got her as a pup, and she's been a good companion. It'll be hard when it comes time to say goodbye. It doesn't seem fair that they can't live as long as we do."

"How long?"

"Twelve or thirteen years. Longer, if she doesn't get sick or hurt."

Lily held back a gasp. "Twelve years? But that's only a minute."

"Seems like it," Jake said. "That's why I try to make each day I have with her count. I had another dog that I lost not long ago. Didn't realize the time would pass so quickly, so I tend to spoil this one." He went quiet and turned his focus to his meal, taking a few hearty bites.

Lily ran a hand over Sierra's head, the same as she'd seen Jake do. She already felt affection for the animal, much the same as she felt for Cinder. "I'm sorry you were unable to find your horse," she said to Jake, meaning it. She knew he must be equally fond of all his animals.

Jake swallowed a mouthful of chowder. "I'm sure Cannon is back home by now. Probably even found his way into the barn and got himself fed."

"Animals can be resourceful when need be," Lily commented. She was pleased to see Jake enjoying his meal. "Have some bread, too," she urged, pushing the plate over in front of him. She'd already piled a few slices on her own plate and had slathered each with the honey butter until it was thick from side to side.

Jake took a couple slices of bread for himself, but he used none of the butter. He broke a piece off one slice and tucked it into his mouth with another spoonful of chowder.

"The butter is most delightful. You should try it," Lily said.

Jake relented and spread a small amount on a piece of bread. Then he took a bite and nodded. "It's good," he said, "but I prefer my bread plain."

The conversation ended at that. They finished eating, and then Jake went to the sofa to elevate his leg. Sierra followed and was soon napping beside him with her eyes pinched shut. When Lily finally joined them, Jake was perusing a book he'd picked from the bookshelf that had been stocked with some of her favorite reading material. Santa had kindly made sure both she and Cinder had everything they might need during their stay at the cabin.

The book Jake held had been written in the 1800s by the poet William Cullen Bryant, and though it was one of Lily's favorite books of poetry, she thought it a curious choice for a man like Jake. She would have guessed him to be more of an adventurous sort. "Do you enjoy poetry?" she had to ask.

"Not particularly," Jake said. "This book looked so old, I was more curious than anything. I probably shouldn't even be touching it." He handed it to Lily, saying, "I noticed an inscription in the front. Did the book belong to your grandmother... or maybe your great-grandmother?"

"Something like that," Lily said. She remembered poet Bryant fondly and knew the inscription by heart. *"Dearest Liliana, May you treasure this book the way I have always treasured our friendship. Love, William."*

Mr. Bryant had been her very first assignment as a Christmas fairy, and it was a simple task of lending an ear so he could vent about life's injustices. Being a young fairy, she hadn't thought this to be a very good use of a Christmas fairy's talents, but after spending time with Mr. Bryant, she knew better. All assignments given by Santa were important. And if she hadn't taken her time with the young poet, he might have given up on his writing and gone on to do something else less valuable. That in itself would have been an injustice.

"Is there a story behind the inscription?" Jake asked.

"There is, but I doubt it would be of interest to you," Lily said.

"Try me."

"Okay," Lily said. She took a breath, thinking of how she could modify the story so it wouldn't be such a stretch of the truth. Finally, she began. "Poet Bryant was a young man when he and my grandmother met. They quickly became good friends and spent a lot of time together talking about life and politics and such. Then one snowy Christmas Eve, the young poet invited my grandmother over for a splendid dinner of roast goose with all the trimmings."

She smiled a small smile. "Of course, my grandmother didn't sample the goose, but there were plenty of other treats to be had, and it was a most delightful meal."

"I take it you come from a long line of non-meat eaters," Jake commented.

"Yes," Lily said. "But back to the inscription… this book," she continued, pressing the book gently to her chest, "was Mr. Bryant's first signed copy, and upon presenting it to my grandmother, he told her he hoped she would keep it with her always as a reminder of their friendship."

Jake arched an eyebrow. "Your grandmother must have been very special to him if he gave her his first signed copy."

Lily turned and placed the book back on the shelf. "As I said, my grandmother and Mr. Bryant were friends. Nothing more."

"But why do I get the feeling you've left out a big piece of the story?"

Lily's face warmed. She preferred not to delve any deeper into a subject that would only require more untruths. As it was, her conscience already suffered from the deception. "If there be more to the story, it would be for my grandmother to tell, and unfortunately, she's not here." She skimmed her fingers lightly over the spines of the books on the shelf. "I'm sorry there's nothing here for you to enjoy."

"No need to apologize. I'm a rancher. Ranchers don't tend to have much time for reading."

Lily met his gaze, her curiosity piqued. "A rancher? Like in the Old West?"

"Not quite. I have what you'd call a working ranch, and folks come and pay for the privilege of helping me drive my cattle from one pasture to another."

"That sounds like it could be fun," Lily said.

"It can be," Jake agreed. "Problem is city folk arrive thinking they'll have a swell time riding horses and taking nature walks, with plenty of martini breaks. Then, when they find out cattle driving is real physical labor, it hits them hard. Day one goes fine. Everyone is excited to be doing something new and different. But by day three, some don't even show up for breakfast. I find them curled up on their bunks in the fetal position." He laughed. "I suspect they're suffering from culture shock. Though I'll admit, over the years, I've had a few surprises. Some of the folks enjoy the experience so much that by the end of their stay, they vow that once they're home, they'll get their own plot of land, along with a few head of cattle to chase."

"Challenge can be good for the spirit," Lily said.

"I guess that depends on whose perspective it is. If you ask me, cattle would be happy if they could skip being chased and just spend their entire lives hanging out in a pasture with a trough of cold water and a big block of salt."

"What about you?" Lily asked. "What makes *you* happy? Do you have family living nearby that you can spend time with during the holidays?"

Jake shook his head. "My parents moved to Florida when their bones began to creak with age, so no. But that doesn't mean I'm not happy. My animals keep me so busy I don't have much time to think about being *un*happy."

"So, other than your animals, you're alone?"

"I don't see it that way. And anyway, what's wrong with being alone? You came here to be alone, didn't you?"

"Yes, but it's just until Christmas. Then, I go back… home."

"You don't sound so sure," Jake said. "I don't mean to pry into your business, but you don't strike me as someone who would voluntarily forgo the lights and gift buying and everything else that makes people go crazy this time of year. I know you said you wanted to do something different, but why come here?"

Lily fought to keep her wings still. It was far too soon to tell Jake she was a Christmas fairy and that she was here on assignment from the big boss at the North Pole. That truth would have to come later. Clasping her hands together, she forced herself to think about other things, like all the twinkling lights she could be looking at right now if she were in New York City. Or perhaps she'd be attending a Christmas party, there were so many, with carolers and gift exchanges, and oh, how she loved shopping for gifts. Plus, there would be ice-skating and tree decorating and—.

"Lily? Did you hear me?"

A rush of heat filled Lily's cheeks as she realized she'd gotten so lost in thought she hadn't heard Jake talking to her. "I must apologize. I was just thinking about Christmas in the city. I do enjoy it. But I promise you, I'm quite happy spending Christmas here in this cabin. I like the peacefulness and beauty of it." She took a small breath. "Back to you. Winter can be long when you have no one to talk to, and with your parents so far away, I hope you at least have friends to keep you company during the holidays."

"I have friends," Jake said. "But I've gotten pretty good at resisting their invitations, and I suppose one day they'll just stop asking." He shrugged. "I like being alone."

"I see," Lily said. Though she didn't see at all.

"If my mom had her way," Jake continued, "I'd be running a bed-and-breakfast for folks who might be looking for a special Christmas getaway. A bed-and-breakfast was something she'd always wanted to do. She even went so far as to have my dad build a guest cabin on our property. But then, before she could put it to use, she and my dad moved to Florida, and that was the end of that idea. So there's a cabin, but the only folks who use it are the ones who come to chase my cattle. Other than that, it stays empty. Which is too bad because it's a real nice place for a winter retreat."

"*You* could run the bed-and-breakfast," Lily suggested.

"I could. It would take a lot of effort, but I suppose I could get some of the local kids to help out. I give them work when I need the occasional extra hand, and I'm sure they wouldn't mind earning some additional money for Christmas."

"And what would you do to make your bed-and-breakfast special for the holidays?"

"I haven't given it much thought, but I'd probably do the usual… serve fattening food, have a tree lighting, maybe even offer sleigh rides. My parents had an old sleigh they bought when

I was young, and they left it in the barn when they moved away. I still have it. All it needs is a fresh coat of paint and a horse to pull it. My old quarter horse is a bit long in the tooth to be dragging a sleigh around, but I have a couple younger horses that might do the job. Or maybe I'd go and get myself a couple reindeer."

"Yes, and then after having them pull your sleigh, you could roast them over an open fire," Lily said, her tone sharp. She'd tried to forget about him being a reindeer hunter, but the image of him aiming his rifle at the young reindeer in the forest was still fresh in her mind, and every time she thought about it, she was angry all over again.

Jake pressed his lips together. "You didn't believe me when I told you I wasn't going to shoot that reindeer."

"I wanted to," Lily said. "But I know what I saw."

"You know what you *think* you saw," Jake said, his temper flaring. "Things aren't always as they seem." He gave her an assessing look. "Let me guess, you belong to PETA, and you donate a good chunk of every paycheck to Save the Whales. You probably even spend all your spare time helping out at your local animal shelter."

Helping out at an animal shelter? What a great thing to do! Lily tucked that idea away for later use.

"Look," Jake continued, "I would no more shoot a reindeer than I would my own dog. In fact, I wasn't going to shoot anything." He gave a shallow sigh. "It was a wolf. And all I'd intended to do was scare him off so he wouldn't go after the reindeer."

Lily gave him a doubtful look. "I saw no wolf."

"Trust me. It was there."

"What did this wolf look like?"

"Like a wolf. Gray fur, bushy tail. He was hiding in the brush not far from where the reindeer stood."

"Gray fur and a bushy tail? That sounds more like a squirrel to me."

"I think I know a wolf when I see one," Jake said.

Lily was quiet for a few moments, then relented, saying,

"Perhaps." Because he probably did.

Jake grinned. "Don't tell me you're actually agreeing with me. We might become friends yet."

Something stirred inside Lily. It was the way Jake was smiling at her. It made her uncomfortable. So uncomfortable her wings vibrated. Then the vibrating turned into an all-out flutter, and before she could stop it, a flurry of delicate snowflakes appeared and swirled to the floor around them.

"What the—!" Jake jumped to his feet and spun around, his eyes searching. But the flurry had already ended. He looked at Lily. "Did you see that?"

Lily did her best to remain calm, to keep her wings from releasing more snow. "See what?"

"The snow! It just snowed in here!"

Lily's eyes went wide. "I don't think so. That would be impossible."

"I don't care how impossible it would be. I saw snow!" Jake walked in a circle, his eyes focused on the ceiling.

Lily kept her wings contained. "It's been a long day. Maybe you're tired and need to lie down."

"It hasn't been *that* long," Jake said. He swiped a hand over his head, and it came away damp. "My hair is wet. So is yours. How do you explain that?"

"We were outside."

Jake gave her a steady gaze. "That was a while ago."

This was not going well, Lily thought. She had no plausible explanation for the snow inside the cabin, or their hair being wet. "Maybe you have a fever. Do you feel sick?" She reached for his forehead, but he brushed her hand away.

"Stop. I'm not tired, and I'm not sick. Are you seriously telling me you didn't see it snowing in here?"

"It's an old roof. It probably needs repairing."

"Never mind the roof! It was *snowing* in here!"

"Maybe it's your eyesight," Lily offered.

Jake groaned. "It's not my eyesight. I have perfect vision." His gaze went to the floor. "There!" he said, pointing. "I dare you to tell me you don't see water on the floor!"

Lily didn't have to look. She knew he was pointing at the puddles from the melted snow. Her wings tingled, but she managed to keep them still. "I don't know what you want me to say. Your boots were wet when you came inside," she said, trying to sound reasonable. But no matter how reasonable she sounded, she knew he would continue pressing her until she lost control of her wings again. She had to do something to prevent that from happening, something that would give her time to think. With a sweep of her hand, she released enough fairy dust to cover him from head to toe, and in an instant, he froze.

"Oh, my, this can't be good," Vivienne said, appearing beside Lily. "Don't tell me you and the human have already had your first spat."

"He was asking questions," Lily said. "Why does he have to ask so many questions?"

"He's human. It's what they do." Vivienne tipped her head back to look at the ceiling. "I see you haven't hung the mistletoe."

"Forget the mistletoe! I've been busy!" Lily said, her voice rising. She shot Jake a despairing glance. "What do I do with him now that he's frozen?"

Vivienne grinned. "What would you *like* to do?"

"Make him forget what he's seen."

"Ah, had a little snow mishap, did you?"

Lily nodded, hating admitting anything to Vivienne.

"The solution is simple," Vivienne said. "Go back to the moment before things went awry and change course."

"Change course?"

"Yes. Go back. Rewind. *Faire plus.*"

"I can do that?"

Vivienne gave a quiet cackle. "Oh, my dear, sometimes I forget how young you are and that you still have so much to learn about being a Christmas fairy. It's *your* fairy dust. You can do whatever you want while the human is under its spell. That's what fairy dust is for, to get oneself out of sticky situations." She directed her gaze at Jake and sighed. "He really is quite a treat for the eyes, isn't he? Too bad he's a hunter."

Lily looked at Jake, all frozen and pointing at the floor with his mouth agape. At the moment, he didn't look to be that much of a treat.

"Anyhoo," Vivienne continued, "I mustn't dally. Coma man is about to ask that nurse I was telling you about if she'd like to help him decorate for Christmas, and I want to be there to make sure it includes a sprig of mistletoe. Speaking of…" She looked up at the ceiling again, and then back to Lily. "Good luck with the hunter." And with a flip of her hand, she was gone.

Chapter Eight

Lily was ready to rewind. She'd wiped the floor dry, and she'd rubbed a towel over Jake's head until his hair was dry. All she needed to do now was take herself and Jake back to the moment before she lost control of her wings. Standing before him, she waved a hand to release him from his frozen state, and then she waited a moment before restarting the conversation they'd been having about the wolf. As soon as Jake looked up from the floor, she said, "I'm sorry if it was because of me you fell into the lake. I couldn't help but shout when I thought you were going to harm that poor reindeer."

"It wasn't your shouting that caused me to fall. I just slipped," Jake said. His focus went to his arms. He held them out in front of himself. They were sparkling with fairy dust. "Where did all this glitter come from?" he asked. Then his gaze went back to the floor, where there was even more sparkle than what he had on his arms.

Lily joined him in looking at the floor. What a mess she'd made. A lovely *sparkly* mess, but still a mess. "Goodness," she said, "I don't know, but it sure is pretty, isn't it?" She shrugged. "It's not important. Let's talk about the wolf. I'm so glad he didn't get the reindeer."

"Yeah, well, you can't blame a wolf for wanting to eat. It's the way of the wild. Reindeer are prey. Wolves are predators. Wolves eat prey. It's that simple."

"If that's how you feel, why would you care if the wolf was going after the reindeer?"

"I didn't want him going after *that* reindeer."

Lily smiled. "You sound like you might have a special interest in *that* reindeer."

"You could say he and I share a history."

Interesting, Lily thought. "Tell me more," she said, eager to hear how Jake came to have a reindeer under his protective custody. She had a feeling it was going to be a good story. She went to the sofa and curled up on one of the cushions, and Jake followed, sitting beside her. He stretched out his legs and made himself comfortable. It was as if he'd completely forgotten about his arms being covered in glitter, which didn't bother Lily at all. The fewer untruths she was forced to tell, the better.

"It's not that exciting," Jake warned. "Are you sure you want to hear it?"

"I shared my story about the book, now it's your turn," Lily said.

Jake laughed. "Fair enough. I'll try to keep it short." He took a moment to gather his thoughts, and then he began, saying, "It was one of those ink-black nights when Mother Nature let all hell break loose in my part of the world. Hail struck the ground with chunks of ice the size of golf balls, and the wind tossed everything that wasn't nailed down into the next county. A lot of folks lost power, and some even had trees come down on their homes. I had one come down myself, over the fence at the back of my property. It wasn't much of a loss, it was an old fence, but it left an escape route for my cattle, and I had to spend half the night rounding them up." He paused. "Bored yet?"

"Not at all," Lily said truthfully.

Jake continued. "By the time I had every cow accounted for, I was dead tired and ready for sleep. But before heading back to the house, I had one last look around, and I saw something moving on the ground that turned out to be a reindeer calf covered in hail. Musta only been a few days old, he was so small. If I hadn't seen him move, I would've stepped on him."

"Poor thing," Lily said. "He's lucky you found him. You didn't see his mama anywhere around?"

Jake shook his head. "She might've run off when she saw me coming to fix the fence and would've come back. Or maybe she got hurt. There was no way to know. And I couldn't just leave the little guy, shivering on the ground, waiting for her to return. So I wrapped him in a towel, put him in the front seat of my truck, and took him home with me. Fast-forward several months, and the little fella was grown and grazing right alongside my cattle like he was part of the herd."

"Maybe he thinks he's a cow," Lily offered.

"Maybe," Jake said. "In any case, being the one who took him in, I've always felt responsible for his well-being. And that's why I was in the forest. I'd heard reports of a wolf hanging around closer in than what was usual, maybe looking for easy prey, and it started me thinking I should go out and see if Frost had gotten himself into trouble." He smiled. "'Course, when I found him, he looked good. Happy. I wasn't even intending on bringing him back home with me. But then I saw the wolf hiding in the brush, looking like he might be considering having himself a meal of reindeer meat." He gave Lily a look. "I was only going to scare the wolf. I didn't want to see Frost get hurt."

Lily smiled, happy she'd been wrong about Jake. He had a gentle kindness about him that was beginning to shine through, and she wondered what unhappy event had occurred in his life to turn him against Christmas. Discovering that would be the key to successfully completing her assignment. "Frost seems an appropriate name for your reindeer," she said. "He's quite a handsome animal."

"I think so," Jake agreed. He looked to the window. "I sure hope he's okay out there."

Lily hoped so, too. Should Jake's reindeer come to any harm, she would never forgive herself for interfering with his effort to protect him. "I'm sorry I scared Frost away," she said. "And I'm sorry you fell and hurt yourself so that you can't even go out looking for him. I should go see if I can find him. It's the least I can do after chasing him off."

"You did nothing wrong," Jake said, quick to reassure her, "and it's not a good idea for you to be out there by yourself with the possibility of a hungry wolf lurking around. Soon enough, I'll be able to get out and have another look."

Soon enough? What did that mean? Jake's lack of urgency had Lily hoping he intended to stick around awhile. At least until he found Frost. Though she couldn't let herself think about what might happen between her and Jake when he was so worried about his reindeer. And all this talk of a wolf lurking about had her once again concerned for Cinder. First chance she got, she needed to make sure her own reindeer was still safe.

Jake got up from the sofa to add a piece of wood to the fire, though it wasn't really needed, and Lily suspected he was just restless and wanted something to do. Having a lot of animals to care for, he probably wasn't used to sitting around, not doing much. She hoped his boredom wouldn't push him into leaving before they had a chance to get to know each other better or before she could finish her assignment. She thought for a minute about what she might do to prevent that from happening.

"I have an idea," she said to Jake. "Do you like to play games?"

"Depends on the game," Jake said. "I hope you're not planning on bringing out Monopoly. I've played that game enough to last me a lifetime."

"Not Monopoly," Lily said. "Something much more fun. It's called Truth or Dare."

Jake gave her a look. "Isn't that usually played by couples, or a group of people who already know each other and want to see who they can get to embarrass themselves?"

Lily shrugged. "Perhaps if you and I play, it will help us get to know each other better."

Jake smiled thinly. "I have a better idea. How about you just ask me what whatever it is you want to know. That way, we can skip any embarrassing dares."

"Okay," Lily relented, her nose wrinkling. "But do you mind if I ask *two* questions?"

"Including the one you just asked, that would make three, but go ahead."

Lily had hoped for more, but she would make the most of this opportunity. If she asked the right questions, it might lead to an answer that would give her a hint as to why he didn't "do" Christmas. Could be any number of reasons, from a bad break-up to just not being in the mood to celebrate due to his parents living so far away. Though she suspected it wouldn't be something that simple.

Studying Jake's face, she did a bit of pondering. After several moments, she had her first question. "Do you ever get lonely?" she asked.

Jake hesitated briefly, and then nodded. "I do. But it never lasts. I'm always able to find something to keep myself busy until the loneliness passes."

"But doesn't it come back?"

"Sometimes."

"Then what?"

"Then I call a friend, and we go have a beer."

"But what if none of your friends want to go have a beer?"

"Then, I guess I'm out of luck."

"And then what?"

Jake held up a hand. "By my calculation, you've exceeded your question limit. Now, I have a question for you. Why did you want to spend Christmas here in the forest all by yourself?"

"I already told you why. I wanted a change."

"From what?"

Lily hadn't an answer. She hadn't expected the question. She was stuck, and she could see by the look on Jake's face that he knew she was stuck.

"Tell you what," Jake said, "I'll ask you something easier. Where are you from?"

Lily pressed her lips together. That was a much easier question. Though she couldn't possibly tell him *exactly* where she was from—not that he'd believe her, anyway. "North," she answered, thinking it sufficient.

Jake raised an eyebrow. "North covers a lot of territory. Care to be more specific?"

"Far north," Lily answered.

"Canada?" Jake asked.

Lily grinned. "I'm sorry, but I believe you've exceeded your question limit."

The question-and-answer session hadn't gone the way Lily had hoped. Nor had it revealed much. She sat in her room, disappointed in herself for not thinking things through and asking the right questions. But if Jake gave her another opportunity, she would do better. She lay on the bed thinking of what she might ask the next time they played question-and-answer until, finally, she remembered she needed to go check on Cinder.

Peering into the other room, she saw Jake lying still on the sofa. He appeared to be asleep, so she quietly made her way to the door, waving to Sierra as she did so, and they both snuck out of the cabin. The winter air was so refreshing, Lily had to pause so she could soak up the glow of the moon that hung like a big blue ornament in the night sky. But only for a moment. Then it was on to the barn.

"Hello, fair reindeer," Lily said as she approached Cinder's stall. She ran a hand over Cinder's fur to see if Cinder was in need of another brushing. Finding she wasn't, Lily turned over an empty bucket to sit on, wanting just to be near her reindeer companion for a while. Sierra sat beside Lily, leaning her head against Lily's legs and looking up at her like she wouldn't mind a good ear scratch. Lily happily obliged, enjoying her time with Sierra. Though she'd never had a dog of her own, she had many fond memories of assignments that involved the helping of animals, and Jake's comment about working at an animal shelter was definitely something to keep in mind should she one day live in the human world.

After giving Sierra's ears a good scratch, Lily sat quietly, and as the minutes passed, her eyes grew heavy, and it wasn't long before she was dreaming of fairy life and Christmas joy and all things wonderful. When she finally opened her eyes, it seemed only a few moments had gone by, but there were slices of blue peeking through the spaces between the boards that made up the barn walls and she knew it was already morning.

Chapter Nine

When Lily opened the cabin door, Jake was standing in front of the fireplace. He wouldn't even look at her. He was arms-crossed, mouth-tight, and not looking at all like the man she'd shared such enjoyable conversation with the night before. She waited, wondering if or when he would begin the conversation. Wondering, too, how she would respond.

"You were out there without a coat and no shoes," Jake finally said, though it was more of an accusation.

"Yes," Lily admitted. She could hardly deny it.

Jake turned to her. "I'm sure you have some explanation for your ability to be out in the cold wearing practically nothing, but you do know, don't you, that it's not normal?"

Lily's wings vibrated at her back. Jake's opinion of her mattered, and right now, he was looking at her like he expected her to say something reasonable. She took a moment to think of a response he might accept. She didn't know what that might be, so she decided to keep it as honest as possible. "The cold doesn't bother me much. Your dog seemed to want to go outside, and I thought it would be nice for her to play in the snow—"

Jake held up a hand. "I get it. You and my dog are crazy about the snow. Now, mind if we talk about our food situation?"

"Food?"

"Yeah, you know, the stuff we eat to stay alive? I had a look inside the cupboards while you and my dog were outside, and except for baking supplies, we have nothing. I'm not even sure how you've been coming up with the ingredients for the meals you've prepared. So, unless you have a secret stash somewhere that I don't know about, we might be in trouble."

Lily swallowed, thinking fast. "I'm not sure where you looked, but we're not out of supplies. We have plenty to eat." She went to one of the cupboards and opened it. "See?" She stood back so he could see it was full. Then she opened another cupboard, and it, too, was full.

Jake's brow furrowed. "That's impossible." He stepped up to a third cupboard and opened it. It was full of dried goods. He tried another. Full. Then he went to the refrigerator and yanked open the door. Fully stocked. He closed the door and quickly opened it again. Still full. He swallowed and rubbed a hand along the side of his face. "I don't know what's going on here, but I'm telling you, I looked in every one of those cupboards not a half-hour ago, and they were all empty! So was the refrigerator!"

Lily spread her hands. "I don't know what to say. You must have looked in *those* cupboards." She pointed at the last two that were still closed. She opened them, and the shelves were bare.

Jake looked back and forth several times between the full cupboards and the empty ones. "No. That's impossible," he said. "I checked all of them. I know I did. They were empty."

"But as you can plainly see, they are not," Lily said.

Jake looked at the fully stocked cupboards again, then he turned to leave the kitchen. "I think I need to sit down." He made his way into the other room and dropped heavily onto the sofa. "I'm sure I checked all the cupboards. They were empty," he repeated as he stared at the floor.

Lily caught her lip in her teeth. Poor man. She'd broken him. But maybe he could be fixed. She looked around at the cabin's drab, bare walls that lent nothing to the spirit of the season and wondered if a few decorations might help his state of mind. She gave some thought to what she might do to brighten things up, and then she remembered seeing a box of ornaments in the bedroom closet, along with a supply of craft paper, which she could use to make a colorful chain. But what good was a chain if they didn't have a tree?

She glanced over at Jake. His eyes were now closed. She knelt next to him and whispered close to his ear. "Jake? Are you falling asleep?"

He cracked open an eye. "Hardly."

"Good," Lily said, "because I was thinking…."

Jake opened both eyes. "About what?"

"Decorating."

"Why?"

"Because it's almost Christmas," Lily said, laughing lightly.

Jake shrugged. "It's your cabin. You don't need my permission."

"I wouldn't want to do anything that might make you uncomfortable."

"Such as?"

"I'd like to put up a small tree. It would fit perfectly right over there." She pointed to a corner of the room that was just the right spot, far away from the fireplace.

Jake looked to where she was pointing and seemed to be considering her idea. But then he shook his head, saying, "No. No tree."

"I'll come with you and help you carry it," she offered.

"I don't need any help to carry a tree. I just don't want one. If I had my way, I'd be at home right now, watching football and chugging a beer."

"You won't have to decorate it if that's what you're worried about," Lily persisted. "I've had much experience decorating Christmas trees. You can just sit and watch."

"Like I said, it's your cabin. You can decorate it however you want. But I'm not the least bit interested in going out to get a tree."

Lily's shoulders sagged with her disappointment. But she wasn't going to take Jake's rejection of a tree personal. He wasn't the first human she'd run into who was less than enthusiastic about decorating for the holidays. Though such an adamant refusal was concerning. Perhaps she'd stumbled upon a clue that would tell her why he'd lost his Christmas spirit. This was something that deserved further examination.

"Would you like to talk about it?" she asked Jake.

Jake cut his eyes to her. "Talk about what?"

"Why you hate Christmas."

"I never said I *hated* it. I just don't see any reason to celebrate a holiday that causes more anguish than it does joy."

Anguish? She'd never heard anyone use that word before when speaking of Christmas. Now, she was even more curious. "Sometimes, it helps to talk," she said.

Jake rolled his head in her direction. "And sometimes, it doesn't."

"And sometimes, it does," Lily countered, determined. If she was going to help him, she had to know his story. Even if it meant angering him.

Jake looked at her for a long minute. "You're not going to leave me alone about this, are you?"

"Maybe… if you share," Lily said with a slight smile.

Jake sighed. "If I tell you my story, you need to let me get it out and then leave it alone. Do you think you can do that?"

She nodded.

Jake gave her a doubtful look, then said, "I should probably warn you, nothing about my story is feel-good. So, if you don't want me putting a damper on your holiday cheer, maybe you'd better rethink wanting to know why I don't care to celebrate Christmas."

"Don't worry about me," Lily said. She'd been sent there to help him and help him she would, if at all possible. She made herself comfortable, sitting next to him on the sofa.

Jake stared ahead into the fire for a minute with the light dancing in his eyes. As Lily waited for him to begin, she wondered if she was asking too much. She didn't want to pry, yet she needed him to share.

"It was the winter I turned ten," Jake finally began. "We had a lot of snow that year, same as this year, and I was so busy helping my dad with the cattle that I didn't have time to think about what I wanted for Christmas, let alone getting a tree. But I had a younger sister, and getting a tree was all she talked about. It wasn't even Thanksgiving yet, and every morning, over breakfast, she would ask if it was finally time for us to get a tree." He laughed lightly. "She was relentless. I thought I'd go crazy listening to her."

"Children get so excited this time of year," Lily said, smiling.

Jake nodded. "Anyway, one morning, when I was in a bad mood from having to get up so early to tend to the cattle, I got to teasing Josie and I told her the day had finally arrived. After me and Dad finished with the cows, we would be bringing home a tree. And, no, she couldn't come because she was too little to be of any help." He looked to the fire, pausing. "It was mean of me. I should have known better. She was just a kid."

"You were a child, too," Lily reminded him.

"Yeah," Jake said quietly, "but I still should have known better." He took a settling breath. "To finish, it was a little more than an hour after my dad and I left the house when we heard my mom yelling, sounding hysterical. We hurried back, but we were at the far corner of the pasture, and it took us several minutes. By that time, my mom could barely get the words out. She'd left my sister in front of the television watching cartoons while she went up to make the beds, and when she came back downstairs, the front door was open and Josie was gone." He swallowed, looked pained. "My mom found Josie behind the barn, no coat, no shoes. She did her best to get Josie warmed up, but my sister had been fighting a bad cold for a week and after being out in the freezing snow, she got even sicker. Came down with pneumonia. The doctor said she had no more fight."

Lily drew in a breath, feeling Jake's sorrow. Now, she understood his discomfort at seeing her improperly clothed for the weather. "I'm so sorry," she said, resting a hand on his arm.

"Me, too," Jake said, sounding tired. "So, now you know why

I don't celebrate Christmas. And I'm sure it's also why my parents moved away. My dad probably felt it was what he needed to do for my mom." He smiled thinly. "I could have followed them, I suppose, but staying here makes me feel closer to Josie. This is where my memories of her are and I don't know that I could ever bring myself to leave them behind." He looked to the window for a long minute, then added, "I think maybe my sister is the reason that darn reindeer is so important to me. The night I found him, it was her birthday, and I managed to convince myself it was her sending me a sign that she was okay." He shrugged. "Maybe that's what I needed to believe to ease my guilt."

"I'm sure you know what happened to your sister was an accident," Lily offered gently.

Jake nodded. "I do. Most of the time. But the holidays tend to be hard. This time of year, everything reminds me of Josie and what we all went through that day. The sorrow, hearing my mom cry, seeing the anguish in my dad's eyes." He shook his head. "Every Christmas, it's like I relive all that pain."

Lily stayed quiet for a minute, giving him time. Finally, she spoke, choosing her words carefully. "I hope you won't mind me saying this, but if you'd rather be near your parents, you mustn't feel as though you're leaving your sister behind. Memories of those we love aren't tied to one certain place. They're in our hearts and our minds, and as long as we continue to remember them, they are never really gone. Your sister will always be with you, no matter where you choose to live."

"I appreciate that," Jake said. His eyes strayed to the window again, where big white flakes filled the sky. "I think I'll go for a walk and get some fresh air before it turns into a blizzard out there." He stood and put his weight evenly on both feet without wincing. His lips tilted up at the corners. "Looks like I might be able to walk out of here pretty soon, after all."

Lily didn't want him to go. But she'd come to know him well enough, and his desire to be alone seemed to be his way of dealing with whatever might be bothering him. She just hoped he wouldn't be gone long.

Chapter Ten

After a short hour of tromping around in the snow, Jake's ankle was throbbing and he had to stop and rest. As he stood there in the muffled silence of the forest, several snowflakes fell through the trees and landed on his face, which made him think of his sister. After all this time, he could still picture her just as she was: a tiny girl with big eyes that made her look like some kind of doll, or maybe an angel, with a head of curls that seemed to float aimlessly about her face. Sometimes, he could even still hear her voice, all giggly and happy about some little thing. Especially if it had anything to do with Christmas. And if she were here with him right now, she would be begging him to help her find the "perfect" Christmas tree.

He smiled at the thought, and it felt strange. But it also felt good, and he figured that was because of the woman back at the cabin. She'd made him see that it might be time to let go of the pain, that it was okay to be happy, and that Christmas wasn't the reason he'd lost his sister. In fact, the more time he spent with Lily, the less angry he was about being stuck at the cabin with her, and was even finding he enjoyed her company. She had a way about her that made him feel comfortable, like he was the most interesting person she'd ever met. She was also the kind of woman who, under different circumstances, might have had him entertaining *what if?* Though he had no idea why. She was so much a mystery that it would take a lifetime to figure her out. Plus, she had the worst diet and she——. But he didn't have time to come up with anything else because he'd just found the "perfect" Christmas tree.

Alone again, Lily fell into thinking how much of a challenge this assignment had become. It wasn't like she could magically return Jake's sister to him. And if she couldn't do that, how would she change his feelings about Christmas? About all she could do was help him see that leaving the past behind didn't mean he had to forget his sister. It simply meant he could move on. Be happy. Let go of the hurt that the loss of his sister had caused everyone in his family.

First things first, though. Jake may have rejected her idea of a tree, but that didn't mean she couldn't come up with something else to bring Christmas alive in the sorry cabin. She looked about at the bare walls again. They needed something. But what?

After giving it some thought, the only thing she could think of that would cheerify the cabin was snow. Which they already had plenty of outside. But if she made dozens of beautiful, glittery snowflakes to hang everywhere, even from the ceiling, it would be a winter wonderland inside, too. And each snowflake could be different, the same as what Mother Nature provided.

Happy with her idea, Lily did a quick and completely unscientific calculation to come up with the number of snowflakes that would be needed to transform the cabin. Approximately two hundred, give or take a couple dozen. And with that many snowflakes to be made, she needed to get started so she could be finished by the time Jake returned.

Twirling her way into the bedroom, Lily left in her wake a stream of snowflakes that immediately melted into tiny puddles

Lily put on the sweater and jeans, and then she stood before the closet, looking for anything else that might help. She glanced at the bedpost where she'd placed the hat she'd worn into the forest. But then a pair of earmuffs caught her eye, and she picked them up, rubbing the faux fur between her fingers. The elves sometimes wore earmuffs, and they never had cold ears, though they did look rather silly, like they had two furry lumps growing out the sides of their heads.

Silly or not, she slipped the earmuffs on and then moved in front of the full-length mirror that hung on the back of the bedroom door to have a look. "Oh!" she said, laughing and putting her hands to her face. And as she stood there, staring at herself and continuing to laugh, she heard the cabin door open.

Chapter Eleven

Lily tore the earmuffs from her head and tossed them aside as she ran to the other room. She didn't want to miss the look on Jake's face when he saw all the snowflakes. But when she entered the room, instead of Jake, she saw green branches filling the cabin doorway, with Sierra wiggling her way from one side to the other, trying to find her person.

"Outta the way, girl," came Jake's voice from the back of the branches. Then he finally appeared. He shut the door with the heel of his boot and nodded toward the corner of the room. "Is that where you want this thing?"

"Oh, yes, that would be perfect!" Lily said, clapping her hands together in delight. She moved quickly to push a stool out of the way, then she stood back as Jake dragged the tree across the floor. She could hardly believe it. A tree was the last thing she expected after the conversation they'd had.

When Jake had the tree placed so that its best side was facing out from the corner, he eyed the firewood stacked on the hearth. "If you'll hand me a few pieces of wood, I think I can make a stand that'll hold this thing."

Lily was happy to help in any way she could. She hurried to

hand Jake three pieces, glad that she'd thought to replenish the wood supply while he was away.

It took only a moment for Jake to place the wood so that it formed a sturdy triangle around the tree's trunk. Then he let go and stepped back, assessing. "I didn't realize it had so many bare spots," he said. "It looked great out in the forest among all the snags, but now, after shaking off all the snow, I'm afraid it's lost some of its charm."

Lily stood next to him, smiling. "Not at all. It's a good tree. All it needs is to be decorated." The truth was, she'd seen prettier. But with a little TLC, the small fir would do just fine. "I'll get the box of paper from the other room," she continued. "We can use it to make a colorful chain." She left Jake standing there, still eyeing the tree, and when she returned, dragging both the box of paper and a box of ornaments behind her, she found Jake staring at the walls.

"What happened in here?" he asked, turning full circle. "Looks like you and my dog had a party while I was gone."

"I decorated," Lily said. "Isn't it wonderful?" She spread her arms, embracing the moment. She was far too happy to worry he might not approve.

Jake's focus went to the floor, where silver and gold glitter winked up at him from between the floorboards. His gaze came to rest on Sierra, who still had glitter stuck in the fur at the top of her head.

Lily pointed at the box of ornaments by way of avoiding having to explain. "Shall we take a look?" she asked as she sat on the sofa, eager to get started.

"I'm okay just watching," Jake said. He sat next to her and made himself comfortable.

Even though Jake didn't want to help, Lily felt this was progress. At least he hadn't walked out after seeing the walls plastered with paper snowflakes.

Taking each ornament from the box, she handled them with care, not wanting to break any, they were so old and fragile looking. Then, setting them aside, she took three strands of lights from the box. They, too, had seen a lot of years and needed untangling before they could be used.

Jake still seemed comfortable just watching, so she proceeded with the untangling herself, which took a while, but she was finally ready to begin decorating the little tree. Starting at the bottom, she wound the lights around and around until she'd used all three strands. Unfortunately, they only went two-thirds of the way up. And even after hanging the ornaments, there were still a lot of bare spots. Then she got an idea. If she used plenty of glitter when making the chain, the sparkle might make the tree appear to have more lights, Plus, the chain would help hide any remaining imperfections.

She pulled the box of craft paper over in front of herself and selected several sheets. Then she pushed the box over to Jake, hoping he'd dig in and help. When he didn't make a move, she thought a little subtle nudging might be in order. "This is going to take a while," she said. "I won't mind at all if you'd like to help." She didn't wait for his response, just shoved a pair of scissors toward him, along with a few tubes of glitter. Then she got busy with her own pile of craft supplies.

While she worked, she kept an eye on Jake. He didn't even look inside the box. He seemed more interested in studying the flames of the fire. But by the time she'd put together a three-foot-long chain section, he had scissors in hand and was working on his own section of chain.

Happy, Lily quietly hummed Christmas carols while she continued making colorful loops. Jake didn't seem to mind her humming, and the lines on his forehead even softened after a while.

With both of them making loops, it wasn't long before they had several sparkling sections that, when attached, made a chain that was plenty long to decorate the tree, top to bottom. Jake helped with that, too, holding one end and feeding her the rest while she wound it around the tree. Then, when she got near the top and had difficulty reaching, Jake took over and finished. Lily couldn't help but smile when she stood back to admire the tree they'd decorated together.

"It seems all that's left is to plug in the lights," Jake observed.

"Oh, no," Lily said. "There is so much more to this event than just plugging in lights. We need to sing. We need to light candles. We need to have hot chocolate!"

"Do we even *have* candles?" Jake asked.

"I believe we do," Lily said. She hurried to the kitchen and returned with an entire box of tea candles, which she spread about the room and lit. The effect was that of being in the middle of a forest cathedral. She contemplated adding a little snow, which she could easily produce with just the slightest flutter of her wings, but she doubted it would go over well. Besides, they had enough snow in the form of paper snowflakes.

"What now?" Jake asked.

"Now, we drink hot chocolate!" Lily said. She returned to the kitchen, and while she stirred the hot chocolate to perfection, she stole a glance at Jake and caught him adjusting the chain.

More progress.

Handing Jake his hot chocolate, she stood by his side, and they sipped from their mugs with paper snowflakes dangling about their heads. Delighted with how everything was going, she was eager to get on with the rest of the tree-lighting ceremony.

"I think we're ready for Christmas carols," she announced, turning to Jake. "Do you have a favorite you'd like to sing?"

"Oh, I don't think you want to hear me sing," Jake said. "This is your thing. I got us a tree and helped with the decorating, so I think I've earned the right to stand back and listen while *you* sing."

Lily didn't want to push him. He really had done enough. She gave it some thought and finally decided on an appropriate song for the moment—"Oh, Christmas Tree." She didn't often sing solo, but she knew the song well and thought she could get through it without embarrassing herself. Taking a few breaths to settle her nerves, she began, and when she was finished, she caught Jake staring at her in such a way that it caused a funny tickle in her stomach.

"You sing very well, like a songbird," Jake said gently.

Lily's cheeks warmed at his compliment. "That's kind of you to say," she told him. The tickle in her stomach continued and now her pulse was racing. It was uncomfortable, but it was also nice. "I think it's time we plug in the lights," she said quietly. "And since I sang, I'll let you have that honor."

"That much I can do," Jake said.

Lily watched and held her breath in anticipation as Jake reached for the end of the light strand. But then his arm brushed against hers and it gave her another strange sensation, which made her pulse race even faster. She did her best to ignore it, but she was afraid if it went on much longer, she might lose control of her wings.

"Here we go," Jake said as he pushed the plug into the wall socket. When nothing happened, he jiggled the lights and tried again. Still nothing. He looked closely at all three strands, examining several of the bulbs, and even took a couple out of their sockets, then plugged them back in. Again nothing. "Sorry," he said, his lips tight, "but I think we might be out of luck with the lights. I'm not surprised. Those strands look to be pretty old."

Disappointed, but not yet ready to give up, Lily examined the lights herself. She was grateful for the distraction, and as she looked at each strand, her fear of losing control of her wings dissipated. She closed her eyes and imagined every bulb on every strand brightly lit and even twinkling. And when she opened her eyes, the tree was pure joy! So full of color, it lit the entire cabin with good cheer.

"Guess I was wrong," Jake said, standing back.

"Oh, Jake, it's absolutely beautiful!" Lily said, clapping her hands together and feeling so good, it made her want to hug someone. And since Jake was the only someone in the room, she tossed her arms around his neck and squeezed him tight. "Thank you for this," she said. "A million times, thank you!"

Jake circled his arms around her, returning her hug, and Lily was hit with an unexpected jolt that was both exciting and scary. Then, before she could stop it, her wings fluttered and she and

Jake were instantly surrounded by tiny white flakes.

"What the blazes!" Jake said, whirling away from her. He looked to the door, saw it was closed, then turned back to her. "Did you see that?"

"See what?" Lily asked.

"The snow! It was coming down all around us!"

Lily laughed a nervous laugh. "Snow? Here in the cabin? Well, now, that's quite impossible, isn't it?"

"Impossible or not, it just snowed in here! Don't tell me you didn't see it!"

Lily continued fighting to keep her wings still. If she couldn't, she and Jake might find themselves standing in the middle of a blizzard. Going into pure panic mode, all she could think to do was use her fairy dust to go back to the moment just after she lost control. It was for the good of the assignment, she told herself as she waved a hand to release a large amount of fairy dust over Jake.

In an instant, the moment was rewound, and once again, she and Jake were doused with snow. But this time, when Jake whirled about, the cabin door was wide open, and a fierce gust of wind was blowing even *more* snow into the cabin.

"I must not have closed the door all the way when I came in with the tree," Jake said as he hurried to secure the door. Then he looked about at all the snow that was already melting on the floor. "Sorry about the mess."

"It's okay," Lily said. "The floor will dry." She watched as Sierra spun around, wagging her tail at all the commotion. Glitter was everywhere. In the air, on the floor, but mostly all over Jake, who had his arms held out in front of himself as he looked at the sparkling mess.

"What's going on here?" he asked. "Where did all this glitter come from?"

Lily caught her lip in her teeth. She'd used far too much fairy dust. "I guess I got carried away making these," she said as she batted aside one of the hanging snowflakes.

"I don't get it," Jake continued, still looking at his arms.

"That's twice we've been in the middle of a conversation, then all of a sudden, I'm covered in glitter." He looked at Lily's arms. "But you don't have any on you."

Lily's wings were on the verge of releasing more snow. She held out her arms and pretended to look for glitter she already knew wasn't there. Her pulse pounded at her temples as she struggled to come up with a reasonable response. But she had nothing.

Panicked, she tried to think of how she could fix things. It was the hug. It shouldn't have happened. She had to try once more to go back. But this time, she would take herself and Jake back to the moment just before she put her arms around him. It was the only solution, the only way to salvage things. Then she and Jake could enjoy the rest of their evening together.

Jake was still looking at his arms when Lily raised her hand to release more fairy dust. But before she was able to let loose, an urgent pounding came at the cabin door.

"Expecting company?" Jake asked, looking surprised.

Lily shook her head. She held her breath as Jake went to the door. She only hoped it wasn't Vivienne popping in for another visit.

Chapter Twelve

A man whose head was at the same level as Jake's stomach stood at the open doorway. He wore shiny black boots, a bulky green coat, a green knit hat, and red mittens that matched the color in his cheeks. "I am here to see my princess," he announced to Jake.

Lily recognized the voice, but it couldn't possibly be. She peered around the edge of the door to get a better look at the little man. "Enar? Is it really you?" she asked.

"It is indeed. Hello, my princess," the little man said, peering back at her from under Jake's arm.

Jake stepped aside, and Sierra eyed the little man, back fur raised. Jake held up a hand, indicating she should stay put, and she did.

Lily eased forward. "Enar, what are you doing here?"

Jake looked from the little man to Lily. "You know this man?"

"Of course, she knows me," Enar said. "How do you think she knows my name?"

"He's an old friend," Lily explained. "Why are you here?" she asked Enar again.

Enar inched his way inside and spoke quietly. "I came to defend your honor and to plead with you not to do anything foolish."

Lily straightened. "I can assure you, I do not need to have my honor defended. Nor do I intend to do anything foolish."

Enar looked Jake up one way and down the other, his eyes surveying. "This man has been a gentleman?" he asked Lily.

"A *perfect* gentleman," Lily assured him.

Enar sniffed. "I suppose I'll have to take your word for it, as I lack the experience you have with such people."

"Such people?" Jake asked, edging into the conversation.

Enar continued speaking to Lily, saying, "Too, I know you would never allow yourself to be compromised."

"That is right, Enar. I would not," Lily said. She gave Jake a scant glance. He was in his arms-crossed, none-too-happy stance. Everything was falling apart. In a hundred years, she would not be able to explain Enar's presence. Then again, perhaps now would be a good time to tell Jake she was a Christmas fairy… right after she found out the real reason for Enar's visit. "Shall we go outside and talk?" she suggested to Enar. She was already stuffing her feet into the boots by the door. She grabbed the puffy coat and put it on as she nudged Enar out onto the porch. Before shutting the door, she gave Jake a small smile. "I'll only be a minute," she told him, though she dreaded the questions that were sure to follow when she returned.

"I hope you don't mind my dropping in like this," Enar said as soon as the door was closed.

Lily shuffled away from the door so Jake wouldn't hear their conversation. "Of course, I'm always happy to see you, but don't give me any nonsense about wanting to protect my honor. Tell me the truth. Did Vivienne send you?"

Enar's mouth dropped open, and his breath hung in a frosty white cloud about his head. "She did not! I have told you why I am here. To keep you from making a mistake." He took one of her hands in his, and his eyes were drawn to it. "Your hand! It's nearly frozen! What is wrong with it?"

Lily pulled away from him and tucked her hand into the pocket of the puffy coat. Her fingers were already tingling from being exposed to the freezing air. It wouldn't be long before she grew those ugly bumps again. "Nothing is wrong," she said. "I just seem to be having a hard time adjusting to the weather here."

"Nonsense!" Enar said. "It's no colder here than it is at the North Pole. You must be ill. I beg you to return home with me immediately."

"No need to worry. I'm fine," Lily said. Though she didn't feel fine at all, and returning to the North Pole would be of no help. "You were saying… something about wanting to keep me from making a mistake?"

"Oh, yes," Enar said, "the reason for my visit. I'm afraid perhaps I haven't made it clear how I feel about you, and that is why you're here." His tone softened. "You needn't run away to find love, my princess. You have already found it. With me. I have loved you from the very first moment I saw you. In fact, my feelings for you have grown so strong, I spoke with Santa, and he has granted me permission to build a home at the top of the hill that overlooks the reindeer meadow. I know how that spot pleases you. Or if that is not a suitable place, I'm sure I can find another location that is equally nice. I would never expect you to come live with me at the elf quarters with all the other elves."

Lily caught herself before she broke out into laughter. Living at the elf quarters was not something she could ever imagine. She loved them all dearly, but they were a wild bunch, and she would never be able to keep up with their antics. She placed a gentle hand on Enar's shoulder. "My dear friend, I am flattered beyond measure. A home overlooking the reindeer meadow is a most perfect place. But, Enar, as much as I care for you, I think you know my wish is to find love with a *human* man."

Enar dipped his head. "Yes. I understand that is your Christmas wish. But since that has been your wish for a good number of years, and Santa has yet to allow it, I was hoping you might have changed your mind."

"I'm sorry, Enar, I have not."

"But why would you continue to ask for something, knowing it will only end in disappointment?"

"This year, I may not be disappointed," Lily said. "Santa has finally agreed to consider granting my wish. He is to give me his decision once I have completed my assignment."

"After Christmas Eve? But that will be too late!"

It was the same as Vivienne had told her, but Lily believed in Santa's word. "Santa is making an exception for me this year."

"I see. And if his decision is that you are to remain at the North Pole?"

The very idea filled Lily's chest with a dull ache. She was not ready to say goodbye to the opportunity to fall in love, and she was especially not ready to say goodbye to Jake. Not when she'd begun to have such strange, yet pleasurable, feelings inside whenever he was near. And though she cared deeply for Enar, he did not make her heart soar, nor did he cause bubbles to burst inside her stomach the same as Jake did. And, oh, how she loved those bubbles. Though she didn't think it necessary to go into such detail with Enar, and probably he wouldn't appreciate hearing it. "If Santa determines I must remain at the North Pole, it will be difficult to hear," she told Enar. "But if that is what must be, I will accept it."

"Then you are once again prepared to go without a Christmas wish?" Enar asked.

"I am," Lily said, nodding.

"It's not too late to ask for something else," Enar said. "There is no shame in changing your mind." He paused, thinking, and then continued. "I know you've always enjoyed experiencing new things, so if it's simply a little excitement you are looking for, might I make a suggestion?"

"Such as?"

"You could learn how to fly Santa's sleigh. Why, he might even be willing to let you ride along with him on Christmas Eve while he delivers toys."

Lily shook her head. "I have no desire to fly Santa's sleigh. I get so confused by all the lights and knobs. I fear I would be a danger in the sky."

"Then what about teaching the reindeer a few new tricks? I could help you, and we could put on a show for everyone in the town center on Christmas morning."

"I'm sorry, Enar, but that also does not interest me. We both know I'm no good at training reindeer. They barely listen to me. Cupid is the worst. I think she is jealous of my relationship with Santa. Whenever I enter her stall, she corners me with her antlers. I could be injured."

"Don't worry about Cupid. I'll have a chat with her."

"No. Don't. Cupid and I will manage. Besides, if I were to become a member of the human world, it wouldn't matter how Cupid feels about me."

Enar stared down at his feet, where a dusting of new snow had already settled on the tops of his boots. Finally, he raised his head and met her gaze. "What about your wings? I don't believe I've ever heard of a human with wings. And if you have no wings, how will you make it snow?"

"Perhaps I will still have my imagination to make snow," Lily reasoned.

Enar looked doubtful. "I believe that gift belongs only to Christmas fairies."

Lily felt a painful zing in her chest. She knew Enar was right. By entering the human world, she would lose her ability to make snow. And it made sense. No human she'd ever encountered could produce snow, no matter how hard they wished it to happen. But as difficult as that was to even think about, it was a sacrifice she was willing to make if it meant she would find love. "I suppose I will have to leave snow-making to the other fairies," she told Enar. "Or Mother Nature. You know how fond she is of surprising humans with a sudden burst of weather."

"As if she doesn't already have enough to do," Enar grumbled. He was quiet for a minute, then said, "I've heard living among humans isn't easy. They're full of emotion. It's like they're on a roller coaster ride every second of every minute of every day. Think of how exhausting that must be."

"I'm sure that's an exaggeration," Lily remarked.

"Perhaps," Enar said, his shoulders sagging. Then his brow drew tight. "There is one other thing to consider. To be human means you will die."

Lily knew Enar was reaching for anything that might convince her to rethink her wish. But that wasn't going to happen. The joy she'd witnessed during her assignments when two people fell in love was so great, it mattered not that her life would one day come to an end. She wanted to experience all, both joy and sorrow. And she wanted to experience those things for a lifetime, not just during a single holiday season.

"Yes, as a human, I will die someday," she told Enar softly. "But my hope is that *some*day will be a very long time from now."

"Humans do not live as long as we do," Enar said. "For them, someday is an instant. Many humans only have a life span of seven or eight decades."

"Eight decades is hardly an instant," she reasoned.

"But at the North Pole, you could live for five thousand years or more."

"Goodness!" Lily's eyes went wide. "I have never thought about living so long."

"Yes, and think of all you could accomplish in that much time. With me," Enar said. "You and I could become the North Pole's power couple."

Lily laughed. "I believe the North Pole already has a power couple. Santa and Mrs. Claus."

"True," Enar said. He shuffled his feet and kicked at the snow, looking defeated.

Lily felt bad for her friend. She tried thinking of how she might explain so he would understand. "Sit with me," she said as she brushed frozen snow off the chairs next to the door. Enar sat and gazed at her with adoring eyes, which didn't help at all with what she was about to say. Still, she had to speak her truth. "Dearest, Enar," she began, "do you recall how you felt last month when you knew Vivienne was upset about that nutcracker you gave her?"

Enar nodded. "It was most unpleasant. As soon as I heard her footsteps approaching the Toy Room, I dashed away to the farthest corner and hid behind a big stuffed bear. My stomach felt like it was full of nuts and bolts. I tried to tell her I did not mean for the nutcracker's sword to rip her dress, but she refused to hear me. And in my defense, I did warn her that it was more sophisticated than the others, and that she should use care when handling it."

Lily stifled a laugh. "Yes, I remember you warning her, but as we both know, Vivienne does not always listen." She laid a hand on Enar's arm. "Now, imagine the opposite of how you felt that day. What would that be like?"

Enar's mouth stretched into a wide smile. "Oh, my princess, it would be like sitting next to you every morning watching the sun rise over the reindeer meadow! It would be like seeing every name removed from Santa's Naughty List! It would be like having ten Christmas wishes granted all at once!"

"Exactly!" Lily said. "And that's how I imagine it feels to fall in love. It would be like new snow and hot chocolate and everything wonderful that one could possibly imagine all tied together with a big red bow!"

Enar's eyes gleamed in the light of the moon. "And that is how I feel about you. It is how I have *always* felt about you."

"But, Enar, it is not how *I* feel," Lily said, the sound of her voice floating softly on the night air. She had hoped to let him down as gently as possible, but it was evident by the look in his eyes that she had to be more direct. She drew in a slow breath and continued. "You have been a good friend to me for many years, and I wish I could tell you what you want to hear. But I cannot. And even if given time—another two or three hundred years—I will only see you as a friend. Nothing more. I am sorry if that hurts you. But it is what is, and I cannot change it."

Enar swallowed and held her gaze. "So, it is your intention to stay here with the human and not return to the North Pole?"

"If my wish is granted, yes."

Enar tipped his head at the cabin door. "Do you love the human?"

Lily warmed at the question. "My feelings are strong," she answered.

Enar's face turned dark with disappointment. "The human's feelings are also strong. I can tell. But if he has yet to profess his love, there remains hope." He paused, giving her a tender look. "I will allow you your time with the human, though I will think positive thoughts and hope that you will come to change your mind." He stood. "It's late, and I must be on my way. But I wonder if I may see Cinder before I depart. Gormar asked me to check on her. You know how serious he takes the reindeer's grooming."

"Of course," Lily said, glad now that she'd taken the time to brush Cinder.

Chapter Thirteen

Cinder had a visitor. Frost. Lily recognized him by the white fur that trailed from his muzzle all the way to his hindquarters. Her immediate thought was to run back to the cabin and tell Jake she'd found his reindeer, but her next thought was that she should first finish her visit with Enar.

"I was not aware Santa had sent two reindeer to accompany you on your assignment," Enar said, looking closely at Frost. "I'm not familiar with this animal. Did he come from the reindeer meadow?"

"No," Lily said. "This reindeer belongs to Jake. His name is Frost. I'm not sure what he's doing here, but it seems he and Cinder have become friends."

"Looks to be so," Enar said as he continued examining Frost, looking him over from head to tail and even peering inside his mouth. Frost nibbled at Enar's coat pocket, the same as Prancer did whenever he thought the result might be a treat, and Enar drew a carrot from his pocket and broke it into two pieces, one for each reindeer.

Lily also looked the young reindeer over. Now that she had a chance to see him up close, he was even more handsome than her original assessment.

"He appears to be comfortable with us," Enar continued, turning to Lily, "and he looks healthy. Do you think he might enjoy flying? I'll bet he would learn quickly."

"I don't know," Lily said. "But Santa has so many reindeer already. I'm sure he has all the help he needs."

"Santa is always looking for new talent. We could take this youngster back to the North Pole and let Santa have a look at him."

Lily shook her head. "I have already told you, this is Jake's reindeer. It wouldn't be right to take him. And we talked about me coming back to the North Pole. It is my hope I will not be returning."

The barn was silent for several minutes as she and Enar stood side by side, watching the two reindeer take turns nuzzling each other. Then Frost moved away from Cinder, barely making a sound as he left the barn through a gap in the boards. Cinder made a low grunting noise at his departure.

"Will he return?" Enar asked.

"Perhaps," Lily said. She hoped so.

"Cinder does seem smitten with the young bull," Enar said. "It will be unsettling for her to leave him when your assignment is over and she must return to the North Pole."

Lily moved closer to Cinder, resting a protective arm over her back. "I would like to keep Cinder here with me if possible."

Enar laughed. "That would make two wishes you hope to have granted. And I'm afraid keeping Cinder is a lot to ask. She is next in line to become an active participant on Santa's sleigh team."

"Santa's reindeer are all healthy. Cinder will not be needed," Lily countered. But even as she spoke the words, her throat tightened, and her eyes became moist. She hadn't thought about ever having to say goodbye to Cinder, though it made sense that Cinder would eventually return to the North Pole. Enar was right. Many hours had been spent on her training as a backup reindeer, and she was a valued member of the sleigh team.

"Injury is always a possibility when Santa delivers gifts," Enar continued. "Or even during the off-season when the reindeer run free in the meadow. All that running about and kicking up of their hooves could easily result in an unexpected mishap."

"Yes," Lily agreed, her throat tightening ever more. "I know one of Santa's reindeer could get hurt. But why must you torture me so by reminding me of that possibility?" She fought to keep the moisture in her eyes from turning into real tears, but feeling such emotion was new to her and she was helpless to stop several fat drops from forming and escaping down her cheeks.

Enar gave her a concerned look. "Are you weeping?"

Lily nodded, still trying to stifle her tears.

"I have never seen this," Enar said.

"I know," Lily said, sniffing and wiping her face with the sleeve of the puffy coat. "It is most disturbing. I don't seem to be able to control it. It just happens, whether I want it to or not."

Enar stared at her for a minute before saying, "I am sorry to sadden you, my princess. But the things I have told you, you must already know. Santa only trains the best reindeer, and Cinder is at the top of her class. She will be the first chosen should the need arise." His tone softened. "If you would only reconsider returning with me to the North Pole, then you would not have to give a moment's thought to Cinder's departure. I know I'm not the most handsome elf, but you have always owned my heart, and I cannot imagine loving any other. I vow to always put you first, and I will bring you more than your fair share of sugar plums… even chocolates from Switzerland if that's what it would take to make you happy."

"Oh, Enar…"

"Please, allow me to finish," Enar said. He cleared his throat. "Only a few days remain until Christmas. It may be too late for you to find love with the human. But you can still have love. With me. Say you'll return to the North Pole once you have completed this assignment. Then we will go to Santa together and tell him you've changed your mind about your wish."

"But I have not," Lily said. "Enar, please, I know this is hard for you, but I cannot allow you false hope. We have been friends now for more than one hundred years. If we were going to become more, don't you think it would have happened by now?"

Enar smiled a reluctant smile. "One hundred and seven, to be exact. Oh, how quickly time does pass." His voice wavered, and he paused to gain control, then continued. "I suppose you are right. And I know I must accept your decision to stay here. For now. But know this… if I receive word that the human is not treating you as he should, he will have to answer to me."

Lily wiped the last of her tears away. She was thankful for the blessing of having such a good friend. Of everyone at the North Pole, if Santa were to grant her wish, she would miss Enar the most. "I appreciate your devotion," she told Enar, "though I'm not sure I'm worthy."

"Let me worry about that," Enar said. He took one of Lily's hands in his. "For as long as snow falls from the sky, that's how long I will love you. And even if Santa does decide to grant your request, and you do not return to the North Pole, I will wish you luck and happiness for all the days of your human life."

"Do you mean that?" Lily asked.

"I do," Enar said, and he kissed the back of her hand. "Farewell, my princess." Then with a snap of his fingers, he was gone.

"Goodbye, my friend," Lily whispered into the crisp barn air. Then she turned her attention back to Cinder, wanting to give the reindeer one last hug before she returned to the cabin and told Jake *his* reindeer was safe. Though that would mean she would also have to tell him about Cinder, which seemed unfavorable, as it would only lead to more questions she could not yet answer.

She ruffled the fur on Cinder's neck. "What do you think, Cinder? Shall I report seeing the handsome reindeer to the man in the cabin, or shall I keep his visit here a secret?"

Cinder grunted, and it didn't sound like a grunt of approval. More like a *let's keep the boy reindeer to ourselves* kind of grunt.

Lily sighed. "That's what I thought you'd say. Very well. Perhaps it is best we keep Frost's appearance to ourselves for the time being. At least you and I know he's safe and healthy."

The moment Lily left the barn, she felt chilled. Even so, the snow was so incredibly beautiful and the temptation too great; she couldn't resist kicking off her boots. It would only be for a quick minute, she promised herself. And perhaps burrowing her feet into the cold, invigorating snow would clear her mind so that she would have easy answers for Jake's questions about Enar.

As the snow squished between her toes, she smiled, thinking this was just what she needed. But when something sharp and prickly attacked the soles of her feet, she cried out and hurried over to the porch steps, fully expecting to see some small creature with its fangs sunk into her flesh. But all she saw when she turned up her feet to examine them was that they'd turned deep red, like the color of Santa's suit.

"Oh, my, this does not seem right," she said, feeling panicked to have the cold affecting her this way again. She rubbed her feet vigorously, but they went from cold to burning, and she found little relief.

"What did you expect would happen when you kicked your boots off?"

Lily looked up to see Jake standing in the cabin doorway. Then, all at once, his arms were around her, and she could feel him practically vibrating with anger as he carried her inside. He dropped her on the sofa, then covered her with a wool blanket, and she remained quiet, waiting for him to say something. Sierra sat next to her, her tail barely twitching as they both watched Jake standing in the middle of the room, looking like he didn't know what he should do next. Finally, he grabbed his coat and hat and went out the door.

"Jake, wait!" Lily called to him. When he kept going, she scrambled away from the warmth of the blanket and went to the open doorway to see him making his way through the snow toward the forest. She called to him once more, but he didn't look back before he disappeared into the trees.

Sierra rested her head against Lily's leg, and Lily rubbed Sierra's warm fur. "Don't worry, girl. I'm sure he'll be back soon. He just needs to… think… or something." But, really, she had no idea what Jake needed to do.

After standing at the door for a long minute, Lily stepped back inside and sank into a chair, feeling lost. Any ideas she'd had about her and Jake becoming a couple were quickly vanishing. Why, oh, why had she let herself be tempted by the snow? Why couldn't she have kept her vow to never again let him see her outside in her bare feet? Over and over, she scolded herself for being so careless until she heard a sneeze, and then Vivienne appeared beside her, holding a tissue to her nose.

Lily gave her a scant glance. "Bless you," she said half-heartedly.

"You'll never believe the weather where I just came from," Vivienne said. "All it does is rain. Every day it's rain, rain, and more rain."

"Seattle," Lily said plainly. She was well familiar with the area.

"Honestly, I don't know how the people there stand it. Would you believe they actually have several different terms for the wet stuff, depending on its consistency? Drizzle… scattered showers… mist… sprinkles." Vivienne wiped her nose one last time, and then the tissue disappeared into thin air. "I have a mind to send them a few snow showers just to mix things up a bit. Though I suppose that would pose a problem for anyone who doesn't own a truck or an SUV, and then I'd be blamed for parents not being able to get out and finish their Christmas shopping."

Lily made no comment. She wasn't up for visitors. Especially when the visitor was named Vivienne.

"Oh, dear," Vivienne said, looking about the cabin, "someone has had an accident with the glitter."

"There was no accident," Lily said. "I decorated."

"Hmm… bored, were you? And where's the human?"

"Gone."

"What do you mean gone? Gone where?" Vivienne asked.

"Away from me," Lily said.

Vivienne ran her gaze over Lily. "I can't imagine why, what with you being so fashionably dressed."

"I was cold," Lily said, frowning.

"Then make yourself a hot toddy. Or even a pot of hot chocolate. In fact, I wouldn't mind having a cup, myself." Vivienne went and sat at the table, and with a flourish of her hand, she produced two mugs of steaming hot chocolate. She batted a low-hanging snowflake away from her face and commented, "Really, one or two snowflakes would have been enough. This is excessive even for you."

Lily looked about at all the snowflakes. "I like them. I think it's just the right amount."

"You would," Vivienne said. "But never mind that. Come and sit and tell me more about this being cold business."

Lily went to the table and sat, but she wasn't in the mood for hot chocolate or explaining anything to Vivienne. Though if she didn't, Vivienne would continue sitting there sipping her hot chocolate and gloating. So explain she would. "It's odd," she began, "one minute, I was outside enjoying myself, and the next, I became so chilled, I grew unsightly bumps all over my arms. Plus, my teeth began clacking together." She *clack, clack, clacked* to demonstrate. "As you can imagine, it was a most unsettling experience." Remembering how uncomfortable she'd been, she finally took several large sips of her hot chocolate.

"Not to mention so very unfairylike," Vivienne added. "So, what did you do?"

"I ran back inside and put some clothes on, of course!" Lily looked down at the sweater, at Santa smoking a cigar. "I guess I could have chosen something more flattering. But at the moment, all I cared about was being warm."

Vivienne pushed her lips into a smarmy grin. "Oh, dear, I do believe I know what's happening to you. You're falling for the human! Another day or two stuck in this cabin together, and you may find yourself covered head to toe in unflattering apparel all year round." Her eyes gleamed. "It looks like we may both be getting what we wish for this Christmas. All you need to do now is seal the deal with a kiss!"

Lily peered at Vivienne over the rim of her mug. "A kiss won't necessarily mean the deal is sealed. And even if I were to hang the mistletoe, how do you propose I get a kiss from Jake when he's gone?"

"He'll be back," Vivienne said. She waved a hand in Sierra's direction. "Is that not his dog over there by the fire?"

Lily looked to Sierra, who was basking belly-up in the glow of the burning embers. "It is," she told Vivienne.

"So, all you need to do is hang the mistletoe and be ready to pucker up when the human returns."

"I don't know. Even if Jake comes back, I can't see him being overcome with desire to kiss me. Strangle me would be more like it."

"Why are you being so negative?" Vivienne asked. "You've obviously become fond of the human, so isn't it possible he's also become fond of you? And even if he hasn't, the mistletoe will take care of that. Just one glance is all it usually takes for most humans to react."

"Jake isn't most humans," Lily remarked.

Vivienne raised an eyebrow. "This isn't like you. You're always so hopeful and optimistic. It's really quite sickening." She assessed Lily's attire once more. "Have you changed your mind? Is it the clothes? Is the idea of wearing such outerwear completely abhorrent to you? Surely, you didn't think you would remain immune to the cold if you joined the human world. There's a price to pay for wanting to have it all, my dear. You need to ask yourself if the human is worth that price."

"It's not the clothes!" Lily said, her voice rising. "I just don't think mistletoe will do any good at this point. Jake caught me out in the snow barefoot!"

Vivienne scoffed. "So he thinks you've got a tiny screw loose. It means nothing. I've seen very few men who can stand beneath the twig and resist kissing the nearest woman. Chances are, the human has already been thinking about it and is just waiting for an opportunity. Consider mistletoe that opportunity."

"You don't understand! You know nothing about Jake, or his situation. Letting him see me out in the snow was a costly mistake. At this point, I don't even know if I'll be successful with my assignment."

"Forget the assignment!" Vivienne spouted. She got to her feet. "We fairies can't fix everyone's woes! You need to think about yourself! Unless you want to risk receiving the Unable to Grant Stamp and lose all your wishes for the next hundred years, you need to *hang the mistletoe!*" She ducked her head around another low-hanging snowflake and pointed to a bare beam on the ceiling. "There," she said. "That looks like the perfect spot."

Lily looked up at the beam. It did seem a good place to hang mistletoe.

"If you fail at getting yourself kissed," Vivienne continued, "it won't be because the hunter has no interest. It'll be because you didn't pucker your sour lips!" She turned her wristband up and tapped it. "Goodness, look at the time. I'm sure I have somewhere more interesting to be." And she was gone.

Chapter Fourteen

Lily sat at the table for several minutes, contemplating Vivienne's advice to hang the mistletoe. As exasperating as the elder fairy could be, she did occasionally make sense. Wishing and hoping for a kiss might be a fine way to go if one had all the time in the world, but she didn't, and sometimes, a person did need a nudge. Still, if Jake had no interest in kissing her, mistletoe would have no influence over him, and that would be that. Any possibility of them becoming a couple would be at an end.

But what if it wasn't the end? What if Jake did want to kiss her?

Lily's heart pounded wildly in her chest at the idea of Jake pressing his mouth to hers. No man, human or otherwise, had ever done so. But from what she'd witnessed, kissing was a most pleasurable activity, and if Jake were to be her first, she would be a willing participant.

Before she could talk herself out of it, she hurried to once again retrieve the box from the bedroom closet. Then, removing the greenery, she closed her eyes, and it was done. The mistletoe was in full view, hanging from the beam. Now, all she needed was for Jake to return. And, hopefully, when he did, he'd stand in just the right spot and not still be angry with her. Though the way he left, she thought that to be more than a slim possibility.

Giving up a sigh, she began pacing, and Sierra left her place by the fire and paced right along with her. It was somehow comforting. Then, as the two of them started their third round of pacing, from kitchen to living room, Sierra's ears perked and she turned to the door, growling.

"What is it, girl?" Lily asked. She rubbed Sierra's head as they both faced the door, waiting for it to open. When it did, Jake rushed in, out of breath.

"I saw the wolf again," he said.

"Where?" Lily asked. A shiver rippled through her, thinking about Cinder all alone in the barn. She went to the window and peered out, but all she saw was a haze of white. It had been snowing since before Jake left, and it showed no signs of stopping.

Jake came up beside her. "Not far. I think it may have been a female. She was thin. I got the feeling she was tracking me, and I didn't have my rifle, so I wasn't about to stick around and ask questions."

As they stood there, Sierra turned to the door and growled again. The hair on her back stood on end.

"She knows the wolf is out there," Jake said. He stepped away from the window, looking around the room. "Where's my rifle?"

"You don't intend to go out there and shoot the poor animal, do you?" Lily asked.

"No, but I'd like to have my rifle nearby, where I can easily get to it, if need be."

"It's in the bedroom, in the closet," Lily said. She'd put it away so she wouldn't have to look at it all the time.

As soon as Jake was in the other room, Lily put on the puffy coat and boots. She had to go check on Cinder. She went to the door, opening it just enough for her to slip out, but Sierra slipped through the door, too, racing ahead into the snow before Lily could stop her.

Hurrying down the porch steps, Lily's feet sank into the deep snow. She couldn't see more than a few yards in front of her face, but she was able to make out Sierra's tracks, and she followed them. The last thing she needed was to lose Jake's dog, or worse, have Sierra confronted by a wolf.

Halfway between the cabin and the barn, Lily heard a growl. She stopped, and Sierra appeared at her side. Every hair on Sierra's back was standing on end. Another low growl came from in front of them, and Lily stared straight ahead into the blinding snow at two yellow eyes that seemed to glow in the dark.

Sierra let out a menacing growl of her own, and Lily stroked the fur on her back to try and calm her. She didn't want Sierra going after the wolf, who didn't seem at all concerned about facing an angry dog.

"Shoo!" Lily said, thrusting a hand at the glowing eyes. She had no reason to be afraid, she assured herself.

The wolf didn't budge.

Sierra became more agitated at the wolf's boldness. She growled again and snapped viciously at the snow.

Lily went into full panic mode. She clenched her fists tightly at her sides, and could practically feel the blood rushing through her veins. She knew if she didn't do something, she wouldn't be able to hold Sierra back. She looked about for something to use against the wolf, but all she saw was snow. Everywhere she looked, it was white powder. She took a breath to steady herself, then reached down and grabbed a handful. Wearing no gloves, the icy cold burned her skin, but she didn't care. She packed the snow into a tight ball, and threw it in the direction of the glowing eyes.

Again, the wolf stood firm.

Lily wasn't about to give up. She packed another ball, even larger than the last, and threw it as hard as she could at the wolf. The moment the snow left her hand, the blast from a rifle echoed off the trees that surrounded the cabin, and the wolf finally fled.

Relief washed over Lily. She turned to see Jake plowing through the snow toward her. When he reached her, he grabbed her by the shoulders. He looked wild, angrier than she'd ever seen him. "What were you thinking coming out here?" he demanded to know. "You could have gotten yourself killed!"

Lily's mouth went dry. She hadn't considered the danger. Her only concern had been to check on Cinder, and then get Sierra back inside. But Jake was right. She'd not only put herself at risk, she'd also put Jake's dog at risk. She looked down at Sierra, glad to see she was safe. And Jake was safe. And though his hands were still squeezing her shoulders, it was a welcome warmth. But as the seconds ticked off and the adrenaline fueling her energy subsided, she began to feel the full effect of facing such danger. The threat had been real. She could have been killed. Eaten by a wolf. Her eyelids fluttered, and everything went dark.

Lily had no idea how much time had passed. All she knew was that she was on the sofa, and Jake was talking to her like he was upset about something. Then she remembered. She'd been outside in the blinding snow, throwing snowballs at a wolf. *A wolf!* No wonder Jake was upset. She opened her eyes, and took him in. He still looked angry. Even so, she was happy to have him there at her side.

"Hi," she whispered and tried to sit up.

"You need to relax for a few more minutes," Jake said. He pushed her gently back so that she was prone again. "Honest to God, Lily," he continued, "I'm going to need some kind of explanation for what went on out there. How could you put yourself in danger like that? And how could you possibly think throwing a snowball at a wolf would save you?"

Lily swallowed. She knew what she wanted to say, but she couldn't get the words out. And even if she could, it was likely Jake wouldn't believe her. Though from the look on his face, she needed to try. He wasn't giving her a pass this time. He expected answers.

"Well?" Jake pressed.

"Do you promise to listen with an open mind?" she asked.

Jake looked at her with cool reserve. "How about I just promise to listen?"

Her heartbeat had returned to normal. She sat up and took a moment to consider what she could say that wouldn't have him either laughing at how ridiculous she sounded or looking at her like she'd lost her mind. Keeping it simple was probably best. Though at the moment, even simple seemed impossible. Still, it was time.

Taking a small breath, she whispered, "I'm a Christmas fairy," afraid if she said it too loud, he might walk out again.

Jake raised his eyebrows. "Excuse me?"

"I'm a Christmas fairy. From the North Pole. And I was certain the wolf would not harm me because Christmas fairies are friend to all animals."

Jake stared at the floor, his jaw tense, and Lily laced her fingers together, afraid she'd made things worse. But if he would just hear her out, it would all make sense. She was sure of it.

"I can only imagine what you must be thinking," she continued, "but I promise, if you give me a chance, I can explain everything… the wolf, the glitter on your arms, the little man at the door—his name is Enar, by the way, and he's an elf."

"An elf," Jake said, his eyes meeting hers. "And you're a fairy."

"Yes," Lily said. "We both live at the North Pole and work for Santa."

Jake held up a hand. "Before you say anything more, I should probably tell you I stopped believing in fairy tales and Santa Claus a long time ago." He pressed his lips together. "I told you I would listen. And I will. But I'd appreciate it if you would at least be serious with me. No more fooling around. I need answers."

"I *am* being serious. I'm a Christmas fairy from the North Pole. I know it sounds impossible, but it's true."

Jake dragged a hand across the back of his neck. "I guess it all makes sense then, doesn't it?"

"It does?" Lily felt a sudden flood of relief. Maybe this was going to work out, after all.

"Of course," Jake said. "I even understand your fondness for sweets now. Everyone knows fairies love sugar."

"They *do?*" Lily asked, delighted with how the conversation was going. She had no idea humans knew about a fairy's need for sugar.

"Absolutely! That's why you've been baking all those pies and cookies." He nodded toward the kitchen, where there were still a half dozen plates of cookies, a candy cane pie, and a fruitcake, which was getting drier by the hour.

"Yes!" Lily said. "Fairies are like hummingbirds. We need a constant supply of sugar to refuel our energy and keep our metabolism going."

Jake shook his head. "And here I was wondering how you've managed to keep all your teeth."

Lily giggled and waved a hand. "No need to worry about that. Fairies don't get cavities."

"Of course they don't," Jake agreed. "But here's the thing… fairies aren't real! Neither is Santa Claus or the Easter bunny or elves! Though, I'll admit your friend's pointed ears did have me going for a minute."

"But you just said—"

"Never mind what I said! I was being sarcastic!" Jake pushed himself up off the sofa and moved away from her. "You really think I believe you're a fairy? And that your little friend was an elf?"

Lily felt a tightening in her chest. Human conversation was hard enough to decipher without adding the element of sarcasm. She'd known it was going to be difficult to explain, but she had no idea human men could be so frustrating. And why expend more energy talking if Jake was going to doubt everything she told him?

"It's late, and I'm tired," she said, getting up from the sofa. "Perhaps we should finish this discussion in the morning."

"No!" Jake said, grabbing her by the arm. "We're going to finish now!"

Lily's brow pulled into a frown. She looked at her flesh being squeezed by his hand. It caused her a discomfort she'd never felt before. Her wings vibrated, but she managed to keep them under control. Having another snow incident would definitely make things worse. She drew in a breath to calm herself and said, "Please unhand me."

"Then don't walk away," Jake said. He let her go.

"Why should I stay? You've already made it clear you're not open-minded enough to believe anything I'm saying."

"That's not true," Jake said. "I'm as open-minded as anyone. I'd just like to hear something that's at least halfway believable."

Lily's wings vibrated again at his tone, and again she was able to calm them. "If you can sit there and listen without becoming disagreeable, I'll continue. Then, when I'm finished, you'll be free to ask questions. Those are my terms," she said, with a tilt of her chin. "Shall I continue, or not?"

Jake's eyes sparked, but he did the zipper thing across his lips.

Lily took the zipper thing as a sign he was willing to listen. Though, that could change at any moment. Still, if he was willing to try, she was, too. She settled, hands in lap, and began. "I want you to know I'm aware that some of what I'm about to tell you will sound so fantastical, it'll be near impossible to believe. But I promise you, it's all true." She waited for a moment to see if he had anything to say. When he remained silent, she continued. "Like I already told you, I'm a Christmas fairy from the North Pole, and my job is to help enrich the lives of humans during the holiday season. It might be something as simple as making it snow for a child who has never seen snow, or I might reunite a person with a loved one they'd worried was lost to them forever. Sometimes, I even help lost pets find their way home."

Jake was still listening, but his eyes were full of doubt.

"Shall I go on?" she asked.

Jake nodded. "Please do."

Lily took a moment to think, determined to tell him everything, though she thought it best to get the easier parts said first. "When I'm sent to help someone, it's called an assignment. This year, my assignment location was this cabin. As you pointed out, I'm not the type to enjoy spending the holidays alone in a place such as this. But then I went into the frozen forest, and it was so beautiful... and, well, I met you." She smiled. "I'll admit, when I first came to believe you were my assignment, I was taken aback. I couldn't understand why Santa would want me to help a hunter of reindeer. But then you explained—"

"Wait—help me with what?" Jake asked.

"Finding your way back."

"From where?"

"From wherever you went after you lost your sister. You see, in losing Josie, you also lost your enjoyment for life. So, that's why I'm here. I imagine Santa felt if I could somehow help you regain your Christmas spirit, your heart might begin to heal." She touched his hand lightly. "Everyone deserves to be happy, Jake."

Jake looked around the room, at all the paper snowflakes and the tree, then his gaze settled back on her. "So, all this, all your decorating, was part of some big plan to help me enjoy Christmas again?"

"I had no plan. The cabin was so dreary, I thought it needed cheering up."

"And you thought by cheering the cabin up, it would help me?"

"Maybe. Did it work?"

"I don't know that I'm ready to go Christmas caroling or join in the town's festivities, but I'd say me bringing you a tree and helping you decorate it is definitely proof you've made a difference."

Lily's lips drew into a small smile. "Then perhaps I have been successful in my assignment."

"If you say so," Jake said, skepticism still edging his voice. He was quiet for a minute before continuing. "I have to be honest. I'm not even sure what to say at this point. I'm a reasonable man, but the things you've told me are pretty hard to believe."

"Understandably," Lily said. "But think about everything that's happened. The glitter on your arms… Enar showing up here…. And how do you suppose he got here in all that snow?" She gestured toward the window, where the snow was still coming down.

"Good question. How *did* he get here?" Jake asked.

Finally, Lily thought, something she could easily answer. "Christmas fairies and elves can travel to all parts of the world in an instant," she explained. "It's much the same way Santa travels on Christmas Eve. Except we don't use a sleigh pulled by reindeer. That would be too cumbersome. All we need do is imagine where we want to go, and it happens."

Jake leveled a gaze at her. "Is that why you're able to walk around in the snow without a coat and in your bare feet? Because you're a fairy?"

Lily nodded. "Fairies must be comfortable in their environment at the North Pole, so they are immune to the cold." Though she had yet to solve the mystery of why her recent venture out into the snow had caused her such discomfort. But she saw no reason to burden Jake with that. And now the look on his face made her question whether or not she should tell him the rest, that she believed him to be her Christmas wish. Would he continue to listen? Or would he walk out the door again and not return? The idea saddened her, but she had to take the chance. "If you're not feeling too overwhelmed, there is one more thing I should probably tell you," she said.

"Sure. Why stop now." Jake settled in a chair at the kitchen table, ready to hear what she had to say.

Lily sat across from him. She hadn't expected they would be having this conversation so soon, so she didn't feel entirely prepared. She quickly gathered her thoughts, and then began. "As enjoyable as it is creating happiness for others, it's still hard work. So, as a reward, every year, Santa allows each fairy and elf at the North Pole the opportunity to ask for one special wish, something that no one else might think to give us." She paused, hoping she wasn't making a mistake telling him everything all in one sitting. Though she'd made it this far, so there was no going back now. "This year," she continued, "my wish was to be given the chance to find love."

"Fairies aren't allowed to fall in love?" Jake asked.

Lily felt a flutter of hope. Jake's question gave her the encouragement she needed to go on. "We can certainly find someone to spend our lives with, but it's more a practical arrangement. You see, if fairies were to go through the same emotional ups and downs that humans are exposed to, it would wear us out. We wouldn't be able to bear it for the hundreds of years we might be doing this work. We can be satisfied with what we've accomplished when an assignment is over, but any joy or distress we've experienced does not stay with us." She let out a small sigh. "That is why I wish to find love. I'd like to keep the joy I experience for more than just a single holiday season. I want to keep it for a lifetime."

"I guess I can understand that," Jake said. "Everyone deserves to have someone to love."

"Yes," Lily said. "But do you understand what I'm saying?"

Jake looked at her for a long minute before he finally said, "Why don't you just tell me."

"Okay," Lily said, swallowing. She felt a strong vibration in her wings, but so far so good. "Jake, I believe you are my Christmas wish."

"What!" Jake drew back. *"Me?"*

Lily nodded. "But please don't feel that you have any obligation to me. Certainly, I wouldn't expect—"

"Whoa!" Jake said. He held up a hand. "Is this a joke? How am I supposed to respond to something like that? What do you expect me to say?"

The vibration in Lily's wings grew stronger. She tensed, hoping it would be enough to prevent an outburst of snow. "Say what you want, how you feel."

"Okay," Jake said cautiously. "I'm beginning to think maybe I've been here too long, that I've somehow led you on and you've begun to have ideas about the two of us getting together. I also think it might be better for both of us if I left here right now before this goes any further."

"Please don't," Lily said. "You've done nothing wrong. It's just a wish—*my* wish—and if you and I fail to make a connection, when my assignment here is over, I will go back to the North Pole and I will be happy to go on being a Christmas fairy. It is a good existence, one that brings me immeasurable joy.

And you will be free to do whatever you choose. Like I said, you are under no obligation to me." She dared not reveal that she was in danger of losing her wishes for the next hundred years if they didn't make a connection. She'd come to know him as an honorable man, and she wouldn't take the chance he might feel a duty to help her achieve her goal. Whatever came next, whether he chose to stay or whether he chose to go, she had to accept his decision.

"But then what?" Jake asked. "Do I just go home and forget about you? Forget we ever met?" He swung his arms wide. "Will I even remember being here at this cabin?"

"You may." Lily smiled, though his question caused the pain in her chest to return.

Jake rubbed a hand over the back of his neck, which is something she noticed he did whenever he was presented with something bothersome or that didn't make sense. He'd been rubbing his neck a lot lately. "I can't think straight right now," he said. "I feel like I'm having some kind of weird dream or hallucination or something."

"Perhaps you need some time to yourself," she offered. "We can talk more in the morning, if you like."

"That might be best," Jake agreed.

Lily went to her room and closed the door with a quiet click. A few minutes later, she heard the cabin door open and then shut. Jake was gone again.

Chapter Fifteen

When the morning light crept through the bedroom window, Lily stayed put under the warm covers, rubbing the palm of her hand over her chest, where a steady pain remained. She'd heard Jake return not long after he'd left the night before, but she'd thought it best to let him have some time to himself. Though she'd lain awake half the night, trying to think of what else she might have said to convince him she was telling the truth about who she was. For if he thought her a liar, how could he ever be expected to develop feelings for her? A man didn't willingly fall in love with someone he believed to be a storyteller.

Her vision blurred as the pain in her chest continued, and tears spilled along her cheeks, making a damp spot on her pillow. She reached up to wipe the wet from her face, thinking surely by now she'd lost every bit of liquid in her entire body. Was this how being in love felt? she wondered. If so, it seemed a far worse punishment than losing a century of Christmas wishes.

It all seemed so hopeless. What she needed to do was think of a way to convince Jake that everything she'd told him was true.

Leaving the warmth of the bed, she went to the window and looked out at the morning sky that was still speckled with tiny white flakes. Causing an end to the snow might be enough to convince Jake. But could she do it? It seemed reasonable that if she was becoming vulnerable to the cold, and if she was losing her desire for sweets, then she might also be losing her ability to perform magic.

Only one way to find out, she thought, and closing her eyes, she imagined the snow-producing nimbostratus clouds replaced with a sky of blue, like a field full of beautiful cornflowers. It didn't take long, just a few seconds, and when she felt the sun's rays warming her skin, she opened her eyes to a perfectly clear sky. Not a wisp of a cloud in sight! Nor did she see even one tiny snowflake.

Excited now to get back to her conversation with Jake, she spun away from the window and flung open the bedroom door. And there he was, standing at the cabin door in a ray of sunshine.

"Have you seen this?" he asked as she approached him. He stepped out onto the porch and spread his arms. "It's finally stopped snowing and is actually warm!"

Fifty-two degrees and rising, Lily thought as she stood in the open doorway and listened to the happy chirp of birds greeting the day, along with a *plink, plink, plink* of water from snow that was already melting and dripping into the gutters.

Jake turned to her. "This break in the weather might not last. I think I should try to get out of here while I can."

Oh. Lily's stomach dropped. She hadn't expected him to be in such a hurry to leave. She glanced out at the snow that was glistening in the morning sun. Of course, he wanted to leave. His ankle was much better, and he had cattle to tend to.

And he didn't believe she was a fairy.

As she stood there, one of the paper snowflakes came loose from the ceiling and floated down to land at her feet. She stared at it for a moment, and then she remembered the mistletoe. With all that had happened the night before—the encounter with the wolf and then arguing with Jake—she'd forgotten about it. But was it too late for mistletoe? She hoped not. She turned and took a few steps inside so that she stood directly beneath where it hung.

Jake followed. "Everything okay?"

"Yes," Lily said, "I just hadn't expected we would be saying goodbye this morning. I'd hoped we could talk more and finish the conversation we were having last night."

"I don't see how more talk will change anything," Jake said. He moved closer but stopped short of the ideal spot. "I thought about what you told me last night, and I understand that you believe in fairy tales. But I don't. I don't believe in magic or elves or Santa Claus. I stopped believing in all those things a long time ago." He paused, thinking. "Try to look at this from my perspective. What if I told you I was super human? You never know, I could be Batman or Superman... maybe even the Incredible Hulk. I'm okay now, but don't make me mad, or I might turn into a green giant and bust out of my clothes!"

"That's ridiculous. You'd do no such thing," Lily said, frowning.

"You're right!" Jake said. "I wouldn't! Because those characters aren't real! They're make-believe! Look," he continued, his tone softening, "if you really believe yourself to be a Christmas fairy who lives at the North Pole and is capable of fending off wild animals by tossing snowballs at them, then maybe you need someone to talk to. A professional who can help you cope with whatever issues you're dealing with. I would even be willing to help you find someone. We could leave here right now and—"

"No!" Lily said. She clenched her teeth, determined. "I don't need to talk to anyone. I'm talking to you! I know it's hard to believe, but I *am* a Christmas fairy. If you would just think about all the things that have happened since you've been here... Enar, the wolf, the glitter on your arms, which, by the way, wasn't glitter at all. It was fairy dust that I used to take our conversation back a few minutes."

Jake gave her a wary look. "What are you talking about? Turning back time?"

"Yes," Lily said. "I needed to rewind time, so I wouldn't have to explain why it was snowing in here."

"What snow?"

"Here in the cabin. Remember the water on the floor? That

was from snow. I'm a young fairy, and I don't have complete control over my wings yet. Whenever something happens that makes me excited or nervous or *angry*"—Lily drew her brow tight—"my wings flutter and produce snow."

Jake held up his hands. "Stop. That's crazy talk. You have no wings hanging from your back."

Lily gave a heavy sigh. "They're there. You just can't see them. Humans can only see a fairy's wings if she allows it."

"Okay. Whatever you say." Jake shook his head, looking exasperated. "I've listened to enough of this. I need to get out of here while the weather holds. I know you said you wanted to spend Christmas here, but if you've changed your mind, I'd be happy to take you with me. Or I could send someone back for you. Whatever you want." He grabbed his hat and put on his coat, and Sierra was at his side in an instant, like she knew this was it, time for them to finally go home.

Frustrated at Jake's refusal to consider she might be telling the truth, Lily blurted, "I made it stop snowing."

Jake turned. "What?"

Lily nodded at the open door. "The snow stopped because I *made* it stop."

Jake gave a short laugh. "This gets more fantastic by the minute. Now you're able to control the weather?"

Lily shrugged. "I can use my imagination to get what I want—within reason. I can't use it for personal gain; all of a fairy's needs are provided by Santa. But yes, if need be, I'm able to control the weather."

Jake said nothing, just looked unconvinced.

"I could show you my wings," Lily offered. She'd hoped it wouldn't go this far. The revealing of a fairy's wings was frowned upon. But she saw no other way to convince Jake. She only hoped her wings wouldn't take this moment to be a no-show. She let out a slow, focused breath and was relieved when they unfolded from her back, much like a flower opening its petals. Then, when they were completely open, she fluttered them just enough to release a brief burst of snow.

Jake was slack-jawed as he backed up until he was against the door jamb. But Sierra wasn't bothered at all by the sudden appearance of Lily's wings or seeing snow inside the cabin. She hurried to lap up the snowflakes that were already melting on the floor.

"This can't be real," Jake said. "Either I'm dreaming, or you've slipped me some kind of drug."

"Neither," Lily said. "I told you, I'm a fairy."

"Fairies aren't real," Jake argued. "I obviously fell off my horse and hit my head, and now I'm delusional."

"I promise you, you're not," Lily told him.

Jake focused on the wet streaks on the floor, touching the toe of his boot in a puddle that Sierra had missed. He smeared it around some and then drew his foot back. He gestured to the snow outside. "Are you telling me all that snow out there is because of you? That you flapped your wings and made it snow so you could keep me here?"

"Fairies don't *flap* their wings," Lily said, laughing. "We're more graceful than that. But to answer your question… I could have kept you here with snow if I'd had to. But Mother Nature provided, so I didn't have to do a thing. And I have two ways I can produce snow. I can either flutter my wings, or I can close my eyes and use my imagination. It's the same as when kids play make-believe. Their imagination can take them anywhere they want to go. That's why Santa uses fairies at Christmastime, so we can help those who are struggling with life's difficulties find a little holiday joy."

Jake swallowed. "I'm speechless."

"That's to be expected. Humans—adults mostly—find it difficult to believe in things that make no sense. Children don't have as hard a time. They're more willing to accept what might seem impossible to others."

Jake's brow furrowed. "I'm an adult, and I'm willing to admit the possibility that otherworldly beings exist. But fairies and elves? That's a bit much."

"I agree. It's a lot to take in," Lily said. "And we're not

otherworldly. We're just different. Magical. A little magic helps people keep believing in the wonder of the season. If nothing magical ever happened, Christmas would become just another day, and there would be no further need for Santa or elves… or fairies."

"Yeah. Okay," Jake said, laughing a nervous laugh and still looking doubtful.

"Tell me what I can do to convince you," Lily said.

Jake shook his head. "I have no idea. It all seems so impossible."

Lily pressed her lips together, staying quiet, letting him think.

"So now what?" he finally asked. "Where do we go from here?"

Lily smiled warmly. "This is where you need to make a decision. Stay here with me, or go back to your ranch. As for me, I must remain here until midnight Christmas Eve. That's when my assignment is officially over."

Jake looked out the door, stared at the glistening snow for a minute, then turned back to her, saying, "This is hard."

"I know," Lily acknowledged.

Jake took another quick glance out the door and back. "I'm sorry, but I think it's time I go home."

Lily dipped her head. "I understand."

Chapter Sixteen

The Toy Room bustled with energy as Santa took his daily stroll past every workstation, taking inventory and making notes. He liked what he saw. Sisette and her team were busy at the Baby Doll Assembly Line, making sure each doll was in perfect condition before being boxed and wrapped. Then there was Victor, at the head of the Retro Toy Assembly Line, directing several of the junior elves as they pieced together sections of what looked to be a complicated train set. Next was Arild at the Technology Station, using his engineering skills to build a new and improved replica of NASA's Mars Explorer. And finally, Minchin, one of the elder elves, stood at the Innovative Toy Station, working a remote control to test a small airplane that he claimed could do aerial tricks.

Santa couldn't help but smile. The elves had outdone themselves this year, coming up with so many new toys and amazing gadgets that it was sure to be a happy Christmas for all. And everything was right on schedule.

He took one more look at the Innovative Toy Station, where Minchin appeared to be struggling with the small airplane. It didn't seem to want to perform any tricks. Oh, well. Perhaps by next year, Minchin would have all the kinks worked out, and then the plane would be a big hit with kids of all ages.

Finally moving on, Santa reached the overhead balcony, where he stopped to gaze out over the entire room. He had only one last item to check on, a name on the Nice List. And for that, he needed to speak with Dalyor, the Toy Room Supervisor. But at the moment, Dalyor was talking to an elf who seemed to be having a problem with a remote-controlled car that would only go in reverse.

Santa watched as Dalyor worked with the car for a minute, mumbling as he did so. Finally, he set the car on the floor, and it sped off in forward motion. Satisfied it was now working properly, Dalyor handed the remote-control to another elf, then he ran up the ramp to Santa.

"Greetings, sir," Dalyor said. "I see you have your Nice List with you. Is there a problem?"

"Not at all," Santa said. "I just thought we should take a minute to discuss one of the names recently added. Do you have time?"

"My time is yours," Dalyor said.

Santa traced a finger down the list until he came to the name Bradford Montgomery. Young Bradford had been on the Naughty List the previous two years, but word this year was he'd turned things around, and now his name was near the top of the Nice List. But wanting to make sure it wasn't a mistake, Santa put his finger to Bradford's name to get an impression of how things were currently going at the Montgomery household. Very well, it seemed. Satisfied, he turned to Dalyor. "If I may ask, what gift do you suggest for young Bradford Montgomery this year?"

"Ah, Bradford, isn't that the boy who put a mouse in Suzie Hanson's lunch box last year?"

Santa chuckled. "Yes, young Bradford can be quite the trickster. All in good fun, I'm sure."

"As I recall, he also put purple dye in his sister's shampoo bottle," Dalyor reminded Santa.

"Purple is a nice color," Santa commented.

"Perhaps, but his sister didn't think so at the time," Dalyor said.

Santa tapped Bradford's name. "The boy has been making a real effort to get along with others this year. I think we should reward that behavior with something special, don't you?"

"Of course," Dalyor relented. He gave it some thought, then said, "How about a puppy for young Bradford?"

Santa arched an eyebrow. "You know we can only give puppies to children whose parents consent. Otherwise, the poor animal may be in need of a new home by Easter. And what does that mean for the child, Dalyor?"

Dalyor sighed. "Tears. Lots of tears." Then he perked up. "But what if the dog needs no care?" He looked about the room and pointed at a toy that had just come off the Technology Station Assembly Line. "Over there, the Techno Pup. He doesn't eat a thing, and he's techno cool. He can be taught all kinds of tricks, and he has blue eyes that are not only soothing but can also light up a room, which we all know is important to kids who are afraid of the dark. Plus, the child who receives him can give him a name, and he'll even come when called. And when the child sends in for the dog's papers, he or she will get a certificate of ownership."

"The same as when people register a living dog!" Santa said, his eyes twinkling.

Dalyor nodded. "I dare say the Techno Pup is one of this year's hottest new toys. The mailroom is overflowing with letters from kids asking to find one under their tree."

"You may be on to something," Santa said. He patted Dalyor on the back, and Dalyor grinned and tugged proudly at his suspenders.

"Watch out! Incoming!" someone shouted to Dalyor and Santa as a small toy airplane headed straight for them.

Santa and Dalyor both ducked to avoid getting hit, and when Santa looked down to the main floor, he saw Minchin holding the controller for the plane.

"My apologies," Minchin called up to Santa, looking sheepish. He landed the plane a few feet from where Dalyor and Santa stood.

"No problem," Santa called to Minchin. "How's it going?"

Minchin's eyes lit up. "I think it might finally be ready. Would you like a demonstration?"

"Yes, that would be a real treat," Santa said. He and Dalyor stood back while Minchin worked the remote control to make the plane take off again. The start was shaky, but then, as the plane gained altitude, it flew several smooth laps around the Toy Room and even completed a few tight loops. Then, just as it began its final lap, it went into a tailspin.

Santa kept an eye on the plane, waiting to see where it was going to come down so he could get out of the way, if need be. Then, after a few tense moments, the plane finally hit the main floor with a loud *thunk!* Which resulted in one of the wings breaking off and shattering into several small pieces. Everyone in the room heard the crash, and all eyes were on the broken plane.

"Oh, my," Santa said, staring down at the pieces of wing scattered about.

"I'm just glad it didn't come down on top of us," Dalyor remarked.

"It seems to still need a little fine-tuning," Santa called to Minchin. He felt bad for the elf, but that was the nature of toy production. Some toys worked, and some didn't.

"I guess I should make the wings sturdier," Minchin said, sounding frustrated. He quickly went to work with a dustpan and broom, and everyone else in the room went back to work on their own projects.

"I bet it'll make a lot of boys and girls happy… perhaps next year," Santa said. He gave Minchin a thumbs-up, and then he turned to Dalyor. "As for the Techno Pup, I like your suggestion. I'll be looking forward to delivering one of them to young Bradford this year."

Dalyor tugged at his suspenders again and bid Santa a good evening.

Pleased with how everything was going, Santa was ready to be on his way. But first, he had an announcement to make. He made his way back down the ramp to the main floor, then, in a booming voice that filled the room, he said. "Attention, please, everyone!" He paused to make sure everyone was listening, and when all eyes were turned to him, he continued. "You've all done a wonderful job this year, and I know it's been difficult keeping up with so many new names added to the Nice List. So, to show my appreciation for your hard work, you will all be getting extra time off after this holiday season. Plus, come Christmas morning, each of you will find a generous bonus in your stocking!"

The expansive room exploded with loud cheers and thunderous clapping until Santa held up a white-gloved hand. "One more thing," he said. "A few of you have still not put in your wish request. I need you to get those to me by midnight tomorrow so that I have time to give each wish special consideration. Understood?"

"Understood," every elf replied in unison.

With a twinkle in his eye, Santa waved goodbye to the room and was almost to the door when he heard a voice calling to him. He looked and saw Enar waving to him from the balcony. "Yes, Enar, what is it?" Santa asked, having to raise his voice so he could be heard over the toy assembly lines.

"If you have time, sir," Enar shouted, loud enough that anyone who might be interested could hear, "I was hoping I might have a word with you. It's about Liliana. I was wondering if you intend to grant her Christmas wish this year?"

A train that was being tested came to a screeching halt, and all faces in the Toy Room turned toward Santa to see what his answer might be.

"Back to work," Santa told everyone. And then to Enar, he said, "Now, Enar, you know that Christmas wishes are private, discussed only if the elf or fairy making the wish wants to share. I suggest you wait and talk to Liliana herself when she returns from her assignment."

Enar spread his hands. "But I have already spoken to her, and I am concerned. From her lips, she hopes to finish her assignment and then continue living as a human. Which means she does not expect to return here to the North Pole."

Great gasps sounded throughout the Toy Room, and all assembly lines came to a dead stop as every elf waited to hear more. To become human was a rare event. In the last two hundred years, it had only happened a half dozen times, and only four of those had been successful thus far. The other two were never talked about, and the fairies involved had never returned to fairy duty.

Santa calmed the room with a pumping of his hands. "Now, now, let's not spread rumors. I know Liliana is friend to everyone here, but nothing has been made final yet. If she chooses to leave the North Pole, you will all be informed of any change in her address. Right now, though, I need each of you continuing to give your full effort to ensure a successful holiday season."

Enar ran down the ramp, leaving the balcony, to stand at Santa's side. He spoke quietly, saying, "I apologize, sir. I did not mean to cause a disruption to the production line. I just wanted to know if you were aware of any progress Liliana has made toward her goal."

"No harm done," Santa said. He placed a hand on Enar's shoulder. "I am aware of your feelings for Liliana, but as I said, her Christmas wish is a private matter, and I cannot discuss it with you."

"I wouldn't lose any sleep just yet, little man," a voice behind Enar said. There was a sudden chill in the air as Vivienne stepped up beside him. "Liliana may be returning to us sooner than expected. If not, I hear the fairy Isla has been asking about you."

"Vivienne!" Santa addressed her sternly. "Did you not just hear what I said about spreading rumors? I do not want either of you speaking of things that don't concern you." He looked from her to Enar. "I have a mind to send you both to Human Resources for further sensitivity training."

"But, sir," Vivienne said, "I, too, have been to see Liliana, and she seems to be in a bit of a muddle. I have tried advising her, but as you know, she can be stubborn, and I fear not only will she fail to successfully complete her assignment, but she may also fail at getting her wish. It's the human, sir. He's stubborn and has shown no interest in Liliana."

Santa's spectacles slid down his nose and practically fell to the floor. He grabbed them just in time and fumbled to put them back on. His bushy white eyebrows arched. "If the human is not interested in Liliana, it is his right. And if Liliana is in a muddle, that's to be expected. She has made a life-changing wish, and I'm sure she may even be having second thoughts. And that is *her* right. But I have complete faith in her, and I'm sure she will not let anything get in the way of her assignment. Speaking of… perhaps you should be paying more attention to your *own* assignment. I've heard there have been complications."

Vivienne dipped her head. "The complications are few, nothing that will prevent success."

"Good to hear," Santa said. "I won't keep you, then." He turned to Enar. "I won't keep you, either. I'm sure you also have much to do before the big night."

"Yes, much," Enar said.

With a nod, Santa turned and left the Toy Room, excited that it was finally time for lunch. Not that he was looking forward to having salad for the umpteenth day in a row, but Mrs. Claus had promised him three chocolate chip cookies if he cleaned his plate, and he could already taste every delicious morsel of chocolate melting in his mouth. And once he finished delivering toys on Christmas Eve, he intended to end the salad diet and enjoy three chocolate chip cookies after *every* meal.

As soon as the door shut after Santa, Enar swiveled around and faced Vivienne. "What have you done?"

"Don't look at me like that," Vivienne said, her top lip curling. "It gives me the willies. No wonder little Miss Goody Goodness is looking elsewhere for romance."

"Answer the question!" Enar said, his tone sharp.

Vivienne gave him a blank stare. "Can you be more specific?"

"Don't play dumb. Why have you been visiting Liliana?"

"Why have *you* been visiting her?" Vivienne asked.

Enar straightened. "I happen to have genuine concern for her well-being."

"As do I."

"That's debatable."

Vivienne yawned. "Goodness, I'm so bored, I could fall asleep."

"Don't change the subject. What are you up to with Liliana? Why would you want to help her? It's no secret you and she don't get along."

Vivienne squinted her eyes at him until they were mere slits. "If you must know, I've been giving our Liliana a few much-needed pep talks. It seems she knows absolutely nothing about getting herself kissed." Her lips pulled into a wide grin. "But that's what you're hoping, isn't it? You don't want Liliana to receive a kiss from anyone but you."

Enar worked his jaw until it was a tight knot. "This has nothing to do with me. I want only happiness for Liliana. And why do *you* care if she gets kissed? You're already in a win-win situation. If Liliana is successful with the human, she'll be gone, and you'll be named Head Christmas Fairy. And if she *isn't* successful, she'll return to us and be miserable once again having you for a roommate."

"*Au contraire*, little man. When I am named Head Christmas Fairy, Liliana will be looking for a *new* roommate, for *I* intend to have the elves build me a cottage of my own atop the hill that overlooks the reindeer meadow."

"I dare say not!" Enar sputtered. "Santa has granted me that land so I can build a home there for my bride!"

"Yes, but your intended bride seems to have someone else in mind to become her groom, doesn't she?" Vivienne made *tsk, tsk* sounds. "Looks like you might be spending all eternity alone. Of course, there is that boring little fairy Isla. I hear she can make snow angels like nobody's business."

Sputtering something unintelligible, Enar's face turned the color of a ripe plum. His fists were tight against his sides. Vivienne almost laughed. Poor elf. He was about to have an aneurysm right there in front of her. Though if that were to happen, an explanation might be necessary, and she had other, more important things to do at the moment than answer nonsensical questions.

"Good talk, little man," she said, patting the top of Enar's head. "Now, if you don't mind, I really do need to be off so I can pay a visit to my assignment. Wouldn't want to upset Santa, would we?"

"You think you have it all figured out," Enar said, finally able to speak.

"As a matter of fact, I do," Vivienne said. "And how perceptive of you."

Enar grinned, suddenly and completely in control. "I wonder… has anyone ever told you that if you were to assist Liliana with gaining her wish, it would benefit you, as well? Beyond being named Head Christmas Fairy?"

Vivienne snapped herself out of another yawn. "What are you talking about?"

Enar's eyes were gleaming. "It's really very simple. If Liliana's wish were to be granted, due to your help, your own wishes would be restored."

A wretched noise that mimicked the sound of fingernails scraping against a chalkboard came from Vivienne's throat as she tried to speak. Finally, she got the words out. "You lie! I have never heard such a thing!"

Enar shrugged. "It's true. Help Liliana, help yourself." And he walked away.

Vivienne kept her eyes on him until he was back up on the balcony. She had a mind to make the little toad trip and tumble headfirst over the rail. But such thoughts were improper, and with it being so close to Christmas, she didn't dare do anything that might hinder her chances at being named Head Christmas Fairy.

Jaw clenched, she left the Toy Room. As she moved down the hall, her mind was like a whirlwind, with her thoughts being tossed around all over the place. Here, she'd come up with the perfect plan to thwart little Liliana's Christmas wish by giving her magic mistletoe, which would ensure keeping her as the resident cookie creator. But, now, she had to get back to that dreary cabin *tout de suite* to make sure that pathetic little fairy didn't do something stupid, like get herself kissed! And if that wasn't bothersome enough, she had to actually *help* little Liliana get her man.

"*Grr!*" a growl bubbled from Vivienne's throat as two young elves on their way to the Toy Room walked past her. She shoved them aside, screaming, "Out of the way!" She hadn't a moment to waste.

Chapter Seventeen

When Jake left, Lily was sure she'd seen the last of him. This time, he'd taken his dog. But ten minutes later, he was back and asking questions—*What's it like to live at the North Pole? Does it always snow? Can I, a mere mortal, go there?*

Lily was happy he was so curious, and she was overjoyed at his return. This meant that their time together wasn't over and that maybe they had a real chance. She gave some thought to his questions and then started by telling him how beautiful it was at the North Pole. And peaceful. A place unaffected by the trials of civilization. And yes, he could go there, but only if she, or someone else from the North Pole, took him. Or he could go on an expedition with a guide. But all he'd see is an expansive, flat sheet of ice.

"Ice? That's all it is?" Jake asked.

"No. But since Santa's home and workshop are invisible to humans, that's what scientists believe," Lily said. She lowered her voice to a whisper. "My goodness, could you imagine what might happen if people were actually able to see Santa's home? It would soon be overrun with tourists!"

"Makes sense," Jake agreed. "The only thing that might keep

people away is the cold. It must be hard to live in such a climate."

"It's not so bad," Lily said. "Because of the Arctic Ocean, it's surprisingly warmer than the South Pole. In July, it's not unheard of for the temperature to reach a balmy thirty-two degrees Fahrenheit." She smiled. "We even have wildlife… the occasional arctic fox and a few species of seabirds, like the kittiwake and the snow bunting. You might also see walruses, seals, and a polar bear or two. Though polar bears are another thing scientists don't seem to know much about. Until a group of explorers came along and saw for themselves, the North Pole was believed to be polar-bear free."

"What about dogs?" Jake asked. He glanced at Sierra, who had settled in her spot near the fireplace and was making soft snoring sounds.

Lily shook her head. "We have none. I wish we did. I would love to have a dog like Sierra. She's a fun companion."

"Yeah, I think she's pretty great," Jake said. He seemed lost in thought for a minute, and then he had another question. "So, what do you and everyone else—the elves and other fairies—do during the off-season?"

Lily smiled broadly as she considered the days ahead when the holidays would be over, and activity at the North Pole would wind down to a much slower pace. "It's a special time for everyone," she said. "It's a time for rejuvenation and growth, reflection and rest. The reindeer are put out to their meadow, and everyone is free to do whatever they please. Santa and Mrs. Claus love to vacation in the tropics—as do some of the elves. But many of the fairies—myself included—stay at the North Pole to enjoy the quiet. I get caught up on my reading and take plenty of naps. And of course, I spend a lot of time in the main kitchen testing new cookie recipes." Though, she wondered, with her need for sugar now waning, would her enjoyment of baking also wane? No, she couldn't see that happening.

"Sounds like fairy life isn't half bad," Jake commented. "I'm having a hard time understanding why you can't have everything you want living at the North Pole. Including love. Doesn't Santa love his wife?"

"Oh, yes, most definitely. But then, he *is* human."

Jake's eyes widened. "How can he be human? Isn't he like a thousand years old?"

"At least!" Lily said. "But I assure you, he's as human as you are. And I can't answer how he has lived so long. That's something you would have to ask him yourself." She paused. "May I ask… have you ever been in love?"

"A couple of times," Jake admitted. "Though, the first time, I was so young, it probably doesn't count."

"Love always counts, no matter the age."

"I suppose. But since I was only in the second grade, I was pretty clueless about stuff like that."

"May I ask about this girl who caught your heart at such a young age?"

Jake grinned, looking to the fire, the reflection of the flame dancing in his eyes. "Her name was Amanda," he began, "and we were the best of friends for most of our childhood. At least that's what *I* thought we were until one day when Amanda did something so shocking it almost ruined our friendship."

Lily sat forward, listening intently. She was genuinely interested in hearing about Jake's first love interest.

Jake's smile broadened as he continued. "It was a school day, during recess, and me and Amanda were chasing each other around the playground. Then I made the mistake of running behind the baseball backstop, thinking I could catch my breath. But Amanda followed me, and before I knew what was happening, she had her lips pushed up against mine, and I was helpless to stop it. It was so horrible I thought I was going to be sick. But then I began to think it was nice." He laughed. "Honestly, I don't know what it was. Unexpected mostly."

Lily laughed with him. "Oh, Jake, I think perhaps you wanted to be kissed, or you wouldn't have let Amanda catch you."

"Maybe," Jake agreed. "But that doesn't mean I wasn't traumatized. The moment Amanda's lips touched mine, all I wanted was to be swallowed into the ground. Kissing a girl wasn't something I'd even *thought* about doing. I was more into stuff like fishing with my dad, or catching frogs in the creek. Or even mutton busting. I sure wasn't interested in kissing girls on the mouth." He laughed again.

Lily liked the way Jake looked when he was happy. She also liked the way the firelight flickered in his eyes, making them appear to change color, and she especially liked the way his voice sounded when he wasn't concerning himself with things that made no sense. Just being near him filled her heart, and she wanted to know everything there was to know about him.

"Please, tell me more," she said, hoping their conversation would continue.

"About Amanda?"

"No. About *you*. Tell me about your childhood. What is mutton busting?" She'd never heard of such a thing.

Jake settled back, looking even more relaxed. "Mutton are sheep," he explained. "And mutton busting is something kids do when they're too young to ride broncs or bulls. It's what me and my friends did to pass the time when we weren't helping our parents with chores. We all thought we were destined to become rodeo stars. But being that we were so young, we had to make do with riding sheep, and at my house, it was this poor old sheep named Ronny. We'd had him most of my life, so he was more a pet than anything, and I'm sure he didn't expect that I'd ever want to ride him. Though he got the message pretty quick after me and my friends started taking turns climbing on his back." Jake shook his head. "I don't think I've ever seen a sheep get as mad as old Ronny got. I swear he had steam coming out his ears."

"Did any of you ever graduate to riding bigger animals?" Lily asked.

"A couple of my friends did, but most, me included, went on to pursue other activities. Though my decision to move on wasn't *my* choice. That was all my mom. She didn't like what was going on with Ronny, and she had a talk with my dad, telling him that my time might be better spent chasing cows. She said it was safer than me gettin' thrown off the back of an angry bull someday and having my head cracked open. But I think, mostly, it was that she had a soft spot for old Ronny. She didn't want to see him get hurt, either." Jake shrugged. "So, that was the end of me becoming a rodeo star. And it was probably for the best since I tend to do a fair job of gettin' myself hurt without inviting it to happen." He smiled, looking at Lily. "What about you? What did you do for fun as a child?"

"The usual," Lily said. She didn't think it the time to tell him her childhood was a couple of centuries ago.

Jake's gaze went to the window, and she wondered if he was reconsidering staying. She hoped so. It felt as though they'd finally turned a corner and it was comfortable and encouraging and she wanted their time together to continue. She imagined this was how it would be if she and Jake were a couple. They would sit together after a long day and share stories about what'd happened during the hours they'd been apart. It was such a simple thing, but it was just what she wanted. A relationship full of sharing and being close to someone special.

"I've enjoyed our conversation," Jake continued. "I'm glad I came back, and I appreciate you answering all my questions, but I should probably be going."

"Okay," Lily said, hiding her disappointment.

"I have just one more question. Actually, it's more a request. I don't suppose you could use your magic to make my horse return so I can ride out of here?"

"My powers are limited," Lily said.

"Guess I'll be taking a long walk home, then," Jake said. He reached and gave Sierra a pat, and they both headed for the door.

Lily followed. Watching him prepare to leave again was even harder this time than the last, and she cast her gaze to the floor, not wanting him to see the tears that had suddenly filled her eyes.

Jake touched her arm. "Are you going to be okay here by yourself?"

She nodded and brushed away her tears. "It's just hard to keep saying goodbye. I hadn't expected to see you again. I didn't think you believed any of what I'd told you. But then you were here and you seemed different somehow, like maybe you'd decided being stuck here with me at this cabin wasn't so bad, after all."

Jake smiled. "It's not. If I could stay longer, I would."

"But you have animals to care for."

"That's right."

"Can I ask why you came back?"

"Once I was out in the fresh air and was able to clear my head, I started thinking about all the things that had happened. There was no logical explanation for any of it, and I suppose my curiosity got the better of me. I had to come back so we could talk, so I could leave here feeling better about everything." He paused. "I guess that was pretty selfish of me."

"No." Lily shook her head. "Just honest."

A stretch of silence followed, and Lily glanced up at the mistletoe nestled among the paper snowflakes. She so wanted to get a kiss from Jake, something to remember him by. "Will you have one more cup of hot chocolate with me before you go?" she asked.

"I suppose one more won't hurt," Jake said. "I have to admit, I'm going to miss your hot chocolate. It's about the best I've ever had." He stood at the counter, exactly where Lily had hoped he would. Then, as he watched her prepare the hot chocolate, another paper snowflake came loose from the ceiling and fell to the floor, landing at his feet. He and Lily both stared at it. Lily hadn't caused it to happen, but it was just the kind of luck she needed right then.

"It looks like your decorations are coming down," Jake said, tilting his head back so that his eyes were focused on the ceiling.

Lily held her breath, sure that Jake was looking at the mistletoe. Finally, his gaze met hers, though his eyes held a strange twinkle. Then he reached for her. "Forget about the hot chocolate," he said. "I've heard it's bad luck not to kiss when you find yourself standing under mistletoe."

Jake's sudden change in demeanor had Lily putting a hand to his chest. "Are you all right?" she asked.

"I'm fine. How about that kiss?" He reached for her again and tried to draw her in, but she backed away. Then, all at once, he was covered in gold glitter and looked to be frozen.

"Jake?" Lily said, waving a hand in front of his face.

"Goodness, I hope I didn't overdo it," Vivienne said, appearing at Jake's side. Though she was nearly invisible, dressed in a flowing gown with gold sequins that matched the color of the glitter. Her gaze went to the ceiling, and she pointed at the mistletoe. "I'm going to need that back."

Lily frowned, looking up at the mistletoe. It looked fine where it was. She ducked away from Jake and faced Vivienne. "What are you doing here?"

Vivienne let out a soft sigh. "If you must know, I've come to right a wrong." She narrowed her eyes. "The hunter didn't already kiss you by chance, did he?"

The corners of Lily's mouth turned down. She was only half glad whatever was going on with Jake had been interrupted. "Unfortunately, we didn't get that far. But I think that was his intention until you doused him with fairy dust."

"Yes, well, pardon the interruption, but I've been presented with an opportunity, and like I said, I need to take back the mistletoe. So, if you don't mind, I'll just—"

"You'll just nothing!" Lily said. "Not until you tell me what's going on."

"Details," Vivienne said. "Not that it should concern you, but it seems I may have an opportunity to have my wishes restored. All I need do is help you achieve your goal of finding love—*be still my heart*—and the powers that be will correct the wrong that was done to me so very long ago."

Lily was hands on hips. "That makes no sense. If you're here to help me, why would you take back the mistletoe?"

"Explanations are so boring," Vivienne said. "Why bother?"

Lily was still hands on hips, holding her ground.

"*Hmmph*," Vivienne said, raising her chin. "If you're going to be that way, Miss Sassy Pants, I'll tell you. Not that I'm admitting to any wrongdoing, but there's a teensy problem with that sprig of mistletoe you've attached to your ceiling. As it turns out, it's tainted with magic, and as you know, the use of magic isn't allowed for the purpose of attaining a Christmas wish. Terribly sorry about that."

Lily sucked in a breath. "*Magic?* You gave me magic *mistletoe?*"

Vivienne splayed her hands. "What can I say? I was having a moment."

"An evil moment!" Lily said. "I don't know what I was thinking, trusting you! How could you do this to me?"

"Oh, *please*," Vivienne said with a roll of her eyes. "Don't act like this is all *my* fault. You're the one with a tainted twig hanging from your ceiling."

"Because *you* insisted I hang it! Plus, you told me it was completely natural! You lied!"

"Oh, boohoo. There, now I've said I'm sorry twice. What more do you want?"

"Nothing! I don't want anything more from you. Ever!" Lily said, fuming. "And I don't accept your apology. I should have known when Jake looked at me the way he did that he had no control over his actions." She crossed her arms and turned away from Vivienne so Vivienne couldn't see the liquid gathering in her eyes.

Vivienne groaned. "Before you fall into complete despair, let me remind you that you still have until midnight Christmas Eve to entice the human to kiss you. So, you see, all is not lost—yet."

Lily wiped her eyes and turned back to Vivienne. "It wouldn't matter if I had until Christmas Eve a *year* from now. As soon as you release Jake from his frozen state, he'll leave and go back to his life, and I'll never see him again." She pushed her face into her hands. "This is all so hard. I know nothing about falling in love or enticing a man to kiss me."

Vivienne's brow drew high on her forehead. "For the love of all things Christmas, it's not brain surgery. You've obviously captivated the hunter with your wholesome, witty charm, or he wouldn't still be here. Honestly, you need to get a grip!"

"*You* get a grip!" Lily said. "I had a grip, and then I lost it. I told Jake everything—the truth and nothing but, and now he wants no part of me." Just saying it made her heart ache, and she put a hand to her chest.

"Yes, well, it's unfortunate you couldn't have kept your trap shut just a little longer," Vivienne said. "Christmas Eve is still a few days away. Whatever possessed you to tell the human the truth so soon?"

"I had no choice. He was asking questions, wanting me to explain all the strange things that had been happening. What was I to do? I couldn't keep lying." Lily slumped into a chair. She tried to sniff back her tears, but it was hopeless. Big fat drops slid from her eyes and made watery tracks down her cheeks until they dripped from her chin.

"Oh, my, are you *crying?*" Vivienne asked, looking appropriately shocked. Then with a flip of her hand, she produced a tissue and handed it to Lily. "Here… before you drown us."

Taking the tissue, Lily used it to first wipe her eyes, and then to blow her nose. Then she held the tissue out to Vivienne.

Vivienne's face set in a scowl. "Please. You don't really expect me to take that nasty thing back, do you?"

Lily gave her a look as she tossed the tissue over her shoulder. It disintegrated before it hit the floor.

"Now," Vivienne said, "if you've finished honking your hooter, hear me out. I told you I came to right a wrong, and if you do as I say, I think an arrangement could still work out between you and Mr. Handsome Human."

Lily wrinkled her nose, giving Vivienne a scant glance. "You lied to me. Why would I ever trust you again?"

Vivienne did a palms-up. "Trust me or don't. But if you're willing to give up on the hunter so quickly, perhaps he isn't the human for you. Perhaps another human will come along and fall in love with you."

Lily threw up her hands. "In the next couple of *days?* Have you gone *mad?*"

"This isn't the time to cast insults. I didn't say it would be easy. But too bad you've never taken Enar's feelings for you seriously. You could be back at the North Pole right now, making arrangements to become *Mrs.* Enar. Poor elf. Word is that boring gnat Isla has been making herself available, and I think he might actually be interested."

This got Lily's attention. "Isla? But I thought…."

"What? That if you gave Enar the brush-off, he'd keep to himself in the Toy Room and spend all his time making toy trains for the kiddies until his fingers fell off?"

"Well… no. It's just that… well… he said he loved me."

"Exactly," Vivienne said. "*Loved.* Past tense." She tipped her head and looked up at the tainted mistletoe. "You know, this can easily be fixed." She held out her hand. In it lay a fresh sprig of mistletoe. "All you have to do is let me replace that nasty twig you have hanging from your ceiling with this magic-free sprig of garden variety mistletoe. I plucked it from the North Pole garden just before coming here. Say the word, and it'll be done. Then I'll unfreeze the human, and the two of you can continue where you left off."

Lily swallowed, eying the replacement mistletoe. She had two choices, neither of them fabulous. But with time moving ever closer to the stroke of midnight Christmas Eve, she had to make a decision. She could forget about her feelings for Jake and go back to the North Pole with no wishes to look forward to for the next century, or she could trust Vivienne and hope everything worked out in her favor.

"Well?" Vivienne said, waving the fresh mistletoe in Lily's face.

"How do I know it's not magic?" Lily asked, grinding her teeth together. "You told me you picked the *last* sprig from the North Pole garden."

"Yes, but as I also told you, I was having a moment. And fortunately for you, the moment has passed. I truly am here to help."

Lily hesitated. She so wanted to believe there was still a chance for her and Jake. That he would kiss her and that they had a future together that included a happily ever after. But did she dare risk believing Vivienne again?

"Tick tock," Vivienne said. "Need I remind you about the

Unable to Grant Stamp?"

"Fine. Do it," Lily relented.

"Atta girl," Vivienne said. Then with a flip of her hand, the replacement sprig was in place, and the magic mistletoe was no more.

"Now what?" Lily asked.

Vivienne smiled, though it looked more like a baby passing gas. "Now, my dear, it's all up to you." She took a quick look at her wristband. "Oh, look at the time, I really must be going. I was given another assignment, and I dare say it's turned out to be a tricky one that involves the stopping of wedding vows."

"Sounds complicated," Lily said.

"Yes, well, that's the very definition of love. But not to worry, I have a few ideas. If I can manage to throw a wrench into the bride and groom's special day, it should all work out splendidly." She tipped back her head and cackled to the ceiling. "I do so deserve to be Head Christmas Fairy, don't I?"

"No comment," Lily said.

"Whatever. Ta-ta for now!" Vivienne said. She nodded at Jake, releasing him from his frozen state, and then she was gone.

Chapter Eighteen

"Well, now, there you are, still looking as well-fed and sassy as ever," Vivienne remarked to Cinder as she approached the reindeer's stall.

Cinder raised her head from her trough and snorted, shooting a mist of reindeer breath straight at Vivienne.

"*Argh!*" Vivienne screeched, backing up fast to fend off the mist. But it was too late. The entire front of her dress was wet. She looked at Cinder and swore she could almost see the beast smiling. But, whatever, she wasn't going to scold Lily's little pet. Not now, when she needed the beast's help. And she could change her dress later.

Stepping close to the stall again, Vivienne kept her eyes focused squarely on Cinder's muzzle, should the reindeer be preparing to let loose another snort of wet breath. When Cinder seemed uninterested in doing more damage, Vivienne relaxed. "Now that you've had your fun, perhaps we can have a civilized chat," she told Cinder.

Cinder was eyes half-closed, looking beyond bored with the conversation.

"Now, don't be like that," Vivienne said. "I have something of great important I'd like to discuss, and I need you to pay attention. I promise, it will be in the best interest of everyone, including your little Miss Liliana."

Cinder blinked her eyes open and gave Vivienne a look that Vivienne took as interest.

"That's more like it," Vivienne said, and she leaned in close to one of Cinder's ears.

The moment Jake came out of his frozen state, he noticed the gold glitter covering his arms. He looked at Lily. "Again? Do I even want to ask?"

"Probably not," Lily said, glad for the reprieve.

"Then I guess I'll be going," he said, and he made a move for the door.

Lily's pulse raced. Had he really forgotten about the mistletoe and that he wanted to kiss her? Or had he simply changed his mind? "Wait," she said, her thoughts all over the place. She wanted him to stay, wanted to use her magic to keep him from leaving. But that wasn't allowed. And even if it was, she didn't want him to stay unless it was his idea. "I'll pack you a lunch," she offered, unable to think of anything else to keep him there.

"Thanks, but that won't be necessary. I don't plan on stopping to eat."

"I wouldn't feel right sending you away without at least packing you a small snack." She went to the kitchen and began stuffing a brown paper bag with a variety of cookies. She also packed several dog biscuits for Sierra, taking her time. Anything to delay the inevitable.

Jake paused when she handed him the bag. He gave her a long look, then he leaned in, which prompted Lily to pucker her lips. She waited and waited, thinking he'd remembered the kiss. But all she got was a hug. The kiss was lost.

"I want to tell you again how much I appreciate your helping me," Jake said, continuing to hold her close. When he finally released her, he lingered at the door.

"Was there something else?" Lily asked, hoping there was.

"You've been patient, answering all my questions. But I'm curious. Are you the reason Frost ran off? Was my coming into the forest to look for him all part of the plan?"

Oh, no, Frost! Lily sucked in a breath. "Oh, Jake, I'm so sorry! I forgot to tell you, I saw him!"

Jake's eyes opened wide. "When? *Where?*"

"It was the other night, when Enar showed up. We found Frost in the barn. I'd intended to tell you, but then you and I argued, and I forgot."

"You *forgot?* How could you forget when you know how worried I've been? And how did he get into your barn?"

"There was a gap in the boards," Lily said. "He was there to see Cinder. She's a reindeer. *My* reindeer. She came here with me from the North Pole, and I've been keeping her hidden from you. I was worried you might want to use her for target practice. But now I know I don't need to worry about that. I'm so sorry," she apologized again. "I promise I was going to tell you about seeing Frost. But at least now you know he's safe."

Jake frowned. "You should have told me sooner." His words were crisp, his anger palpable. He stepped out onto the porch and down into the snow, heading for the barn.

Lily followed, stuffing her feet into the boots and grabbing the puffy coat on her way out the door. "Jake, please!" she called to him from the porch. But he kept walking, pretending he didn't hear her. This was upsetting. Be mad if he must, but don't ignore her. She called to him once more, and when he again pretended he didn't hear, she reached down and scooped up a handful of snow, quickly forming it into an icy ball. Then she tossed it at him, hitting him squarely in the back.

Jake turned. "Really? Now, you're throwing snowballs at me like I'm some kind of wild animal?"

Lily pressed her lips together, suppressing a laugh. "It seemed the only way to get your attention."

Jake spread his hands. "Fine. You got my attention. What?"

"We should talk."

"We did talk. I listened to what you had to say. I don't need to hear anymore."

"So that's it? You're just going to leave and be mad at me because I forgot to tell you about Frost?"

"I'm mad, yes," Jake said. "But I'm leaving because I need to get home." He turned and started toward the barn again.

Lily wasn't having it. She grabbed another handful of snow, packed it tight, and threw it, this time hitting him on the back of his neck.

Jake slapped a hand to his neck, brushing away the cold snow, and spun around. *"Seriously?"*

Lily held her ground. She didn't know who she was angrier with, herself or Jake. She was just angry. "You didn't like it when we were talking, and *I* walked away. Well, I don't like it, either."

Jake's gaze was piercing. "What more is there to say?"

"I don't know. What do you *want* me to say? I made a mistake. I said I was sorry. I can't do much more than that."

"I appreciate the apology. But I still have to go. I just want to have a look inside the barn to see if Frost is in there. Now, if I turn and walk away, you're not going to blast me in the back of the head with another snowball, are you?"

"No," Lily said weakly, her shoulders slumping. She watched him until he disappeared through the barn door, then she went back to the cabin. After a minute, she saw him come out of the barn and she thought he might come back inside. But he didn't. He and Sierra just slogged their way through the snow and entered the forest.

Chapter Nineteen

So you didn't find Frost in the barn, Jake thought as he headed into the forest. Nor had he found any other reindeer in the barn. And that meant what? He had no idea. Except that the farther he got away from the cabin, the more impossible the last several days seemed. Including Lily's story about being a fairy. Maybe he really had taken a fall and hit his head, and the entire week of being cared for by a strange young woman was all just something conjured up by his injured brain.

No. Lily was real. That much he knew. A real *what*, though? And how had she caused it to snow inside the cabin? He'd heard of people using machines to create snow, but Lily hadn't used a machine or anything else that he could see. The snow had just appeared. And what about the man, Enar, showing up at the door? Clearly, he wasn't just some random person out for a walk.

But these were all things he'd considered the last time he was out here. It's why he'd gone back. To get answers. And for the most part, Lily had done a decent job of explaining and making him believe anything was possible. So, why was he now questioning her very existence? As much as he wanted to believe everything she'd told him, it was just too outrageous. Fairies weren't real. They didn't exist, except in the imagination of little girls. And he'd never even *heard* of a Christmas fairy.

He stopped for a moment, looked down at Sierra. "What do you think, girl? Are fairies real?"

Sierra returned his look with a noncommittal *woof.*

Jake gave her a pat on the back. "Yeah, that's what I thought. You girls are always sticking together."

Moving deeper into the forest, he passed beneath a large tree branch, and a clump of snow fell on his hat. With the temperature rising, the snow was wet, and the ground had become mushy. Which made footing more difficult. Which, in turn, made his ankle ache. He'd thought he was done with that, but apparently not. He briefly considered turning around, but going back to the cabin wasn't an option. He needed to be home.

After several more minutes, he arrived at a clearing where he stopped to rest, leaning against a tree that chilled him with its earthy dampness. He listened to his stomach grumble for a minute, then he remembered the cookies Lily had packed. Opening the bag, he chose one that looked to be chocolate chip. As he ate it, he looked around and smiled when he realized he was at the same clearing his mom used to bring he and his sister to for picnics when life got boring. She would hitch their big chestnut-colored horse to a wagon and she'd load the wagon with all kinds of supplies—blankets, games, books, sandwiches, and even homemade root beer—so they could while away the afternoon in the forest. First came lunch, then after eating, his mom would sit with her back against a tree and read a book while he and Josie spent hours playing. He'd collect bugs and frogs, while Josie chased butterflies and looked for secret treasures that their mom assured them had been hidden by forest gnomes among the trees. Josie believed every word, but he was too old for such nonsense.

But was it nonsense? After getting to know Lily, he wasn't sure. Maybe gnomes really did exist.

Jake shook his head, still doubting. He wanted to believe Lily. Had even begun to be fond of her. But a lot of good it would have done him to develop real feelings for her. They couldn't possibly have any kind of relationship. How would he introduce her to his friends? *Hey, Jim, I'd like you to meet my girlfriend, Lily. By the way, if it begins to snow in here, it's because she's a fairy and all she has to do is flutter her wings, and it'll be a total whiteout.*

Sure, he could say that. Then his friends would probably call the men in white coats to take him away.

"But that's not something you'll have to worry about," he said loudly, "because you're leaving all that fairy nonsense behind."

Sierra wiggled over to him, her ears perked with concern at the edge in his voice.

Jake rubbed the top of her head. "Don't worry, everything's okay," he told her. "I think maybe I've just been out here in the forest too long, is all."

Needing a distraction from his thoughts, he did some more looking about and quickly spotted a tall fir that he remembered had the initials JL and JL carved into its bark. He walked up to the tree, and sure enough, the initials were there. JL and JL stood for Jack Longmire and Judith Lawson. They were his parents, and his mom always said she liked coming to this part of the forest just so she could see this tree. She said it was where his dad had proposed marriage to her, that it was a symbol of their love, and it would stand forever.

So far, so good.

His mom was such a romantic.

Jake rubbed his fingers lightly over the initials as he breathed out a sigh. Life was good back then, when he was too young to know better. But life hadn't been good like that for a long time. At least not until he met Lily. Getting to know her was like having the sun come out after a particularly hard winter. And whether or not he believed everything she'd told him, he couldn't help but be envious of her lighthearted nature. She was a lot like his sister, joyous and innocent, small but fierce. Plus, she was so passionate about the holiday season, it was infectious. Though her love for the snow was a bit over the top.

He smiled, thinking about seeing her out in the cold wearing practically nothing while she played with Sierra. It'd reminded him of a scene out of *The Nutcracker*, which his mother had always insisted the entire family see every year. They would all load themselves into the car and head into town to see a local production put on by high school students, which was the most boring thing for a kid to do on a Saturday night. But boring or not, it was mandatory, so he and his dad would sleep through most of it while his mom and sister sat on the edge of their seats, watching every move the Sugar Plum Fairy made.

But the Sugar Plum Fairy was an actress, and odds were she couldn't actually dance around in real snow without proper footwear. For that matter, the only humans he'd ever known to go out into the snow without being properly clothed were those crazies he'd once seen on television who were participating in some polar swim thing. And even they didn't seem to be enjoying themselves all that much. Unlike Lily, who was practically giddy at the sight of every new snowflake. He almost wished he could go back to the cabin and watch her in her happiness for just a while longer. Which wouldn't make any sense at all if he expected to get home before dark.

Pushing aside all thoughts of returning to the cabin, he moved on, with Sierra leading the way. But with her stopping every few yards to investigate small animal tracks, they weren't making a lot of progress and he began to wonder if they would ever make it back home. Eventually, he had to stop for another short rest, and as he stood there listening to his own pained breathing, a twig snapped at his back. Hoping it wasn't the wolf again, he spun around.

It wasn't the wolf. It was Frost.

"Hey, buddy, way to scare the pants off me," Jake said on a relieved breath. "Where you been? I've been worried about you."

Frost stepped close and nudged Jake's hand.

"Sorry," Jake said, "I don't have anything to give you, and I doubt you've been starving." He looked Frost over and gave him an affectionate pat. "I heard you have a lady friend. I'll bet she'd been sharing her meals with you."

Frost responded with a quiet grunt, and Jake ran a hand along Frost's back. He was tempted to climb aboard to ease the ache in his foot, but reindeer were much too small for a man to ride, so he had to be satisfied just using Frost for support.

Frost didn't object to the added weight, so together they walked until Jake stopped once more to get his bearings. With the heavy snowfall over the last few days, everything looked different, and the trees seemed to go on forever. He stood still for a long minute, wondering if he'd somehow gotten turned around and had been going in the wrong direction. Finally, he dropped his head back and laughed at the absurd realization he might be lost.

"Don't tell me you been out here so long you lost your mind," said a voice to his left.

Jake turned and, despite his pain, grinned when he saw his neighbor, Bob, on horseback. Behind him was Jake's horse, Cannon.

Bob dismounted, his eyes taking Jake in from head to toe. "I don't recall ever seeing you look so ragged. Like a drowned squirrel, if you ask me. What in blazes are you doin' out here?" He nodded at Frost. "You ain't been out here all week lookin' for that reindeer, have you?"

Jake continued leaning on Frost. "It's a long story that I might tell you over a cup of coffee one day," he said to Bob, adding, "I see you found my horse."

"Yeah," Bob said. "I stopped by your place to give you a basket of muffins the wife made, and when I saw your horse standin' in the yard looking miffed at wearing a wet saddle, it got me to wonderin' if he run off and left you somewhere in a mound of snow. Thought I better come out here and see if you were in some kind of trouble."

"I appreciate it," Jake said.

A few snowflakes fell from the sky, and Bob looked up. "Looks like we're in for more of the white stuff. I ain't never seen it like this. It's like the heavens are determined to dump everything they have on us."

"Seems so, doesn't it?" Jake said, wincing from the pain in his ankle.

"You hurt?" Bob asked, running his gaze over Jake again.

"I'll live," Jake said.

"Can you ride?"

"I think so." Jake released his hold on Frost and limped over to Cannon. The reliable old quarter horse stood firm while Jake got himself in the saddle, and Jake couldn't help but let out a groan of relief at getting the weight off his leg.

"You sure you're okay to ride?" Bob asked. "Seems like that leg of yours is really botherin' you."

"I'm good," Jake said. He rubbed a hand over Cannon's warm neck and felt a certain comfort knowing that both Frost and his horse were safe. The only thing bothering him now was his memory of the young woman back at the cabin. Was she real or imagined? "Hey, Bob," he said when he and Bob were on their way, "you recall ever seeing a cabin out here anywhere?"

Bob shook his head. "Can't say as much. Let's get you home."

Chapter Twenty

Lily grabbed the blanket from the back of the sofa and pulled it tight about her shoulders. Jake's departure had left a chill in the air and an emptiness in her heart. It wasn't at all how she'd expected love to feel. Where were the butterflies? Where was the joy?

Vivienne was right. She should have had a plan. And she should have refrained from being so forthcoming with Jake. Telling him so much all at once had been too much of a shock. Probably, she should have started with something he could easily digest. Though she hadn't any idea what that might be and likely wouldn't have made any difference. Just like the mistletoe hadn't made any difference. What good had it done to hang it? Jake's leaving had sent a clear message: he wasn't interested in the two of them making a connection. Cinder would have a better chance of receiving a kiss from Frost.

Lily looked to the window, suddenly feeling guilty for not immediately going to check on Cinder after Jake left. Pushing the blanket aside, she hurried to the door. But as soon as she opened it and felt winter's bite, she knew she had to better prepare herself for the weather. She grabbed the puffy coat and put it on. Then she shoved her feet into the ugly boots and laced them tight. When she opened the door again, the cold didn't seem nearly as harsh. Though she wasn't about to dally. She needed to see Cinder. Cinder had been so smitten with Frost, surely, she must be in the barn stuffing herself with lichen.

Quickly making her way to the barn, Lily slipped through the big red door with a ready apology on her lips. But when she shuffled over to Cinder's stall and looked over the gate, all she saw was an empty bed of straw.

Turning full circle, Lily looked to all corners of the barn. It was cobwebs everywhere. But still no Cinder. Lily dashed about the entire barn, doing a more thorough search. Still no reindeer.

Running back outside, Lily looked for tracks and thought she saw some. They led into the forest. She ran to the tree line, calling to Cinder, but her calls were met with silence.

On the edge of panic, Lily stared into the dark wood. If Cinder had gone exploring and were to become lost, she wouldn't know how to take care of herself. Nor would she know how to spot a predator.

Calling to Cinder one last time, and again getting no response, Lily knew she had to go into the forest and look for her friend. Trudging slowly through the mushy snow, she listened for any sounds to indicate Cinder was nearby. But all she heard were her own footsteps. Then, eventually, the sky grew dark, and when she could no longer see the trail, she had to turn around.

As good as boots were against cold, they made walking even harder, and by the time Lily emerged from the forest, she was exhausted and freezing. All she wanted was to go inside and make herself comfortable, sans boots. But first, she had to take one last look in the barn to see if Cinder had returned.

Cinder's stall was still empty, and Lily returned to the cabin and stood by the fire to warm her hands that were like ice from spending so much time out in the cold. She finally understood the human fondness for sitting at fireside.

When her hands and fingers were sufficiently thawed, she lay on the sofa, preferring to remain where Jake had slept rather than retiring to the bedroom. Surrounded by his scent, she quickly fell asleep, and when morning arrived, she woke with the renewed hope that she would find Cinder. But when she went to the barn and saw that Cinder was still missing, her hope turned into heart-wrenching fear that she might never again see the reindeer. And she could only imagine what Santa might say when she returned to the North Pole and gave him the news that she had lost one of his reindeer. *My dear, Liliana, Cinder was in your care. She was your responsibility. If you are incapable of keeping one of my reindeer safe, how am I to be convinced you are ready for such a grown-up wish as forever love?*

Lily gave a small sigh. Indeed, perhaps she wasn't ready for such a grown-up wish. Even so, she was not yet ready to give up hope that Cinder would return before it was time for them to go back to the North Pole.

With the clock ticking off the minutes, bringing her ever closer to the end of her time at her assignment location, Lily decided to spend her remaining hours baking. Not that she had any appetite for sugary treats at the moment, but it was better than spending the day worrying.

She caught her lip in her teeth. No appetite for sugar… becoming vulnerable to the cold…. What could it possibly mean? And might she also be in danger of losing her Christmas spirit?

No, she quickly assured herself. That would never happen.

Chapter Twenty-One

The second morning back in his own bed, Jake's phone buzzed on his nightstand at eight a.m. He was tempted to ignore the call, but when Caller ID showed Robert Miller, a.k.a. Bob, he thought better of it. Since he'd been home, either Bob or Bob's wife, Kate, had been calling to check on him, so if he didn't answer, Bob would likely show up on his doorstep to see if something was wrong. Still half asleep, Jake put the phone to his ear. "Mornin'," he answered.

"Mornin' yerself," Bob said. "Thought I'd better check and make sure you been following Doc Evans' orders. I ran into him at the hardware store, and he said you should be back to your old self in no time, so long as you don't do anything crazy. I took that to mean you might need some help around there. I'd be happy to stop by after I run a couple of errands for the wife."

"Thanks for the offer," Jake said, "but there's not much to do around here right now, and in a few more days, I'll be good as new." It was a lie, of course. There was plenty to do, but he'd get it all done somehow without bothering his neighbors. What he really needed was time alone so he could think. Every hour that passed, he was less and less clear about what'd happened while he was in the forest, and the only thing he knew for sure was that a woman who smelled of pumpkin and spice had taken him in and cared for him in a cabin nobody seemed to know about.

"You sure?" Bob asked. "Kate'll have me sleepin' on the couch if I don't at least come by and see for myself."

"Tell Kate not to worry," Jake said. "I don't mean to cut you off, but I just got up and was about to make myself a cup of coffee. I'll give you a call in another day or two." He clicked off and felt bad for lying to Bob. But at the moment, he wasn't in the mood for visitors. He'd had too many already, folks bringing him food and checking in to make sure he was "still alive." There were plenty of apologies, too, for not noticing he was gone and might be in some kind of trouble. Though that was his own doing, since he'd pretty much made a habit of keeping to himself for some time now.

Fully awake, he got up and waited for the pain in his ankle to hit, but all that remained was a residual tightness that felt like he needed to be moving. He went to the kitchen and looked out the window to see what the day held. The in-coming weather looked fierce, like it might bring heavy rain or even more snow, which they hardly needed. They'd already gotten a half dozen new inches since he'd been home.

Sierra stood by the back door, and he let her out to do her business, after which she took to dashing about in the snow like it was the first she'd ever seen. As Jake watched her antics, he became aware of the steady *drip, drip, drip* coming from his kitchen faucet. It was the same sound he'd heard that last day at the cabin when the weather had changed, and the snow was melting in the gutters… and he was standing on the porch telling Lily he was leaving.

Lily. His mouth tightened. Every minute, every hour, every thought was of her. Which was why he needed to go back into the forest and try to find that cabin. He needed to settle in his mind that what he remembered was real.

A knock at his back door interrupted his thoughts, and then Bob's wife, Kate, was standing in the doorway holding a large basket. "Sorry for the intrusion," she said. "My husband said he talked to you, and you sounded like you might be hungry, so I brought you these." She pulled the towel covering the contents of the basket aside, revealing a bounty of muffins. "If you're in the mood for something more substantial, I'd be happy to fix you a hot breakfast."

Jake forced a smile and felt guilty about it. Bob and Kate were good neighbors and good people. They'd been there for his parents all those difficult years after Josie died, and when his parents moved away, they'd continued checking up on him like he was their own son. Which was appreciated, but sometimes, it was too much. Sometimes, he just wanted to be left alone. "I'm good," he told Kate. "Everyone's been dropping off food and offering to help out, so I'm getting along fine."

"Glad to hear that. But take these, anyway," Kate said, holding the basket out to him. "At least you'll have something to snack on. I put a few homemade dog biscuits in there, too, for Sierra. I don't know how the two of you aren't weak as kittens, surviving all that time out there in the forest by yourselves." She turned and looked at Sierra bounding about in the new snow. "She doesn't seem the worse for it."

Jake wasn't ready to get into any kind of conversation about the time he and his dog spent in the forest. If he admitted they hadn't been alone, it would only raise more questions, and he still had plenty of his own he couldn't answer.

"Thanks for the muffins. I appreciate the thought," he told Kate. He took the basket and grumbled under his breath at Sierra, who hadn't warned him they had company.

"Pardon?" Kate said.

"Oh, nothing," Jake replied. He hobbled over to the table and slumped into a chair, ready for the visit to end.

Kate stepped inside and nodded at his leg. "You should have Doc Evans look at that ankle again. You don't want to end up with a permanent limp."

"No need," Jake said. "I'm sure I'll be feeling better in just a few more days."

"Jake Longmire, don't be so stubborn. There's no need to suffer. And if you're not up to driving yourself, I'll send Bob over, and he can take you into town."

"I can drive. I just don't think I need to see the doctor," Jake said, his voice gruff and unappreciative. "Now, if you don't mind, I have things to do, so if you'll please shut the door on your way out." He hoped to God she would just go.

The door clicked shut, and he watched Kate tromp her way through the snow to her SUV. She gave Sierra a pat on the head, and then shot him a look, before getting in and driving off. This made him feel even worse. He rubbed the back of his neck, imagining what his mother might say. *You've just been rude to a very nice woman. Now, go apologize.*

Maybe he would. But not right now.

He stayed seated, contemplating the basket of muffins, and eventually pulled the towel away to have another look. They were Kate's special breakfast muffins, full of all kinds of healthy stuff like ground flaxseed, walnuts, and zucchini, as well as a good amount of chocolate pieces to help sweeten the healthy parts. But at the moment, the idea of eating a muffin or anything else held not one bit of appeal.

Several minutes ticked off the kitchen clock, and his phone buzzed. He snatched it from the table. "What!"

"No need to snap at people who are trying to help you," Bob said loudly in his ear. "I don't mind so much, but Kate came back here looking like you insulted her cooking."

Jake groaned. "I didn't mean to snap at you… or your wife. It's just that I haven't gotten a lot of sleep since I've been home, and I really don't need any help. All I need is a few more days to myself and for people to stop bringing me food."

"There's a nice way of telling a person that," Bob said.

Jake sat silent for a moment. "You're right," he said, his tone softening. "Tell Kate I'm sorry for being rude to her. And, please, tell her I said thanks again for the muffins."

"I'll tell her. I'm sure she won't hold it against you. But you could tell her yourself if you had a mind to. Anyway, just wanted to let you know, it wouldn't be no trouble if you needed me to take you into town."

"Thanks. I'm good. I'll call if I change my mind."

"One more thing…," Bob said. "Kate noticed you hadn't put up any Christmas decorations, so she wanted me to ask if she could come over and put up a tree for you."

"There's really no need. I think I have a wreath up in the attic. I'll probably just put that on my front door and call it good. I'm not in much of a mood for a tree."

"Well, that's what I figured," Bob said. "But Kate's worried about you bein' all alone for the holidays." He paused. "I understand if you aren't up for it, but Kate's got a tub full of extra ornaments, and I got a feeling if you don't take them, she'll make me put up a second tree here."

Jake tipped his head back and stared at the ceiling, half expecting to see paper snowflakes floating around. But this wasn't the cabin, and Lily wasn't here to do any decorating. All at once, he felt a hollowness the likes of which had hadn't felt since losing his sister.

"Tell Kate to come on over," he told Bob on a heavy breath. "If she wants to make my place look festive, I won't spoil her fun."

"You sure?" Bob asked.

"I'm sure," Jake said, and he clicked off. He shoved the basket of muffins aside and got to his feet, putting most of his weight on the one with the injured ankle. It really did feel better. His limp was more from habit now than anything. Which, to him, meant he was free to do whatever he pleased. Even take a ride through the snow to a cabin on the other side of the forest—if that's what pleased him.

Opening a cupboard, he found a bottle of Extra-Strength Tylenol. He took two, downing them with a few sips of water, and then he put a mug of water for instant coffee in the microwave. While he waited for the water to heat, he stared out the window at the pasture nearest his house and saw Frost and his cows huddled together. The cows didn't look any worse for his having been gone a few days, though they'd probably started to wonder when he and Sierra would return. He liked to think so, anyway. But more than likely, they probably hadn't even noticed his absence, what with the local kids he'd hired to come by and make sure they were fed.

The microwave beeped, and he ignored it. Something strange had caught his eye. Was that another reindeer standing next to Frost? He took a pair of binoculars from a drawer and went to the door, opening it. He focused, and sure enough, two reindeer were hanging out in the pasture with his cows.

"Hey, buddy, who's your friend?" he whispered, and Frost turned his head toward the house like he'd heard.

Jake watched for another minute, and then wanting to get a better look, he pulled on his boots, grabbed his coat, and limped out the door. Upon seeing him, Sierra yapped a happy greeting and accompanied him out to the pasture and through the gate. But then she saw something that piqued her interest more than welcoming a new reindeer to the pasture, and she ran off in another direction.

Patting the cows' rumps as he walked among them, Jake moved slowly toward Frost and the female reindeer. When he got close enough, he reached out and smoothed a hand down Frost's back. The female kept her eyes focused on him, but she seemed okay with his presence, so he reached out to her, too, and she touched her muzzle to his hand.

Smiling, Jake curled his fingers into the fur at her neck and scratched lightly. This had to be Lily's reindeer. Cinder, if he remembered correctly.

That settled it. If he needed a good reason to ignore doctor's orders, this was it. Lily would want to know her reindeer was safe. And with tomorrow being Christmas Eve, if he wanted to see her again, he couldn't wait.

Chapter Twenty-Two

Christmas Eve Day had arrived, but Lily saw no reason to rejoice. With her time at the cabin quickly drawing to an end, such little hope now remained for Jake's return, and, too, the possibility of Cinder showing up also seemed remote.

Wandering into the kitchen, Lily took inventory of all the pies and dozens of cookies she'd baked since arriving at the cabin. There were so many, she'd had to pile one plate on top of another just to fit them all on the counter. And who was going to eat so many treats? Not her, that much was certain. Though she did, at the moment, have a taste for something. She ran her gaze once more over the counter until her eye caught the candy cane pie over in one corner. It looked especially enticing, with bits of crushed red and white candy sprinkled across its top. But she wasn't in the mood for candy cane pie. She needed chocolate—in a mug and piping hot!

Yes! Hot chocolate was just what she needed! Though making it from scratch was too much a chore so, closing her eyes, she imagined a cup full to the brim and topped with marshmallows. Just thinking about that first sip had her smiling. But when she opened her eyes, there was no hot chocolate and no marshmallows.

Just an empty mug sitting on the table. She picked the mug up and turned it upside down. Not one drop of liquid spilled out.

Frustrated and desperate now for a dose of chocolate, she eyed one of the plates of cookies and chose a cookie that looked to be full of chocolaty morsels. She took a bite and wasn't disappointed. The reward was instant, even better than hot chocolate. As she savored the rest of the cookie, she considered what it would mean if she could no longer create food using her imagination. Would she need to take cooking lessons from one of the other fairies? Isla perhaps? Fairy that had captured Enar's attention?

Allegedly.

Lily pressed her lips into a thin line. Learning how to cook was too much to contemplate at the moment. And if it was true, that Enar had moved on and was seeing Isla, she was happy for him. He and Isla would enjoy fabulous home-cooked meals on his plot of land overlooking the reindeer meadow.

But what about Jake? Had he moved on, as well? She hoped that was not the case and, in fact, hoped more than anything that he was missing her very much. Though, perhaps he was lucky to have escaped being stuck with someone whose only domestic ability was the baking of sweets. And even that might soon be in question.

With a sigh, Lily went out to the porch, wondering if she could even still produce snow. Concentrating, she attempted to unfold her wings, and though it took a moment, they eventually spread free from her back. But when she tried to flutter them, they barely twitched. Next, she closed her eyes and imagined a brief burst of snow. But when she opened her eyes, there was nothing. Just the darkening sky that remained clear and bright and full of stars that were twinkling back at her like they were laughing at her foolishness.

Wrapping her arms about herself, she was suddenly overcome with loneliness. Which was strange. Being alone and lonely was not something she'd ever had to endure at the North Pole. There were always other fairies and elves around, not to mention Santa and Mrs. Claus and all the reindeer. It was a community of sharing and friendship and all things good, with so much activity going on that there was never any time to be lonely.

Thinking this, the corners of Lily's mouth lifted slightly. No matter the pain she'd suffered during this assignment, she would go back to the North Pole and she would be surrounded by friends and they would continue their lives together sharing stories while drinking hot chocolate on the hill above the reindeer meadow. And then, before long, her magic would return, and all would be well.

She hoped.

So, why did tears continue to cloud her eyes?

In an attempt to cheer herself, she began singing, going through a medley of Christmas carols that began with "Silent Night" and ended with "The Twelve Days of Christmas." But when she got to the part about five gold rings, she was reminded once more of Jake and marriage and a forever kind of love she might never have—at least not for the next hundred years—and again, her eyes filled.

So much for cheering herself up.

Staring through the haze of her tears at the tree shapes that were growing ever darker against the sky, she saw something move in the shadows. She watched and waited, filled with renewed hope that Jake had finally returned. But as the figure stepped forward into the emerging light of the moon, she saw it was only Enar.

"Hello, my princess," Enar said.

"Enar, what are you doing here?" Lily asked, confused by his presence. This being the biggest eve of the year, all elves would be needed to help with last-minute details that included the completion of wrapping thousands of gifts and then loading them onto Santa's sleigh. And though it was still hours until Santa's departure to deliver toys, no elves could be spared on such an important night.

"I have come to take you home," Enar said.

"To the North Pole?"

"Yes, my princess."

"I don't understand," Lily said. "What about my assignment?"

"Has the human not departed?"

"He has," Lily said, nodding.

"Then you have completed your assignment."

"But… it is not yet midnight."

"No matter," Enar said. "It is close enough."

"It matters to me," Lily said. If even a flicker of hope remained that Jake might return, she wanted to stay.

"You're concerned about your wish," Enar said.

"Yes," Lily said, her lips trembling. "I am sorry. I know that is not what you want to hear."

Enar stood straight. "Not to worry. I have been seeing someone myself—Isla."

So, it was true. Vivienne hadn't spoken an untruth. Not about that, anyway. "I'm happy for you," Lily said, meaning it.

"Yes, well," Enar said, clearing his throat, "it is unfortunate you were not successful with the human."

"There is still time," Lily offered. "I would like to remain here a while longer."

"Did you not break the rules by using tainted mistletoe to obtain a kiss?"

"I did not know it was tainted."

"It matters not," Enar said. "A rule is a rule."

Lily dipped her head. "Yes." It was what she knew he would say.

"We should be going. There is still much to be done back at the North Pole. I trust Cinder is in the barn?"

Lily sucked in air. "Oh, Enar! I have done a terrible thing! I fear I have lost Cinder!"

Enar's eyes widened. "You *lost* her? How could that be?"

"I don't know!" Lily cried. "I went to check on her, and she was gone, I think into the forest. I tried to find her, but… oh, it's been two days now since I last saw her, and I don't know where she could possibly be." She dropped her head into her hands. "Oh, Enar, I've not only lost one of Santa's reindeer, but I may have even failed at my assignment. I'm a terrible Christmas fairy.

I deserve to receive the Unable to Grant Stamp and have Santa take away my wishes for all eternity."

Enar approached Lily and patted her on the back. "There, there. Santa would never take away your wishes. And, too, my princess, what is this stamp you speak of? I have never heard of such a thing."

Lily raised her head from her hands. "It was Vivienne. She told me that if I fail to find love by midnight tonight, as a consequence, I would be given the Unable to Grant Stamp, and I would lose my Christmas wishes for the next hundred years."

"Ah, Vivienne," Enar said, nodding. "You are not to worry. Only this year's wish is forfeited. And only because it is too late for you to make another."

"But what about Vivienne's Christmas wishes? She said she lost them because of her own failure to find love."

Enar laughed, sputtering. "Vivienne? *Love?* Surely, you don't believe it. Oh, she might have *thought* she wanted to be in love, but once the young man she was seeing turned his back on her, she returned to the North Pole, and it was business as usual." He shook his head. "She didn't lose her wishes for failing to find love. She lost her wishes because she was caught stuffing the ballot box when she first ran for Head Christmas Fairy."

"But isn't that title assigned by Santa?" Lily asked.

"It is. *Now.* Everything changed because of the evil fairy, Ailsa. I'm sure you've heard of her." Enar waved a hand. "Anyway, you took a chance, and it didn't work out. Better luck next time."

Next time? Lily put her hand to her chest, where the ache never ceased. She wasn't sure she would survive *this* time. "Vivienne also said that if I were to join the human world, I would lose all memory of my friends at the North Pole and that I might not even believe in Santa or Christmas miracles anymore."

Enar pressed his lips together. "It is truly sad that Vivienne would fill your head with such nonsense. And sad, too, that you would believe such nonsense."

"So I *would* remember?"

"Of course… if you want to," Enar said. "It always helps to

have believers wandering among all the nonbelievers. The more, the better." He looked at his watch. "Are you ready to go?"

"Yes, but what about Cinder?"

"Not to worry. She will find her way home."

"But what if she doesn't?"

"Then you might have something to worry about."

Chapter Twenty-Three

Jake was up early the following morning and swallowed the last of the Extra-Strength Tylenol that he hoped would be enough to get him through being in the saddle all day. Though he figured if he ended up miserable, he could count on Lily to provide him with some pain relief once he got to the cabin. That is if her story about being a fairy with magical powers hadn't been just a wild tale. Though, if it wasn't a tale, why hadn't she provided him with a little pain relief when he'd first gotten hurt? He'd spent nearly a week with her, and all she'd done was advise him to keep his leg elevated while she attempted to fatten him up with cookies and pie.

The memory of it had Jake smiling as he gave Cannon his morning feed that included a generous scoop of Ranch Candy. The Ranch Candy being a bribe to put Cannon in a good frame of mind for a visit from the vet. Not that there was any reason to worry about the old quarter horse—Cannon was tough—but Jake wanted to get the vet's okay before taking his horse out for another long ride in the snow.

The vet finally arrived around midmorning, and he took his time giving Cannon a thorough exam, during which Cannon showed his appreciation by nipping the vet's backside. When the exam was over, the vet told Jake his old horse was good to go, and Jake took pity on the vet and added a decent tip to the bill to atone for Cannon's crankiness, as well as having been asked to make a special trip out on Christmas Eve.

"Your horse is okay, but what about you? I heard you took a fall," the vet said as he stood at his truck, ready to leave.

"That was a while ago. I'm fine now. Good as new," Jake said. Or close enough. It wasn't that he minded the concern, but he didn't have time for a conversation about his health. With the days winter-short, he had only a few more hours of daylight and he needed to get going.

The vet climbed into his old truck and cranked the engine over, and as soon as the truck's license plate became a blur, Jake hurried inside to grab the lunch he'd packed. He had a thermos with coffee and a roast beef sandwich he'd made from a meal one of his neighbors had dropped off. Plus, he'd wrapped up a hunk of meat for Sierra, along with enough kibble to last a day or two—just in case.

By the time he was ready to head out, the temperature had dropped considerably, and the surface of the snow had hardened, so he spent what seemed like hours listening to the monotonous crunch of ice beneath Cannon's hooves until he reached the clearing with the tall fir. There, he dismounted and was glad for a cup of hot coffee. He also ate half a sandwich. Then, he was back in the saddle and pushing on, with Sierra bounding happily along the trail up ahead of him. Her energy had no end.

When he reached the lake where he and Lily met, he considered taking another short break, but instead continued on until he arrived at the tree line where he could see smoke billowing up from the cabin's chimney. In another couple of minutes, he would be standing before Lily, and he had no idea what he would say to her. But it didn't matter. He'd work it out.

He urged Cannon on, and by the time he stepped up onto the cabin's porch, his stomach was tied in knots. He still had no idea what he was going to say when he saw Lily. He just knew he had to see her. But as he went to grab the door handle, he caught himself. It would do neither of them any good if he scared her half to death by barging in without knocking.

After taking a couple deep breaths, he finally raised his hand to the door and barely let his knuckles brush the wood. Sierra wasn't nearly as calm. She was at his side, bouncing on both front paws, not one bit interested in waiting patiently for the door to open. And when it didn't, Jake gave her a look. "Don't worry," he told her, "Lily's probably just busy and didn't hear my knock."

Sierra gave up her bouncing and settled to a sit, and Jake knocked again. Louder, this time. Again getting no response, his own impatience got the better of him, and he cracked open the door. Warm air from inside the cabin greeted him, and he stepped inside to see a fire burning bright in the fireplace. Then he looked to the kitchen, where he saw plates stacked high with cookies covering the kitchen counter.

"Lily!" he called and got no answer.

In her own eagerness to see Lily, Sierra rushed to the bedroom, back-end wiggling and tail wagging. She quickly returned, alone and panting and giving Jake a desperate look. He went to the bedroom to see for himself that Lily wasn't there.

She wasn't.

Disappointed at finding the room empty, he went back to the kitchen and held a hand over the tops of the pies and the stacks of cookies. They'd been there long enough to cool, though the scent of warm cinnamon still hung in the air. He took one cookie that looked to have plenty of chocolate chips and ate it in two bites. As he stuffed a second cookie in his mouth, he looked out at the dark outline of the barn against the night sky.

That's where Lily had to be.

Fifteen minutes later, he was back inside the cabin. He'd left Cannon unsaddled in a stall with water, along with feed from one of the saddlebags, and then he'd had a look around outside the barn for footprints. He hadn't seen any, human or otherwise. It was as if Lily had simply vanished. But why would she stoke the fire and leave? Plus, if he remembered correctly, she'd told him she would be staying until midnight. So, where was she?

Jake settled by the fire to think, and as the clock ticked off the minutes, he became more and more concerned that he was too late. Lily had already returned to the North Pole.

Thinking such a thing, he almost laughed. Would have laughed for sure a couple weeks ago, and even now, it was a hard thing to imagine. But as he ran a hand over his jaw, he couldn't help but wonder how a person might get themselves to the North Pole. And not only get there but find someone who lived there. Lily had told him he could hire a guide to take him, but she'd also said that unless he went with someone who was a resident of the North Pole, all he'd likely see was a big, flat sheet of ice.

It was probably just as well he couldn't hire a guide, he decided. After all, it wasn't like he could tell anyone his reason for wanting to go to the North Pole. But that didn't mean he was ready to go home and forget about Lily. Couldn't even if he wanted to. Meeting her had changed his entire perspective on life. It was because of her he could finally smile again without the pain of the past haunting him or making him feel guilty for being happy.

No, he wasn't about to go home and just forget about Lily.

He grabbed one more cookie, then slumped into a chair and let his mind go to work on a solution to his problem. It stood to reason that if Lily worked at the North Pole, then Santa was the answer in finding her.

He got up to search for pen and paper, laughing out loud at the idea that was forming in his brain. He was going to write his first letter to Santa Claus in more than twenty years. No matter that it was already Christmas Eve, or that he was rusty at letter writing, he just knew it was something he needed to do.

His search for a pen was quick. First place he looked was one of the kitchen drawers. And for paper, he used a piece of leftover craft paper from the bedroom closet. Then he sat at the small table where he and Lily had shared meals and quiet talks. From there, he just stared at the paper, clueless how to proceed. And just as he was about to put his idea to rest, it came to him.

He knew exactly what he wanted to say. The words seemed to write themselves.

Dear Santa,

It's been a while, so I imagine you're surprised to hear from me. But don't worry, I'm not about to ask you for a new truck or a winning lotto ticket. What I need is a favor. I'm trying to find someone, and I think you might know her. Her name is Lily, and she claims she's a Christmas fairy who works for you. Now, I realize you probably have a lot of workers there at the North Pole, so if it helps, here's what I know about her... she loves to go barefoot in the snow, and she's pretty good at making snowballs. She also bakes. A LOT! Cookies and pies, mostly. Which is probably why she walks around smelling of cinnamon and spice. Another thing she likes to do is hum Christmas carols. Though I suppose that might have been part of her plan to get me in the mood for Christmas. Oh, one more thing... wherever she goes, snow follows. All she has to do is flutter her wings, and it's snow time!

So there it is. If you know Lily, and you think I deserve something special for Christmas this year, my wish is for you to send her back to me... because I miss her and I can't imagine life without her. I'd give you my address, but I'm sure you already have it.

Regards,
Jake Longmire
P.S. My dog misses Lily, too!

Jake read his letter twice through. He felt completely silly for writing it, and even sillier after he found an envelope and addressed it to Santa. Not because he still had his doubts, but because he also had no idea how his letter could possibly get to the North Pole in time for Santa to read it. Though he figured if he left the envelope with a plate of cookies on the fireplace mantel, along with a glass of milk, Santa would find them. It's what he'd always done as a kid, and it seemed to work in getting him just about everything he ever wanted for Christmas. Not that he expected Lily to show up sitting under the tree, but he figured Santa would be able to work that part out.

Satisfied he'd done all he could to reconnect with Lily, he settled on the sofa, exhausted and ready for some downtime. Sierra lay beside the sofa, within easy reach of his hand, and he rubbed the fur on her neck until they both fell asleep.

Chapter Twenty-Four

Lily hurried along the brightly lit hallway on her way to see Santa. She was frantic to talk to him before he left to deliver toys. Not only did she need to tell him about Cinder, but she also wanted to ask if he would allow her to return to the cabin before the clock struck midnight. If there was even the slightest chance Jake might show up, she wanted to be there waiting for him.

Arriving at Santa's office door, she saw light coming from within. Good, she thought, feeling just a flicker from her wings. But as she raised her hand to knock, the door opened, and she came face-to-face with Santa's personal assistant, Luvon.

"Not now! I'm in a hurry," Luvon said as he swept past Lily.

Lily poked her head in the door and saw that Santa's office was empty. "Santa?" she called just to be sure, and when she got no response, she turned and ran after Luvon. "Wait! Where is Santa?"

Luvon didn't break stride, just kept walk-running, like he couldn't make up his mind how much of a hurry he was in. "It's too late to make a wish," he said over his shoulder. "You can come back and see Santa in the morning. Or you can talk to him later tonight, at the Christmas Eve Ball. He'll be making an appearance if he returns from delivering toys in time. Which is doubtful because he's already behind schedule!"

Lily did her best to keep up. "I'm not here to ask Santa for a wish. I just need to speak with him. It'll only take a minute. I promise."

Luvon slowed his pace. "What is it you need?"

"I must tell him something."

"About Cinder? He knows," Luvon said. "*Everyone* knows."

Lily caught her lip with the edge of her teeth. "I see. Well, then, I still need to see Santa. I want to ask him a favor."

"I told you, it's too late!" Luvon looked at his watch. "Speaking of… I don't have time to stand around and chitchat. Santa is in the Reindeer Barn waiting for me to bring him these replacement plants." He held up a wad of red velvety fabric that looked large enough to cover a table. "The old man split a seam getting into the sleigh, and I got an eyeful that will take me a hundred years to forget."

A blush warmed Lily's cheeks. "That is something best kept to yourself. I'm sure Santa would not enjoy you sharing such a detail. He has been trying so hard to lose weight."

"He needs to try harder," Luvon said. And then he lowered his voice. "It's the cookies. Everyone has been sneaking him extras, hoping it will influence him to grant their Christmas wish." He shook his head. "Something needs to be done. A new rule needs to be established. If it were up to me, anyone caught trying to bribe Santa with treats would forfeit their wish."

Lily giggled. It was the same every year, with everyone giving Santa an extra cookie or two. And it seemed harmless enough. But the problem with all those extra cookies was that they resulted in extra calories that went straight to Santa's waist, and then his suit needed altering. Which resulted in a baffled Mrs. Claus, who simply couldn't understand how her husband continued to gain weight, despite his being on a strict diet of salad and oranges.

Luvon gave her a sharp look. "You think it's funny that everyone has been trying to bribe Santa?"

"Well, no, but… maybe a little."

Luvon scoffed. "I'll have you know I could be in big trouble over this. *Huge!* I might even lose my job and be sent to work in the Toy Room." He held his hands out to Lily. "Look at my hands. I'm not meant to build things. I organize!"

Lily managed to stifle another giggle. "That's right, Luvon. You organize. And you know Santa could never replace you. You're his right-hand elf, and you keep everything running smoothly."

Luvon sniffed. "I'm glad someone here notices my effort. But it's not Santa I'm worried about. It's *Mrs.* Claus. She's not all sugar and cinnamon, you know. The truth is she can be a real killjoy at times."

This brought a spurt of laughter out of Lily. She'd heard the same thing, mostly from elves or fairies who had been caught doing things they shouldn't. Or from Vivienne, who had a ready complaint on her lips about everything. "Now, then, Luvon, I know it might seem like Santa's wife can be difficult, but she really is a pleasant woman who just wants to make sure everyone is doing their job, and that Santa stays on course. It's because she cares."

"*Hmmph.* I care, too!" Luvon said, shaking the red pants at Lily. "I care that I get these pants to Santa before he takes off without them!" He looked at his watch again. "I have no more time to spare. As I said, you can either talk to Santa tonight at the ball, or you can wait and see him in his office tomorrow morning. Early! He and Mrs. Claus will be boarding a plane for Honolulu at precisely eight a.m." And with that, he turned and continued down the hall, shaking his head and grumbling as he went about how someone needed to come up with a decent no-calorie cookie recipe.

Lily followed, determined to see Santa, with or without his trousers. She moved quietly, with her back pressed tightly to the wall until she saw Luvon turn left at an arrow marked *Reindeer Barn*. But then Luvon disappeared through a double green door that had a sign posted that read *Stop! No admittance!* and Lily dared not go any further. On Christmas Eve, only the elves who were assigned to help load Santa's sleigh were allowed access to the Reindeer Barn. The less confusion, the better when Santa was preparing to depart the North Pole to deliver toys.

With sagging shoulders, Lily turned and went back down the hall. Any chance her Christmas wish might still be granted was slipping away. Her only option was to see Santa later at the ball.

Walking slowly, she followed the red carpet that ran the length of the hallway and would take her to her room. She was doing her best to keep a good attitude, though it wasn't easy. She'd had such high hopes for a different outcome this Christmas. But perhaps she wasn't meant to find love. And maybe next year, she would ask Santa for something else, like her very own chocolate factory right there at the North Pole. Then she could drown herself *and* her broken heart in chocolate. Dark! None of that milk chocolate poison so many of the other fairies favored.

Finally reaching her room, Lily paused to prepare herself in case Vivienne was inside. No telling what snide remarks the elder fairy would have regarding her early return home. She could already hear Vivienne saying mean things and gloating about how she'd failed to even get a simple kiss from Jake. If only it weren't true.

Drawing a deep breath, Lily counted to three and opened the door.

Chapter Twenty-Five

Vivienne wasn't alone. The young fairy, Narissa, was with her, seated at her feet, giving her a pedicure. And by Vivienne's manner of dress—an elegant, full-length emerald-green gown—Lily surmised Vivienne was preparing to go to the Christmas Eve Ball.

"Liliana! Is it really you?" Narissa asked, her eyes lighting. "We were told you may not be coming back to us." She was so excited that her wings let loose a flurry of wet snow. Plus, she accidentally painted one of Vivienne's toes red.

"Argh!" Vivienne screeched, drawing her foot away from Narissa. She stared down at her bloodied toe, aghast. "Look what you've done! My toe looks like it's been nibbled on by the Abominable Snowman! And look at my dress! You've ruined it!"

"So sorry," Narissa said. She immediately gained control of her wings and grabbed a tissue to wipe the snow from Vivienne's dress, but the flakes had already melted and done their damage.

"Stop! Just stop!" Vivienne screeched again. She glared at Narissa and pointed to the door. "Go! Now! I'd like to speak with Liliana alone! But don't go far. I expect you to finish my pedicure when little Liliana and I are done with our business."

Narissa quietly gathered her things and departed the room, visibly relieved she'd been ordered to leave. It was for the best, Lily thought. Narissa was young and impressionable, and it was better she didn't witness the conversation that was about to take place. Ears that young needed to be protected.

Vivienne stood, facing Lily, a smirk playing at her lips. "So, I'm guessing your return means you and the hunter failed to make a love connection. What a pity. He was rather handsome… in a human kind of way."

"You're right. Jake is handsome," Lily said. "Plus, he's kind and good and so unlike you."

"Hmm, how interesting that you would describe a hunter of reindeer as *kind* and *good*. Taken a liking to the dark side, have you?"

"For your information, I misjudged Jake. He wasn't intending to hurt that reindeer. He was trying to protect it from being harmed by a wolf."

"Details," Vivienne said, yawning. "Are we finished here? Because I'm bored." She spun around to face the mirror, turning this way and that to see the damage done to her dress. "Oh!" she scoffed. "Just look at what that pathetic Narissa did to my beautiful gown! Now, what will I wear to the ball?"

"A pointy black hat, perhaps?" Lily offered.

"*Grr*," Vivienne said, her top lip curling as she sent Lily a sharp glare.

"Oh, put your fangs away," Lily said. "And don't blame Narissa for the damage done to your dress. She wasn't expecting to see me. But you were. You knew all along I'd be back because you were the one who gave me that tainted mistletoe. You never wanted me to find love. You wanted me to be miserable, the same as you. I'll bet you even put a curse on that replacement sprig, just to make *sure* Jake wouldn't kiss me."

"My, what an imagination you have," Vivienne said. "Why ever would I want to cause you to have your wish denied if it meant I could have my own wishes restored?"

"Don't pretend you care about wishes! You're old! At this

point, you already have everything you could ever want! All that's left is for you to be named Head Christmas Fairy!"

"Hmm," Vivienne said, putting a finger to her chin, "now that I think about it, you're right. Except for the *old* part. But I'll ignore the insult because I know how miserable you must be. Poor fairy. You didn't play by the rules, and now, not only have you lost the opportunity to experience real love, but you've also forfeited any chance you might've had at being named Head Christmas Fairy. Which leaves Santa with only one option— *moi!*" She pressed a hand to her chest as she admired herself in the mirror.

"That's not what I heard," Lily remarked.

Vivienne swung around. "What are you talking about? Of course, Santa will choose me. I'm perfect for the job."

"I don't think so. You're too mean."

"Sticks and stones," Vivienne said. "And now that we have that settled, send Narissa back in. She needs to finish my nails. I want them perfect for tonight. Word is there's a new *tall* elf called Vulred who will be in attendance, and I hear he has an affinity to us more seasoned fairies."

Lily ignored Vivienne's demand to send Narissa back in, nor did she care about some new tall elf. Her only thought was to give Vivienne a taste of her own nastiness. "You're not only mean, you're also a liar. Enar told me there's no such thing as an Unable to Grant Stamp and that by failing to find love, I have only lost this year's wish."

Vivienne let out a quiet cackle. "Well, now, we all tell an untruth now and then, don't we? Even you. As I recall, you told quite a few untruths to the hunter."

Lily fumed, hating that Vivienne had made a valid point. "You're right, and that's why Santa is no longer considering either of us for Head Christmas Fairy. He's offering the job to Ruth again."

Vivienne's eyebrows shot up to her hairline. "That's ridiculous! Talk about old! Ruth is old *and* boring and… old! Why would he choose her?"

"First, Ruth is not much older than you. And second, Santa has chosen her because he knows it was you who gave me the tainted mistletoe, and word is you are now at the top of his Naughty List."

"Liar!" Vivienne sputtered, a vein bulging in her forehead.

"Sorry, but it's true. Ruth is going to be named Head Christmas Fairy. Again." Lily crossed her fingers behind her back the same as she'd seen humans do at times when they were telling an untruth. "If you don't believe me, go ask Luvon. I spoke with him just a few minutes ago, and he told me Santa has already decided. He'll be announcing it at the ball later tonight, as soon as he returns from delivering toys."

Vivienne's lips twitched. Her face was as red as the smeared polish on her toes. She was breathing so hard the windows were fogging up. "We'll see about that," she said at last, and then she gathered her petticoats and moved to the door, giving Lily a narrow look before swishing out.

Lily smiled. She'd hit Vivienne's last nerve, and it was most pleasing. She went to the door and watched Vivienne make her way down the long hallway. She knew exactly where Vivienne was headed. To find Luvon. And then she'd find out—if she didn't have an aneurysm first—that Ruth was probably *not* going to be named Head Christmas Fairy. Though it certainly served Vivienne right to think otherwise, even if only for a few minutes.

"Is everything okay?" Narissa asked. She'd been waiting patiently just outside the room. "Should I stay and wait for her to return?"

"No," Lily told Narissa. "Vivienne will be a while. You should go and get ready for tonight's ball. Make sure you wear something exquisite. I hear there's a new elf in town named Vulred who might be looking for a dance partner."

Narissa took her leave, and Lily hurried to her closet to find a dress of her own to wear to the ball. Not that she was in any mood to dance and make merry, but if Santa returned from delivering toys in time, there might still be a chance he would allow her to go back to her assignment location. Flinging open the closet door, she did a quick survey of her entire closet, but not one article of clothing stood out that might be suitable for attending a ball. To make sure, she began pulling all of her dresses from their hangers until she finally slumped to the floor of her closet near tears. Everything she had was too old or too plain or just not fabulous enough.

Perhaps it was for the best, she thought as she leaned against the wall, settling in for a good cry. After such an exhaustive search, it was all she had energy for. But then a piece of silky material that still clung to a hanger feathered across her cheek, and she looked up to see a splash of red that was so vibrant and had so much sparkle, it lit the entire closet. And when she tugged the material, and it fell into her lap, her energy was instantly restored. She'd found the perfect dress for attending a ball.

In her excitement, she twirled from the closet, dress in hand, eager to try it on. And just as she slid it over her shoulders, the door burst open, and Vivienne flew back into the room, looking like she might indeed be having an aneurysm.

"You lied to me!" she said. "I found Luvon in the Toy Room, and he had no idea what I was screeching about. And now, thanks to you, I'm going to be late for the ball, and the other fairies will be all over Vulred!"

"Sorry about that," Lily said, not feeling it. "But tell me, did you at least learn something?"

Vivienne squished her lips around some. "As a matter of fact, I did. I learned I can't trust you. That you're as spoiled as that reindeer of yours and that I should have let the hunter kiss you under that blasted mistletoe. Then you would have known what it is to have true heartache!" Her voice wavered, and she swallowed and turned away from Lily.

Lily sucked in a breath. Was that moisture she'd seen in Vivienne's eyes? No, it couldn't be. Fairies didn't cry. Even so, it was clear that Vivienne was in distress, and that's when Lily realized something about her roommate. Vivienne had been hurt. Deeply. And perhaps no one had shown her any compassion when her own dreams of finding love had gone unfulfilled. Or perhaps no one believed she'd been hurt. Enar certainly didn't.

Immediately regretting wanting to get even, Lily moved close to Vivienne. "I'm sorry I told you an untruth," she said, giving Vivienne's shoulder a light touch. "All I wanted was for you to see the damage that can be done by telling even a small lie. I know it's no excuse, but I was so upset when I found out about the mistletoe... and then Jake left, and I was all alone." Lily swallowed. "I just wanted to make you hurt the way I hurt. But now I know it wasn't your fault. It's what was meant to be. So... will you forgive me?"

Vivienne turned back to Lily. The moisture in her eyes had already dissipated. "I suppose I should. I mean, with it being Christmas Eve and all. And I suppose I regret anything I might've done to cause you discomfort. But don't take this to mean we're going to be pals. The last thing I need is a gal-pal who wants to engage in girl talk on Friday nights."

"Of course," Lily said. "I also do not need a pal." She smiled. Some things never changed.

Chapter Twenty-Six

Santa tiptoed past the sleeping man and paused to eat a couple of cookies from the plate he found on the fireplace mantel. He recognized the recipe as being one of Lily's, it was so delicious. Lily had become such a skilled baker the past few years, he'd hoped he could convince her to keep him in good supply of treats if he named her Head Christmas Fairy. Though if he did that, she would be far too busy with other duties to spend time baking him cookies and pies. And even if he didn't name her Head Christmas Fairy, if she was determined to have her wish granted, her time at the North Pole might very well be coming to an end.

Ah, well, it was probably just wishful thinking, anyway. Mrs. Claus was sure to restrict his diet for a good long time when she found out he'd split the seam of his trousers again.

As he reached for a third cookie, he noticed an envelope with his name on it next to the plate. He took the envelope over to the table and made himself comfortable with a glass of real milk, not some substitute like the almond or coconut milk some folks left in an attempt to help him stay healthy. Which he appreciated. But his preference was, and always would be, whole cow's milk.

After brushing cookie crumbs from the front of his suit, he

opened the envelope and smiled as he read the letter he found inside. It had been written by the man sleeping on the sofa, and unlike most letters he received that sometimes included a long, complicated list of items a child wanted to find under his or her tree, the man was asking for only one thing—help in finding the woman he loved.

Santa stroked his beard as he contemplated the man's request. Though no longer a child who still believed in the magic of Christmas, the man was such a good soul, and he'd suffered far too long with the pain of losing his sister. But as deserving as the man might be, Liliana had broken a rule while on this assignment, and rules were meant to be kept.

Nibbling one more cookie, a peanut butter one this time, Santa gave the situation more thought. He knew it hadn't been Liliana's intention to use the magic mistletoe, and he also knew it was Vivienne who had gifted the mistletoe to Liliana. Though he wasn't sure why.

Finishing his cookie, Santa picked up the letter and read it again. That the man had even written such a letter was evidence that Liliana had made significant progress in her assignment. And perhaps the magic mistletoe had nothing to do with the man wanting to kiss her. Perhaps his attraction to her was real and true.

While enjoying one more glass of milk, for the protein, of course, Santa watched the sleeping man for a minute. He didn't so much as stir. His dog, on the other hand, was eyes open and keeping watch from her place by her master's side. "That's a good girl," Santa said. He moved over to where the dog lay and reached a hand down to give her a pat. Then he backed away and stood at the front of the fireplace. To be sure, the man's request deserved special consideration. But at the moment, there were still a great many toys to be delivered.

With a wave of his hand, Santa filled the fireplace with enough fresh firewood for a robust flame that would last through the night. Then he closed his eyes, and in an instant, he was back in his sleigh, urging his team of reindeer into the sky, toward their last stop of the evening—Canada! Oh, how he loved flying over the wintry landscape of the Selkirk mountain range! Such a magnificent sight it was, he never tired of this particular route.

"Hup! Onward, boys and girls!" he said as he shook the reins. A scant minute later, he flew directly over a pasture that was filled with cattle and a couple reindeer—Cinder and her new friend, Frost. Looking down, Santa waved, and then with a *Ho! Ho! Ho!* he continued on, flying his sleigh up to where the stars seemed to be twinkling extra bright on this Christmas Eve night.

Chapter Twenty-Seven

The Christmas Eve Ball was a grand affair, with everyone gathered together to celebrate another year of successful toy building and assignment completion, and Lily couldn't help but smile as she watched her sister fairies and the elves dance the night away in their fancy clothes. Even Mrs. Claus was out on the dance floor, dancing with every elf at least once, though it made a funny sight with them barely able to wrap an arm around her waist.

But where was Vivienne?

Lily scanned the room until she spotted the elder fairy dancing with one of the elves from the Weather Room. She didn't appear to be grinding her teeth, so maybe she'd already gotten over the mishap with her dress.

Grinning, Lily continued looking about until she saw Narissa, who had done particularly well picking out the perfect gown. And who was that tall elf spinning her around the dance floor? Vulred perhaps?

On a sigh, Lily sank against the wall. She had no interest in joining the fun. She still hadn't thought of what she might say to Santa when he confronted her about losing Cinder. A good explanation might be her only hope in being allowed to return to the cabin. Though with the Nice List being so long this year, it was doubtful Santa would return from delivering toys in time. Luvon had said as much. And even if Santa did make an appearance, he might refuse to hear what she had to say. She had not only failed to keep one of his reindeer safe, but she had also left that reindeer behind.

Finally, after many hours of watching everyone in their gaiety, the clock's strike of midnight signaled the end of Lily's torture. Santa hadn't shown, and it was over. Another Christmas Eve had come and gone, and she would spend tomorrow—Christmas Day—in her room. Alone. She would be in no mood to visit or open gifts or even sing Christmas carols. Even now, she was having a hard time sitting and watching all her friends laugh and make merry. Too, she was barely aware of the music that had been playing for the last hour… or that elf Gormar had been standing at her side, talking to her for the last five minutes. But at last, his persistence got her attention.

"Oh, hello, Gormar. Merry Christmas," she said, making a fair attempt at holiday cheer.

"Merry Christmas to you, too, Liliana! But did you hear me?" Gormar asked. "I was wondering if you would like to dance."

"I'm afraid I'm not in the mood for fun, Gormar," she said, looking straight into his eyes. If she were standing, she would be looking down at the top of his bald little head. Not that she held his short stature or that he was bald against him, but it had always seemed awkward dancing with someone whose face pressed against her abdomen.

"But it is Christmas," the portly elf said. "And you're here and, well, even if you're not in the mood, it seems a shame to let good music go to waste. Perhaps a dance will lift your spirits!" He held out his arms to her.

Gormar's enthusiasm was endearing. And he was right about the music. It was lively and joyous and perfect for lifting spirits.

"Perhaps one dance," she relented, smiling at Gormar. She stood, and she and Gormar were belly-to-nose as they danced to

"Christmas Waltz." It was a lovely song, one of the loveliest, in her opinion, but it did nothing for her mood. Then "Jingle Bell Rock" came on, and every elf and fairy who was still seated came out of their chairs and headed for the dance floor.

Lily couldn't help but feel optimistic. She might not have Jake, but she had everything else she needed to be happy. She had many friends there at the North Pole, and she might even be named Head Christmas Fairy one day. Though surely not this year, not after losing Cinder and after using magic mistletoe to gain her Christmas wish… even if not her intention.

As Gormar spun her around, she saw Enar dancing with Isla, who was stunning in a frilly blue gown with sequins that drew everyone's attention in her direction.

Enar caught her looking, and he gave her a nod and a smile, and she smiled back at him. Then she closed her eyes, and as she floated over the dance floor, she imagined herself in Jake's arms, the two of them waltzing the night away. It would have been a perfect end to the year. But with her powers nearly gone, dancing with Jake was now nothing more than a hopeless dream. In fact, she might never again have the ability to close her eyes and imagine anything into being.

A sob filled her throat at such a thought, and the happiness she'd felt only moments before instantly dissipated. Her eyes filled with tears, and try as she might to blink them away, several escaped and dripped onto Gormar's hand.

"Liliana! What is wrong with your eyes?" he asked, immediately releasing her from his arms.

"It is nothing, Gormar," Lily said, wiping away another tear that was sliding down her cheek. "I shouldn't be here. Please forgive me, but I must go." Turning, she hurried from the ballroom, wanting only to be alone with the pain in her heart that had grown to be so unbearable she worried she might never recover.

Down the hall she ran, more tears streaking her face. And her hair, which had been pinned neatly in place, fell and hung over her eyes so that she couldn't even see where she was going. But no matter. Another minute and she would be safely back in her room, where no one could see what a mess she'd become. She raced on at a frantic pace until, all at once, she found herself with a face full of velvety material.

"Oh, my! I'm so sorry!" she cried, backing up and looking to see who it was she'd assaulted. *"Santa?"*

"Well, hello, my dear," Santa said, giving her a jovial smile. "I was hoping I would run into you tonight—though maybe not so literally. But here you are, so do you have time for a chat?"

Chapter Twenty-Eight

Lily twisted her fingers into knots as she stood at the front of Santa's desk. This was it. Santa was about to give her his decision regarding her Christmas wish. Though it could just as easily be that he wanted to scold her for losing Cinder. Either way, she'd already resigned herself to another year of living at the North Pole, with Vivienne for a roommate. Even so, until Santa said the words, she was determined to remain hopeful.

The longer Santa stayed silent, the more concerned she became. And impatient. If the news was bad, a quiet muttering of the word *no* would suffice. And if Santa intended to lecture her about losing Cinder, then why not get on with it?

As she continued waiting, she took in the holiday decorations Mrs. Claus had put up. It was garland and ribbon and lights everywhere, plus a fat tree in one corner that had been adorned with dozens of colorful balls and enough big red bows for two trees. Just looking at all the bright colors filled Lily with quiet optimism. She breathed in the scent of oranges and pine, grateful for something to occupy her mind other than the possibility of a good scolding.

Another minute passed, and she could stand waiting no more

"Santa?" she said, ready for her torment to be over. But the only response she received was a soft snore. Santa had fallen asleep.

Not wanting to startle him but needing to do something, Lily reached over his desk and touched his arm. But when her touching resulted in nothing more than a loud snort, she decided on another approach. Closing her eyes, she imagined a burst of snow with big white flakes that would land on Santa's cheeks and gently kiss him out of his drowsy state—because who doesn't enjoy a gentle kiss every now and then? But when she opened her eyes, the short burst of fat snowflakes she'd intended turned out to be only a spurt of flakes so tiny she doubted Santa would even be able to feel them. Then, as they dissipated, Santa snorted several up his nose, which caused him to jerk his head so that his glasses slipped down and hung precariously from his mustache.

"Oh, my," he sputtered, frowning and looking confused by the droplets of water dripping from his nose. He fumbled to catch his glasses before they fell to the floor.

Lily quickly plucked a tissue from a box at the corner of his desk and handed it to him, saying, "I'm sorry, sir. It's my wings. I've been trying to control them, but they seem to have a mind of their own these days."

Santa wiped his nose and held up a white-gloved hand. "Yes, I'd heard you were having trouble. Enar told me how you brought one of the assembly lines in the Toy Room to a halt week before last. He said it was a real blizzard. I'm just glad it didn't stop toy production." He stared at a water spot on his desk. "I'm not sure how much damage your wings could possibly do, but I trust you will make every effort to keep that from happening again next year. I'm sure you can imagine the result if a child were to find no gifts under their tree on Christmas morning."

Lily dipped her head. "Tears and sadness and a loss of Christmas spirit."

"Indeed. And you know what happens when a child loses his or her Christmas spirit."

"I do, sir," Lily said. She felt the need to explain. "Vivienne and I were having a disagreement about one of the toys the elves were testing, and I know it was silly, but I let her rile me. I promise I will try harder to keep my wings under control from now on, no matter how upset I become." She did her best to look appropriately apologetic, though what she really wanted was to tell Santa how difficult it was having Vivienne for a roommate. That every morning she hogged the bathroom, taking far more time than was necessary for any Christmas fairy to begin her day, and that she chattered endlessly about how things would change around the North Pole once she was named Head Christmas Fairy—and not for the better, in Lily's opinion. But she didn't want to get started on anything that might cause a detour in her conversation with Santa. He knew Vivienne as well as anyone, and he, most certainly, knew what a trial she was.

"It's a shame you and Vivienne do not get along," Santa remarked. "You would think after a hundred years of being roommates, the two of you could work out your differences."

"Vivienne and I get along as well as can be expected," Lily said. "She does her job, I do mine. We're copasetic."

This brought a brief chuckle from Santa. "That's what I like to hear. Now, then, where were we?"

"I'm not sure," Lily said. "I thought you might want to discuss my Christmas wish. And, too, I had hoped to talk to you about going back to my assignment location before you left to deliver toys. Enar came to escort me home, but it wasn't yet midnight, and I wanted to stay in case—"

"Yes, well, it's too late for that now, isn't it?" Santa said as he pushed aside a pile of papers to uncover a small blue notebook. "Before we get into discussing your wish, you wouldn't have a spare cookie or two in your pocket, would you?" He tapped a finger on the edge of a bowl of oranges that sat at one corner of his desk. "It's this diet Mrs. Claus has me on. I don't see how she expects me to get by on only salad and oranges after a full night of delivering toys."

"Oranges are full of vitamin C, good for your skin," Lily reasoned.

"Be that as it may, I'm starving, and oranges are hard to peel." He tapped the edge of the bowl again. "Too, I think my consumption of so much vitamin C has been affecting my ability to concentrate. I need more cookies!"

Lily held out her hands from her red silk dress. "I wish I could be of help, but as you can see, I haven't any pockets. Too, Mrs. Claus gave us all strict orders at the beginning of the holiday season that we were not to feed you. She was worried you wouldn't fit into your suit on Christmas Eve, and she said it had no more material to be let out."

"No more material!" Santa said, huffing. "It seems Mrs. Claus and I need to have a chat. If it were up to me, vegetables and fruit would be banned from the North Pole!"

But it wasn't up to him, and this made Lily so nervous her wings fluttered and released another burst of tiny snowflakes that landed all over Santa's desk.

"Goodness! I'm so sorry," she said as she plucked another tissue from the box at the corner of his desk and handed it to him.

"Relax, child. Snow happens," Santa said. He wiped moisture from the melted snowflakes off the front of his notebook, and then he gestured to the chair at the front of his desk. "Please, sit and make yourself comfortable. And don't worry. I won't hold your refusal to slip me a cookie against you." He took an orange from the bowl and held it out to her. "Here. Perhaps this will help settle your nerves."

Lily shook her head. "I'm sure Mrs. Claus wouldn't approve of me interfering with your diet."

Santa's mouth twisted as he dropped the orange back into the bowl. "The diet is over! The toys have been delivered! I'm free to gain as much weight as I want until *next* Christmas!"

"Yes, sir," Lily said. "But I still don't have any spare cookies."

Santa grumbled under his breath, muttering words Lily couldn't quite hear. When he finished his muttering, he spoke clearly, saying, "Let us get on with this wish of yours, then, shall we?" He focused on the notebook, his gold-rimmed spectacles slipping down as he read his notes. "Oh, my... goodness... interesting," he said as he pushed his spectacles back up onto the bridge of his nose. His gaze met hers. "Is this really your twenty-first request for this particular wish?"

"Yes, sir, it is," Lily answered, her voice wavering. "I had hoped by now, with all my good deeds and after so many successful assignments, you would finally see I am ready for such a wish."

"I see," Santa said, nodding his head and pressing his lips so tight his mustache and beard seemed as one. "What about all your friends here? Will you not miss them? And what about Enar? He is sweet on you, you know."

Lily's fingers tightened around the arms of the chair. Word for word, it was the same conversation she and Santa had every year. And every year, her answers were the same. But perhaps Santa didn't remember. He was always so busy, maybe he needed reminding. "Of course, I will miss everyone here," she said. "Including Enar. But Enar and I are just friends, and that's all we will ever be."

Santa adjusted his glasses and cleared his throat. "May I ask what displeases you about him?"

"It is not a matter of Enar pleasing or not pleasing me," Lily said. "I simply do not have the same feelings for him as Mrs. Claus has for you."

Santa looked at her for a silent moment, like he was weighing the meaning of her words. Finally, he continued. "If I may ask, do you have those feelings for the man from your assignment? Does *he* please you?"

"Well, sir, he is certainly much taller than I. Plus, he has no need for eyewear."

Santa's brow arched. "And why might spectacles be a problem?"

Hope flickered alive in Lily's chest. In all their discussions, Santa had never delved into asking particulars. She straightened in her chair with a ready answer. "It's not that spectacles are a problem. But from what I've observed, Mrs. Claus is always asking the elves if they've seen your glasses, and I fear if it were necessary for me to keep track of another's eyewear, I would not be as patient as Mrs. Claus. It would lead to sour words."

Santa grumbled something unintelligible and then asked, "Anything else?"

"There is one more *little* thing," Lily said, holding up her thumb and index finger. "And though I say it is little, I think it may be the most important quality of all." She clasped her hands together, and her eyes went into a dreamy roll. "The man—Jake—sometimes leaves me so breathless and weak that I think I might lose my ability to remain standing."

Santa's cheeks blossomed with color. "He causes you to feel as though you are going to *faint?*"

Lily nodded. "I believe the correct term is swoon, sir. But yes, my feelings for him have grown to be so strong that I become light-headed whenever he is near." She smiled a big smile. "It really is most pleasurable."

Santa cleared his throat again. "I don't recall Mrs. Claus ever passing out over *my* presence."

"Then perhaps you shouldn't work so hard," Lily offered. "I'm sure Mrs. Claus would enjoy spending more time with you. Perhaps it's time you had an assistant, someone who could relieve you of some of your duties."

"I have Luvon," Santa said, shaking his head. "He's the only assistant I need."

"Yes, but Luvon is so busy keeping everything organized. I wonder if you might need someone who could just assist you with your lists each year. What about Vivienne? Did it not work out well having her help you?"

"Let's just say it worked out," Santa said. "I'm not sure she enjoyed the task as much as you suggested she might. I was worried about the children. Could you imagine what would have happened if the lists had gotten mixed up and no one received the gifts they wanted? The entire holiday would have been complete anarchy. Christmas morning the world over would have been ruined."

"My goodness!" Lily said. "I would never want any child to go without the proper gift." The very idea had her wings fluttering and releasing another burst of snow that was already wet and mushy by the time the flakes hit the floor. "Oh, dear!" she said, jumping up and swiveling around to look at the mess she'd made. "Again, my apologies, sir! Perhaps my wish should have been to have more control over my wings!"

"There, there," Santa said, "calm yourself and sit back down. No need to get so worked up. I'm confident every child received the proper gift." He waved a hand. "Now, then, back to me and the missus. Though I am pleased with your concern for the well-being of our marriage, you needn't worry. Mrs. Claus and I are very happy, even if I do tend to work long hours. But perhaps you are right. Maybe it's time I add another assistant to help me with my lists during the holidays. The Nice List seems to be getting longer and longer each year. Would you happen to know which elf might enjoy such a task?"

Lily doubted Santa would be able to enlist the help of *any* elf. She couldn't think of even one who would enjoy adding names to the Naughty List. Unlike Vivienne, who was perfect for the job. Being the cause of tears was one of her favorite past times. Oh, she might work hard to complete an assignment, but if it wasn't a success, she quickly moved on with no regrets. Too, keeping Vivienne busy was a good way to prevent her from causing trouble for others.

"The elves are already overwhelmed with work in the Toy Room," she told Santa. "I think you should consider keeping Vivienne as your helper. She was even overheard saying that she was glad to have been so busy this year. She's so proficient working her assignments that it sometimes leaves her with too much free time, and she gets bored." Lily crossed her fingers behind her back for safety.

Santa gave a small nod. "Vivienne does tend to become mischievous when she has too much time on her hands. Perhaps that is why you and she haven't been getting along. I wonder, though, if she would want to continue helping with such a task. She's never once asked for an assignment involving the kiddies. I don't know that she's fond of them."

"Oh, I wouldn't worry about that," Lily said, waving a hand.

"I'm sure Vivienne adores children. And I'll bet if you gave her a permanent role working on your lists, she might even be able to complete them without your input."

"I would hope not," Santa said, his mustache drooping.

"I'm sure, though, that you would need to double-check and make sure no mistakes had been made," Lily quickly added, not meaning to make Santa feel he could be replaced.

"Yes, well, it would certainly ensure a happy Christmas for the kids," Santa said. He tipped his chin up. "You may be right about Vivienne. I'll give your suggestion some thought." He smiled, and crinkles formed at the corners of his eyes. "Now, then, let's talk about you and your Christmas wish. But if you could bear with me for a minute, I would like to remind you just once more that if you leave us, Vivienne will be our only option for Head Christmas Fairy. The other fairies are either too young or don't have the same passion that you have for helping others."

"Yes, I am aware," Lily said. "And I am so very sorry. But might you consider naming Ruth again? I hear she is interested in a third term, plus she's been a great leader, and I know she would continue to do the job with much honor. Or what about Calista? She has shown quite an aptitude for leading, and her organizational skills are beyond measure."

Santa gave his head a small shake. "Calista is still finding her way. Just this year, she was asking to be sent somewhere quiet. And Ruth has had her time. It'll be Vivienne. Or perhaps you, should you decide to keep your name in the running."

It was as Lily already knew. But as much as she enjoyed any opportunity to put a bother under Vivienne's wings, being named Head Christmas Fairy held little appeal when her real desire was for everlasting love. If Vivienne were chosen as leader, the fairies would survive. The North Pole would survive. And next year, perhaps Calista or even Narissa would be ready to provide leadership to the other fairies.

"I appreciate your faith in me," she told Santa. "But I think Vivienne might be better suited to lead the other fairies."

Santa let out a full-bellied *Ho, Ho, Ho.* "My dear, you and I both know you don't mean that."

Lily gave a small sigh. "Maybe not. But she *has* completed many more assignments than I, and I think she might enjoy having more responsibility. Plus, she seems to have plenty of enthusiasm for the position."

"Indeed," Santa said. "I'm just not sure she has the proper discipline." He leaned in and lowered his voice so that she could barely hear him. "Between you and me, she has been sneaking me extra cookies every evening, and I have a hunch it is for the purpose of gaining my favor."

Lily fought the urge to agree with Santa's hunch. That would only serve to put her Christmas wish at further risk of being denied. "I'm sure Vivienne means well," she told Santa, then added, "But I also may not have the discipline one should possess to lead the other fairies. Sometimes, without even meaning to, I get myself into trouble. And there are times when I still have difficulty remembering the Christmas Fairy Pledge."

"I sometimes have trouble remembering every reindeer's name," Santa said. "It does not mean I should be replaced, does it?"

"Oh, no, sir. Not at all."

"Pledge aside," Santa continued, "I do not doubt your ability to lead. Other than the time you and your sister fairies got together and poured molasses in the elves' beds, you've been a model citizen here at the North Pole."

Lily pressed her lips into a thin line. The molasses incident wasn't the *only* time she'd participated in such tomfoolery. She was just good at not getting caught. Indeed, she was as full of mischief as the next fairy. There was the time she and Sisette removed every candle from the light posts along North Pole Drive. And once, she and Enar got together and filled Vivienne's Christmas stocking with toads. Even now, thinking about the look on Vivienne's face when she pulled the first toad out and it hopped down her arm was enough to make Lily laugh. It was complete chaos. Vivienne despised the creatures and was so convinced she was in danger of catching warts that she rushed straight away to see elf Nasir, the North Pole's resident doctor, who was forced to prescribe her a placebo cure so that she might have the peace of mind to sleep that night. And though it had all worked out, Lily suspected part of Vivienne's animosity toward her stemmed from that very incident.

"I'm not *always* a good citizen," she told Santa, smiling thinly.

"None of us are perfect," Santa said." He tapped the front of his notebook. "But certainly, if you desire to experience life as a human, or if you are no longer happy here, then you could not possibly be effective in a position such as Head Christmas Fairy."

"It is not my intention to make you feel I do not enjoy my life here."

"But you want more."

"I do."

"Tell me," Santa said, "might there be anything else you would wish for other than to become part of the human world? Your very own gourmet kitchen, perhaps? Or how about a personal assistant? I could assign you one of the young elves."

"I am grateful for the offer," Lily said, "but I have no desire for such things. Love is all I wish for."

"Yes, well, to love means to also know heartache. Maybe even heart*break*. And some hearts do not heal from being broken. Would you be prepared for that?" Santa asked.

Lily placed a hand lightly to her chest, thinking of the pain she had already suffered. But as unpleasant as it was, it also hadn't destroyed her. Life goes on. "I'm not sure one *can* prepare for heartbreak," she told Santa. "And while it would prove difficult, I believe the reward of being in love would be far greater than any discomfort I might ever be forced to endure."

Santa nodded his head and jotted a few notes in his notebook. Then his gaze met hers. "I have only one more question, and it is perhaps the most important of all. So you must think carefully before answering."

Lily swallowed, waiting.

"How do you feel about dying?"

Lily took a small breath. Santa was right. It was a very important question, and the truth was, she would feel positively wrecked. That is, if dying were to happen tomorrow. But as she and Enar had discussed, many humans lived eight or more decades, and that seemed a very good number of years to be in love. And while no one could predict the future, she felt reasonably certain as a human, she would have a fairly long existence.

"To become ill is not something I would look forward to," she told Santa, "but I would eat many oranges and do my best to stay healthy. And death, while not a pleasing thought, is so far in the future, I'm sure I would have plenty of happy years ahead of me."

Santa chuckled under his snowy white beard. "Sounds like a human response if ever I heard one." He cleared his throat and continued, saying, "No matter my question, you seem to have a reasonable answer." He tapped his pen on the open page of the notebook. "I trust you have nothing more to add?"

Lily shook her head. She had made her points, and Santa had made his. All that remained now was to await his decision. She sat quietly while he shuffled papers, scribbled more notes, and mumbled to himself. She dared not interrupt his thought process.

A tall clock in one corner ticked away the minutes, and it seemed like hours before the scribbling stopped and Santa looked up from his notebook. "I have made a decision," he said, though his eyes were void of their usual twinkle.

Chapter Twenty-Nine

Lily had no idea what to expect when Santa stood and approached her. He rested a gentle hand on her shoulder, and she held her breath, hoping for the best.

"Don't be nervous," he began. "What I'm about to say will be mostly painless. I promise."

Lily clenched the arms of the chair. She was beyond nervous.

Santa continued. "I'm sure you know how much Mrs. Claus and I care for you. You have been like a daughter to us, and we had hoped you would want to stay here with us at the North Pole permanently. Or at least a very long time." He paused, smiling. "You do know that Mrs. Claus may require I sleep in the sleigh for many weeks should I agree to grant your wish?"

Lily giggled. "I should hope so. But please, tell Mrs. Claus that I have had a most pleasurable life here at the North Pole. And, sir, I *have* been here for a very long time."

"Yes, well, two hundred years is but a minute in our world. Your life has only just begun, and you've still much to learn about being a Christmas fairy. And though you've had many successful assignments, there is so much more you could do working with humans. So many of them seem to be in need of help these days."

Santa settled against his desk. "I know you would like to experience love, but might there be another reason you wish to leave the North Pole? And would it have anything to do with your roommate or someone else here that might be causing you distress?"

"No, sir," Lily assured him. "My wanting to leave here has nothing to do with Vivienne. Nor does it have anything to do with any of the elves or you or Mrs. Claus, or *anyone*. It's about feeling. Here, we fairies are protected. We come, and we go, and we live for brief moments with humans, and we see the love they share. We see tears of joy, as well as tears of sorrow. But once we leave the human world, we keep only the memory of what we've helped create. The feelings and emotions we experience are lost to us. We come back here to the North Pole, and we start each day anew. And while that's all very nice, it doesn't seem fair."

Santa arched an eyebrow. "Not *fair?* My dear, you have been given a life that allows you to help others without remembering the pain. How is that not fair?" He gave his head a slow shake. "I don't know what's happening to the younger generation these days, always expressing how they're being treated unfairly. It boggles the mind."

"I did not mean for your mind to be boggled," Lily said quickly, afraid she hadn't explained clearly. "It's just hard when we are allowed to enter the human world, and we see such joy, but then we must come back here, to a life that is pain-free—which, as I said, is very nice—but we also do not get to keep the feeling of joy we bring others. I would like to keep that joy for more than just a minute or a holiday season. I would like to keep it for a lifetime." She dipped her head. "I'm sorry if that seems selfish."

"Oh, Liliana, I've never known you to be selfish," Santa said, his tone gentle. "And I do understand your frustration. But as you know, being a Christmas fairy, you are protected from lasting emotion, both joy and pain, for good reason. Experiencing grief can change you, and if you were not shielded from such grief, you might become jaded and weary of helping others. "To put it simply, too many heartaches in one lifetime are not good for a person." He spread his hands. "As for your desire to experience what you've seen shared between human couples, I agree, that is something worth seeking. I cannot imagine how empty my life would have been without the missus. But life here is good, and I would hate for you to leave us before you are ready. That is why I have always hesitated to grant your wish."

"But, sir, I am ready now," Lily said, feeling panicked that he was once again about to deny her wish.

Santa held up a hand. "Not to worry. I promise to further consider everything we've discussed. But you must be prepared for whatever decision I come to, whether I think it best you wait a while longer for such a grown-up wish or whether I give you my blessing and send you on your way."

Lily's shoulders sagged. Though it wasn't a definite "no," it still wasn't a "yes."

"Now," Santa continued, "from what I hear, you left something behind at your assignment location."

"Yes," Lily said, casting her gaze to the floor. "It's Cinder. She wandered off, and though I tried to find her, I fear she is lost."

Santa's lips curved ever so slightly. "Do you think you are the only fairy who has ever lost one of my reindeer?"

"Well…" Lily gave it some thought. She couldn't recall ever hearing of any fairy, or even an elf, losing a reindeer, but that didn't mean it had never happened.

"The answer is yes," Santa said. "It's true. You *are* the first to lose one of my reindeer. Still. That doesn't mean it's the end of the North Pole. It just means you need to return to your assignment location and look for Cinder. Can you imagine how she must be feeling if she thinks you've abandoned her?"

"Oh, I would never abandon Cinder!" With only a twitch of a warning, Lily's wings sprang to life and released a few tiny snowflakes, several of which landed on the tip of Santa's nose.

"So what are you going to do about it?" he asked, taking the burst of snow in stride.

Lily gave it some thought. The answer was easy. "Go find

Cinder and bring her home?" Her wings twitched again, but she was able to calm them before they released more snow.

"Good girl," Santa said.

"But, sir, what if I were to run into a human?" Two hours ago, returning to her assignment location was exactly what she wanted. But now, it was past midnight and too late for any further interaction between herself and the human world. And that included contact with Jake.

"Yes? So?"

"The clock has struck midnight. What about the rule?"

"What rule?"

"The one forbidding fairies to have contact with humans after an assignment is complete."

"Who made such a rule? It doesn't seem very accommodating to me."

"You did, sir."

Santa's eyebrows rose, and he sputtered, saying, "Be that the case, this is an extraordinary circumstance. Cinder is probably afraid and lonely and, well, you need to go find her and bring her back home immediately. Understood?"

"Understood."

Santa continued. "Now, then, I was on my way to the ballroom when I ran into you. I'm a bit late getting back from delivering toys, but as you know, tonight I am to announce my decision on who will be this coming year's Head Christmas Fairy. Since your Christmas wish is still undetermined, it will not be you. And I know you favor Ruth, but I believe I've made the wise choice." He went to the door and held it open. "If you're returning to the ball, please let the others know I'll be there momentarily."

Lily pinched her lips, keeping any further opinion about who he should choose as Head Christmas Fairy to herself. "If you don't mind, I'd like to go to my room," she said. "But, sir, could you tell me how long my punishment will last?"

"What punishment? Why would you ask such a thing?"

"I have lost my magic. And, too, as you've seen, my wings seem to be losing their power. At times, I am barely able to produce a single snowflake, and as you know, one snowflake cannot a snow angel make." She attempted to give Santa a demonstration, but her wings now refused to even make an appearance.

"I wouldn't worry," Santa said. "Losing your magic is not meant as a punishment."

Lily's eyes filled. "But what about my heart?" she asked, pressing both hands to her chest. "I fear it is broken, and if I were to also permanently lose my magic, I might simply crumple to the ground and *die*."

Santa chuffed, looking like he was trying to stifle a laugh. "You have quite a flair for the dramatic, haven't you?"

Lily swallowed, composing herself. "Sorry… sir."

"Never mind," Santa said, the corners of his eyes crinkling. "I promise you, the pain in your heart will subside. And as far as your magic is concerned, only time will tell if it is to return. Either way, it will all work out as it should."

"Yes… but what if it *doesn't* work out? And what if the pain in my heart *never* subsides? What then?"

"Indeed," Santa said. "What then? My dear, only you can answer that."

Chapter Thirty

The early-morning sun shining through the window into Jake's eyes served as an alarm clock. He sat up, disoriented, but quickly remembered where he was. The cabin. He looked to the fire and saw it was still burning bright, with flames that seemed even more robust than when he'd closed his eyes the night before… after he'd finished writing that letter to Santa.

Forcing out a short laugh, he rubbed a hand over his face. He must've been dead tired to have done something like that.

Or desperate.

He looked to the fireplace mantel, to where he'd placed the plate of cookies and the letter, but he didn't see them. He got up to have a closer look. They were gone. He turned and saw that the plate, now empty, was on the table, along with the envelope.

He went to the table, picked up the envelope, and looked inside. The letter he'd written was missing.

He paused to think and retrace his actions from the night before. He'd sat at the table, written a letter to Santa, and then tucked it inside an envelope. Then he'd piled some cookies on a plate, after which he put both the envelope and the plate on the mantel. He was sure of it.

But maybe he hadn't. He was so tired by the time he'd arrived there at the cabin, maybe he'd only *thought* about writing a letter to Santa.

No, as tired as he was last night, he was certain he'd written a letter. So, where was it? He looked in the envelope again, opening it wide. It was still empty. He looked at Sierra. "You saw me write a letter to Santa last night, right?"

Sierra had no comment.

Jake looked to the bedroom door. He couldn't remember if he'd closed it last night, but it was closed now. If Lily had returned during the night, that would explain the missing cookies. Maybe the letter, too. And there'd be no escaping her accusations that he must still believe in Santa, or why would he even write such a letter?

He knocked on the door loud enough that if she were inside and still sleeping, she would be awakened. When his knock got no response, he called through the door, "Lily?" Nothing. "Are you in there?" Again nothing.

He opened the door and saw the bed was empty. He looked in the closet, but she wasn't hiding in there, either.

Returning to the kitchen, he looked at the pies and stacks of cookies covering the counter. There were so many, he couldn't tell if any had been eaten. And other than the empty plate he'd left on the mantel the night before with a stack of cookies, he saw no evidence of anyone having been there while he slept.

Jake eyed the plate he'd taken the cookie from last night. One was all he needed to stop his stomach from rumbling. Then he could think with a clear head about what he wanted to do next.

After eating three cookies, he sat at the table. Maybe his writing that letter had only been a dream. But he knew it wasn't. The crumpled-up pieces of paper on the floor attested to that. And what about the cookies that were missing from the plate he'd left on the mantel? Someone had to have been there last night while he was sleeping. If not Lily, then who? He had no idea. But a person coming into the cabin and making themselves comfortable eating cookies while watching him sleep was disturbing enough that he didn't need to be there any longer.

He got up and doused the fire. Then he gathered his things. His stomach continued to rumble, so he tucked several cookies into his jacket pocket to eat on the ride back home. Shutting the door after himself, he stood on the porch for a long minute, surveying the snow for any trace of footprints. Other than his own and the hoof prints made by Cannon, the snow surrounding the cabin remained undisturbed.

Going to the barn, he had another look around and saw no evidence of anyone having been there. He saddled Cannon and was ready to go. Riding toward the forest, he took one last look over his shoulder. Even though he hadn't found Lily, just being there and seeing the cabin again, he was now certain she hadn't been a creation of his own making.

Chapter Thirty-One

Lily sat on a bench atop the hill that overlooked the reindeer meadow with a warm blanket wrapped around her shoulders and her feet tucked into boots that were just as ugly as the ones she'd worn when she was at the cabin. It was Christmas Day, and she was at the most special place on earth, where it would be nonstop celebrating from now until the stroke of midnight. Even the reindeer seemed to be celebrating the completion of another successful toy delivery. Yes, everyone was happy but her. A void had been left in her heart when she watched Jake walk away from the cabin for the last time, and no amount of caroling or cheerful greetings or exchanging of gifts could fill it. And then to hear that Santa had announced Vivienne as the North Pole's new Head Christmas Fairy—as expected as it was—well, things just couldn't get any drearier.

But thinking about Vivienne was no way for any fairy to begin her day, Lily mused. She'd come to this spot for a few moments of peace and to clear her head before returning to her assignment location, where she was hoping to find Cinder happy and ready to come home. She also hoped that finding Cinder didn't include seeing Jake. She couldn't take another painful goodbye.

She kicked at the snow in her frustration. If only Cinder hadn't run off, and if only things hadn't turned out the way they had, then the day might have been worth rejoicing.

"Upset, are we?" Vivienne said, appearing beside Lily.

A frown darted across Lily's forehead. "Must you be here? I should think you've done enough to ruin my holiday. Wouldn't you rather be at the square this morning, celebrating your victory?"

"I heard you were up here talking to yourself, and I thought I should check to see if you'd lost your mind."

Lily hesitated before answering, not wanting to say something that would only entice Vivienne into further disagreeable conversation. "I have not. Though it's no concern of yours. We're not *pals*, remember?"

Vivienne's mouth spread into a soft smile. "I remember. But even though we're not pals, I do care about you, and as Head Christmas Fairy, your concerns are mine. So, tell me, is there anything I can do to help?"

"No, nothing," Lily said with a shake of her head.

"I've been told Santa wants you to return to your assignment location to find Cinder. I'm sure you will be successful."

"I don't know about that," Lily said, her nose wrinkling. "I've already searched the dark wood, and now, with my powers dwindling to nearly nonexistent, I worry that any further searching might put me in danger of becoming a meal for some large beast."

"Hmm," Vivienne said. She took one of Lily's hands in hers, and Lily tried to take it back, but Vivienne held tight. "Are you sure being eaten by a large beast is your only concern? Or might you also be worried about seeing the man—Jake?"

Lily swallowed. "I might," she said weakly, hating that she was letting Vivienne see her in such a vulnerable state. And before she could blink them away, her eyes filled with tears. "I fear another goodbye might break me."

Vivienne squeezed Lily's hand. "You are stronger than you think, Liliana. Any pain you have suffered will grow softer in time, and any damage done to your heart will become a part of you, and you will be all the wiser for it."

Lily gave Vivienne a sharp look, and she managed to finally yank her hand free from Vivienne's grasp. "Are you saying it'll teach me that I should never allow myself to fall in love?"

Vivienne tipped her head back, laughing lightly. "Not at all, my dear. I'm simply saying you'll learn from any mistakes you've made. It's the part of growing older that isn't always fun, but oh-so-necessary. And worry not about going into the dark wood. No beast would dare tempt fate by eating one of Santa's fairies. As for Cinder, perhaps *she* has found love, and that's why she wandered off. Perhaps she has gone to be with another reindeer."

Lily perked up, feeling a slight twitch in her wings. She hated to agree with anything Vivienne said, but it made sense. Cinder might not be in the dark wood, after all. She might be with Frost—with Frost, at Jake's! "You may be right," she said to Vivienne, adding, "I think I know where I might look for Cinder."

"Splendid!" Vivienne said, pressing her hands together. "If you're ready to go, I can help. I know your magic has been off, so I will see to it that you arrive safely at your destination. And for your journey, I would like to give you something."

Lily waved her hands. "No! Thank you! I want nothing from you. I can do this myself." "Of course, you can," Vivienne said gently. "But trust me, this gift will cause you no trouble." And with a pass of her hand, Lily was dressed head to toe in winter attire any fairy would be proud to wear. Boots with fur at the cuffs, a white wool coat with gold buttons down the front, and soft gloves with lining meant for keeping fingers warm in even the coldest of weather.

Lily took a moment to admire her new winter wear, and then she turned to Vivienne. "Why are you being so nice to me? And what has happened to your voice?"

"I'm not sure," Vivienne said, her face lighting, "but I think it has something to do with Santa choosing me to be Head Christmas Fairy. As soon as he made his announcement, I felt different somehow." She pressed a hand over her heart. "In here."

Lily sniffed. "Congratulations, by the way."

"Thank you," Vivienne said with a slight nod. "I shall do my best to honor the position." She touched Lily's arm. "Are you ready to go?"

Lily hesitated, still doubtful about Vivienne's intentions, though she'd never heard Vivienne's voice so soft or seen such kindness in her eyes. But maybe the elder fairy would be more tolerable now that she'd been chosen for such an important role there at the North Pole.

"I promise you, I will get you to your destination safely," Vivienne said, meeting Lily's doubtful gaze.

Something had definitely changed in Vivienne. Lily didn't know if it was permanent, but she was going to take advantage of the elder fairy's goodwill while it lasted. Setting herself for departure, she told Vivienne, "I'm ready."

Chapter Thirty-Two

It was twilight by the time Lily found Cinder. She was in a pasture surrounded by a great many cows, and Frost was at her side. Jake was there, too, standing outside the fence, talking to another man, while Sierra had her nose shoved deep into a mound of snow, no doubt on the scent of some small creature.

Knowing Cinder was safe and happy filled Lily with gladness. And seeing Jake again caused her such great joy she thought she might remember the feeling forever. But she knew better. Once she took Cinder home to the North Pole, her joy would dissipate, and she would keep only the memory of how her heart free-fell whenever Jake looked at her. It was what must be, she told herself, and she drew in a breath to steady her emotions.

After a few minutes, the man talking to Jake climbed into an old truck and drove off. Then Jake stood alone at the fence for another minute before he finally turned and walked toward a lovely house that was painted a cheerful yellow color with white shutters and a wraparound porch. On the porch was one of those swinging chairs for two that Lily had long admired and hoped to have one day.

The house was unexpected. Lily had always imagined Jake's

taste being more rustic, like the cabin. But then she remembered this was his parents' house, and she thought it a perfect home for a family.

As Jake made his way through the snow, Sierra ran beside him with her entire back-end wagging with unrestrained joy. It must be mealtime, Lily thought, smiling. Jake had no need for a clock as long as he had his dog.

Watching Jake walk away caused a faint stirring of her wings. He'd walked away too many times, and she was afraid this time, if she let him out of her sight, she might never see him again. Hurrying through the snow toward him, she tried to think of something to say. Something profound, perhaps, to keep her in his memory. Though she hadn't any idea what that might be.

When she was but a dozen or so yards from him, Sierra caught sight of her and yipped a greeting that had Jake turning around. His gaze met hers, and her heart trembled like something wild had come to life in her chest. She wanted to run to him, to tell him how much she missed him and that the very sight of him had her wanting to laugh and cry all at the same time. But she dared not. Instead, she gave him a playful smile and said, "Hello, Jake," hoping for at least a grin in return.

"Is it really you?" Jake asked, a mixture of bewilderment and happiness filling his eyes.

Her nod brought him moving swiftly toward her, though Sierra reached her first, and Lily rubbed the top of Sierra's golden head affectionately. Lily hadn't realized until now how much she'd also missed Jake's dog.

Jake finally caught up, and his eyes were drawn to Lily's feet. "Nice boots."

"Thanks," Lily said, her tension eased. "They were a gift. Merry Christmas, by the way."

"Same to you," Jake said. He studied her for a moment. "I don't mean to stare, but I'm feeling a little like I did back at the cabin."

"Which is?"

"Confused." He stepped closer. "I'm not sure what to say. I

didn't expect to see you again. To be honest, after I'd been home a couple of days, I was back to thinking I'd hit my head and had imagined everything about the time we spent together."

Lily smiled. "It wasn't your imagination." She wondered if she'd made a mistake showing herself. She could have simply waited and taken Cinder after Jake went into the house. That would have made it easier for both of them.

"I know," Jake said. "I went back to the cabin yesterday, saw all the cookies you'd baked, but you'd already gone." His gaze steadied on hers. "I was sure you'd told me you weren't leaving until midnight, so I stayed the night, hoping you might show up. But by this morning, when you still hadn't appeared, I figured I'd better come back home. I've only been here a few hours."

"I'm sorry you went all that way for nothing," Lily said. "I had to return…."

"To the North Pole."

"Yes."

"So, why are you here now?"

"I've come for Cinder," she said reluctantly.

Jake's brow furrowed. "That's it? You're not here to see me?"

There it was. The pain. Like someone was standing on her heart. Lily did her best to ignore it. "I'm happy to see you and to know you made it home safely," she admitted, "but I am here for my reindeer." She had so much more to say to him, things that might've made a difference even a day earlier. But none of it mattered now, and it was best to keep it simple.

"I understand that. But when we were at the cabin, you said you believed I was your Christmas wish. Has that changed?"

Lily's throat constricted so that she could barely breathe. "Jake, please don't make this harder than it needs to be."

"I sure will make this hard. I needed to see you. I went back to the cabin, and you were gone! Why didn't you wait?"

"I didn't think you'd be back. When I told you the truth about who I was and what I hoped for, it didn't seem to matter."

"That's not true."

"Then why did you leave?"

"I needed to be home," Jake said. He swung an arm wide, gesturing at the pasture full of cows. "As you can see, I have animals here to care for."

Yes, Lily thought, she knew that. He'd told her about his animals more than once when they were at the cabin. She looked out at all the cows, and at Frost and Cinder. Cinder hadn't even approached her to say hello. It was as if she'd found a home where she intended to stay.

"It wasn't just that," Jake continued. "The truth is I'd only just gotten over thinking you might be on some kind of medication, and then there you were telling me things that couldn't possibly be true. Then, when I found myself covered in glitter again, I guess I panicked. I couldn't let myself believe in magic and fairies with wings that could make it snow. It was too much. I had to get away from you so I could think straight."

Lily felt a quiver at the base of her wings, the strongest in days. And then the sky began spitting out big white flakes.

Jake tipped his head back, looking up. "More snow?" His eyes met Lily's. "Your doing?"

"I'm not sure," Lily said, surprised as Jake was to see the snow. Her teeth began chattering, and she pulled her new wool coat tighter around herself.

Jake was quick to remove his own thick leather coat and wrap it around her shoulders. "Let's go inside," he told her. "I've got a fire burning, and I can even make us some hot chocolate."

Unable to resist, Lily held Jake's arm as he guided her through the snow to the porch. As she followed him inside, her emotions were all over the place. It was as Enar had said, like being on a roller coaster, though she welcomed the ride.

"We can sit in here," Jake said, continuing to lead the way as they passed through a tidy kitchen. They ended up in a large room that was much like the cabin's main living area, only larger and with plenty of comfortable seating that surrounded a big stone fireplace that had a hot flame burning bright. It gave the room a welcoming warmth. There was even a tree that filled the entire corner, with big bows and plenty of tinsel covering every branch.

"Your tree is beautiful," she said, smiling. "I have to admit, I'm surprised."

"That's my neighbor's doing," Jake said. "She saw I hadn't put up any decorations, and she was worried I'd spend Christmas sitting here alone, feeling sorry for myself. I guess she thought the tree might be a good cure for the blues."

"That was kind of her," Lily remarked. She wondered if the *she* Jake spoke of was someone he was close to… or someone he was interested in becoming close to.

"She's a nice lady," Jake said. "She and her husband don't listen so good when I tell them I don't need help or more food, but they're decent people, and I'm glad to have them as neighbors."

She and her husband. Jake's words filled Lily with relief. Though she had no right to be concerned with any relationship he might have with another woman. As she stood there next to him, she caught a whiff of citrus in his hair that was pleasant and so different than what she'd come to know at the cabin. With him sleeping near the fire, his hair and clothes had always had a slightly smoky scent. And whenever he'd gone outside for firewood or to be alone, he'd come back inside smelling of pine and winter air. But the citrus was nice, and now, whenever she made lemon meringue pie, she would think of him.

"I'll get that hot chocolate," Jake said. "Though I have to warn you, it won't be as good as what you made for us at the cabin. Plus, I don't have any marshmallows. But it'll be passable and will warm your insides."

Lily was tempted to tell him her insides were already warm, just being near him, but she hadn't any experience with such conversation between a man and a woman, and the words wouldn't come.

While Jake was out of the room, her gaze trailed over to the tree again, where the lights were blinking bright colors against the wall and doing their part to make the room cheerful. She was anything but cheerful. She turned and focused on the clock that hung above the fireplace, noting that Christmas Day was nearly over. Another year would soon be put to rest, and she and Jake would both begin a new year. Though not with each other. She would go back to the North Pole and continue her duties as a Christmas fairy, and Jake would have his life here. With his animals. She hoped that would be enough, and that he would finally find peace with the loss of his sister. She also hoped he would find love. Even if that love was shared with someone other than her.

When Jake returned with two steaming mugs, he caught her staring at the clock. "You're not going to suddenly disappear on me, are you?" he asked.

"No," Lily said, smiling thinly.

Jake handed her the hot chocolate, saying, "If you're hungry, my refrigerator is full of food that the neighbors keep bringing by. I'm sure there's something in there you might like. I might even have some muffins my neighbor baked. They're supposed to be healthy." He took a step back, toward the kitchen.

"Maybe later," Lily said. She sat on the edge of the sofa, not sure how comfortable she should make herself. "If you don't mind, could we talk?"

"Of course," Jake said, and he sat close to her.

His nearness filled Lily with a wonderful rush, though she was quick to check herself once more. Santa had sent her only to gather Cinder and then return to the North Pole. Any deviation and not even the slightest chance might remain that Santa would consider granting her wish. This year or ever. And though he'd told her he would continue to think about it, she didn't believe his intent was to grant her wish this year.

"I'm sorry you went back to the cabin to find me gone," she said.

Jake set his hot chocolate on the coffee table. "You already apologized, and I've already forgiven you." He paused. "I must be going soft on Christmas because I hated the idea of you being alone on Christmas Eve. But that's only part of why I went back to the cabin. I wanted to let you know your reindeer was here and that she was safe."

"I appreciate that," Lily said. "I saw her out in your pasture with Frost. They seem to really enjoy each other."

"Yeah, it would be a shame to separate them. Frost seems to finally realize he's a reindeer."

"Jake, I—"

"I'd like to say something more," Jake continued. He took a breath, gathering his thoughts. "I know we haven't had a lot of time to get to know each other, but for me, it was enough that I felt changed somehow. Meeting you was like I'd been given a second chance. I'd spent so much time grieving the loss of my sister, I'd forgotten how to live. Then you came along, and it was like I woke up. And for the first time in a long time, I could laugh and feel happy without guilt taking a bite out of me." He paused. "Problem is, it didn't last. Once I was home, I began to sink into that hole again. That's why I had to return to the cabin. I needed to know that everything I'd experienced was real. That *you* were real." He took her hands in his. "You haven't answered my question. Do you still believe I'm your Christmas wish?"

"It doesn't matter what I believe. Christmas has come and gone," Lily explained. "The time for my wish to be granted is over."

"I don't know what that means. Are you saying your wish is no longer valid?"

"It's not a matter of my wish still being valid. There are rules, and they are very clear. For my Christmas wish to be granted, I needed to develop feelings for a human man, and he needed to develop feelings for me. And this had to happen by midnight Christmas Eve."

"But I went back to the cabin, and you were gone."

Lily smiled. "Yes."

"What if I was returning to tell you I love you?" Jake asked.

Lily's eyes opened wide. "Were you?"

"I hadn't thought about it at the time or on those terms. Mostly, I was still trying to figure everything out. When I first got home, everything was such a jumble of thoughts, I couldn't even admit you were real. The only thing I knew for sure was that if you *were* real, I had to see you again. I couldn't just let you walk out of my life."

"Jake, I'm sorry. Perhaps if you'd returned sooner…."

"I know… I should have. But like I said, I was all messed up. Then, with my doctor ordering me to limit my activity for a while, I thought it best I stay put. But the minute I saw another reindeer in the pasture with Frost and my cattle, I knew I had to go back to the cabin and find you. So, I *did* return. You just weren't there."

"I wish I could have stayed," Lily said.

"Me, too," Jake said. Then his eyes lit. "Do you remember what we were about to do before I said goodbye?"

Lily swallowed. "I believe you were going to kiss me." She saw no point in telling him about the magic mistletoe. "I'm surprised *you* remember."

"It's a little murky, but yeah, I remember," Jake said. "So, what if I want to kiss you right now? Is it too late?"

"Oh, Jake," Lily said, shaking her head, "I don't think it's a good idea. It won't change anything."

"Sure it will. We could kiss, and you might be so smitten with me, you won't want to leave." He looked into her eyes. "You could stay… stay here with me," he said, his tone soft and tender. "I know Sierra would love to have you here, too. I think she misses your cooking."

Lily dipped her head. "I can't cook. That was all magic. Except for the hot chocolate. And the cookies and pies… and the fruit cake."

Jake laughed. "Yeah, I don't think I've ever seen so many cookies. You must have spent hours baking after I left."

Lily smiled a small smile. "I needed something to do."

"Anyway," Jake continued, "it doesn't matter that you don't know how to cook. I'm pretty good at turning on the stove and putting things in a pot, and I can teach you."

Lily shook her head. "That all sounds very nice, but I'm a Christmas fairy, and I belong at the North Pole."

"I don't accept that. You were chilled outside, and I know you were becoming vulnerable to the cold when we were at the cabin.

And if you're vulnerable to the cold, doesn't that mean you're becoming human? And if you're becoming human, doesn't it mean you belong here in *my* world?"

"Please, stop… you're confusing me," Lily said. She got up from the sofa and made it halfway across the room before Jake caught her by the arm and forced her to look at him.

"Don't do that. Don't walk away," he said. He let go of her arm and jutted a thumb toward the ceiling. "Didn't we agree it's bad luck not to kiss when you find yourself standing under mistletoe?"

Lily looked and saw a dried sprig of mistletoe overhead, store-bought variety that held no magic. It was plugged into a beam with a nail. She was tempted to give in—what could it hurt? But then, a familiar ping inside her chest reminded her. It could hurt a lot! Because it was too late for her and Jake to make a connection, and she would still have to return to the North Pole.

"I can't," she cried, pushing away from him and rubbing her chest where the ping had turned into an unbearable ache.

"Are you okay?" Jake asked.

"No! My heart hurts!"

"You're having a heart attack?" Jake asked, his eyes wide.

"Yes, my heart is attacking me!" Lily said.

Jake cracked a grin. "I'm no doctor, but I'm pretty sure you're not having a heart attack." He drew her into his arms. "I need to tell you something, and I know it's going to be hard for you to believe, but when I didn't find you at the cabin, I became desperate. And when I become desperate, things get ugly."

Tears filled Lily's eyes. She looked up at him through a haze, unable to imagine him doing anything ugly. "What did you do?" she asked.

"I wrote a letter to Santa."

"But you don't believe in Santa."

Jake shrugged. "Like I said, I was desperate."

"What did you ask for?"

"I asked Santa to help me find you."

"Really?"

"Really," Jake said, his voice tender. "And now here you are, so the least you could do is let me kiss you."

Lily knew what would happen if she allowed his kiss. His lips would be like a soothing balm that would instantly ease her pain. It would be a dream of dreams. It would cause her such great joy, she would never be able to go back. And how could she? How could she go back to the North Pole when all she wanted was to feel Jake kissing her lips for all eternity? Or at the very least, the rest of her life. This was the moment she'd been waiting for… though she could only imagine all the rules she'd be breaking.

"Well?" Jake said, pressing her.

"Kiss me," Lily whispered. Because some rules were meant to be broken.

When Jake's lips met hers, it was as though he'd taken her breath and made it his. His kiss was sweet and honest, and it made her heart soar. And in that fragile moment, when she had given herself over to him completely, she knew without a doubt, Santa had finally granted her Christmas wish. Jake was hers, not just for today and not for a single holiday season. He was hers for as long as she and Jake both lived.

Chapter Thirty-Three

More than a year later…

Lily was baking more than ever these days. And not just cookies and pies for human consumption, but also healthy treats for dogs and cats at the local animal shelter where she now worked. She'd found such fulfillment helping animals that had been neglected or abused find their happy place again, and she'd made it her mission to make sure none of them spent one more minute feeling unloved. Plus, she and Bob's wife, Kate, had joined forces, and each month they put together several baskets to donate to families who were struggling to care for their pets. It was a most rewarding endeavor, and Lily couldn't imagine a better way to spend her time.

Sierra had no complaints with Lily's baking. She'd become Lily's constant companion, waiting patiently for her share of anything Lily wanted to toss her way, and the only time she let Lily out of her sight was when Jake took her along with him to tend to the cows. Though this wasn't one of those days. Jake had left Sierra behind this morning so he could check on Cinder, who was expecting her first calf. "Any day now," Jake had said when he left that morning. So when he returned just a short time later and told Lily to grab her sweater, she knew it was time.

"Hold on," she told Jake. "I just need to take one last tray of biscuits out of the oven."

"Take too long, and Cinder won't wait," Jake warned.

Lily's eyes widened. "Really? Is she that close?"

"Seems so," Jake said. Sierra wagged herself over to him, excited by the tone of his voice. "You can come, too, but you'll have to stay out of the way," he told her.

Lily dropped the sheet of dog biscuits on the stovetop and left her oven mitts on the counter. The biscuits would burn by the time she returned and removed them from the hot sheet, but no matter. She could always bake more biscuits, while the birth of a baby reindeer was something special and not to be missed. Jamming her feet into a pair of shoes that were near the back door, she took Jake's arm so he could help her down the steps. She'd been off-balance the past couple of weeks due to carrying her own precious cargo, and she was nearly as big as the pot-bellied stove Jake had recently installed in the guest cabin.

Sierra wasn't waiting. She was already on her way across the yard, prancing along and wagging her tail like she knew the importance of the occasion. When she neared the barn, she raced ahead and went through the open door, but Lily continued taking her time, and Jake was patient with her.

Once inside the barn, Jake left Lily at the gate to Cinder's stall, where she could watch the birth of Cinder's calf. Lily had been so excited for the big event she'd barely slept the past few nights. The happy occasion of Cinder and Frost becoming parents meant good things for everyone. It brought Jake one step closer to opening the Longmire Bed-and-Breakfast, where folks could come and enjoy a genuine country Christmas experience that included spending time with reindeer, and for Lily, it was the simple pleasure of seeing her family grow. And though she'd seen many newly born reindeer, she'd never witnessed the actual birthing process. That detail had always been handled by Santa and the elves, after which the fairies would put together a celebration, welcoming all the calves into their new home in the reindeer meadow. Once there, the calves were allowed to frolic and play to their heart's content while at the same time being observed to see if any showed promise in becoming backup reindeer to pull Santa's sleigh. For those that lacked the necessary skill, life was still good. They were allowed to live life wherever they chose. Even away from the North Pole, if that's what they desired. Though, most didn't. Being a reindeer at the North Pole meant a life filled with plenty of adventure.

But a reindeer didn't need to live at the North Pole to have a good life. Cinder and Frost were as happy as any of Santa's reindeer. They were well-fed, protected, and happy, and they could come and go as they pleased. Though they mostly seemed pleased to spend their days hanging out with the cows in the pasture. Every once in a while, though, just for a change in scenery, Jake would hitch Cinder and Frost up to the sleigh that his parents had left behind, and they would happily pull it wherever Jake directed them to go. Sometimes, he had them go to the clearing in the forest where he'd gone with his mom and sister on lazy summer afternoons, and sometimes, he just let them go wherever they wanted. Once, he even had them pull the sleigh deep into the forest, and Lily thought he might be trying to find the cabin, though they never found any evidence of it ever having been there.

Lily missed the cabin, and wondered what had become of it, but she was glad for the memory of having spent time there with Jake. She was glad, too, that she hadn't forgotten her friends at the North Pole, or that she'd once been a Christmas fairy. She also thought it possible Cinder remembered life at the North Pole, for there were times when the two reindeer would disappear for a while, and then return, looking as if they'd been given a good grooming. Courtesy of the North Pole's Head Grooming Elf, Gormar, perhaps? It made Lily smile to think so.

"Here we go!" Jake suddenly called out to notify every creature in the barn that it was time for Cinder's calf to make its entrance into the world.

Lily looked over the top of the gate to watch her handsome husband. He was taking charge, as usual, making sure Cinder was comfortable and had everything she needed—a warm blanket, fresh straw, and plenty of water. Frost was a few stalls down, seemingly indifferent to the whole process, but Lily knew he would come around.

Once the birthing began, it went quickly, and Lily was amazed how easy it all seemed. She only hoped *her* child's birth went as easy.

While Cinder spent a few minutes resting, Jake toweled off her calf, rubbing it vigorously until it looked like a bundle of fuzz. Then he stepped out of the stall to let Cinder get acquainted with her newborn, which she did by nuzzling it and making sure it knew she was mama.

"Looks like we just added another girl to our household," Jake said, coming up beside Lily. His hand found hers and held it tight while his other hand rubbed the top of Sierra's head. Sierra had been sitting quietly by Lily's side the entire time.

Lily placed a hand over her belly. What her husband didn't know was that there would soon be yet one more girl added to the household. And if she…. Well, no need to think about that just yet. Even so, Lily couldn't help but wonder who their daughter might take after. Her? Or Jake?

No matter. Whatever the outcome, she and Jake would have their hands full with taking care of two newborns. And she could tell Jake was going to be a doting father. She just had to make sure he didn't overdo his doting. Children needed space to grow and become self-reliant, else they might never venture out into the world and find their true selves.

Jake turned to her. "I wouldn't mind it if you and I had a girl. Especially, if she looked just like you."

Lily squeezed his hand. She leaned into him and smelled the citrus in his hair. At that moment, she was happier than she'd ever been. She could think of nothing more rewarding than being a wife to the man she loved and to have a family grown of that love. Life as a Christmas fairy had been good, but life as a human was even better than she could have ever imagined.

THE END

MRS. CLAUS' CANDY CANE PIE

One 8- or 9-inch pastry shell
12 medium-size candy canes
3 large eggs
One 14-oz can of sweetened condensed milk
1/4 tsp cream of tartar
1/3 cup sugar
1/2 tsp vanilla extract

1. Heat oven to 350 degrees and bake a pastry shell in a pie plate. You can either pick one up from Mrs. Claus at the North Pole or make your own. After baking, place crust on cooling rack, and refrigerate before using.
2. Crush the candy canes into bits and pieces. If you have a reindeer, have them stomp the candy canes with their hooves. Or place the candy canes inside a sealed, gallon-size frozen food storage bag and use a hammer to crush them. A food processor also works well, but it's not as much fun. Set crushed candy aside when sufficiently crushed.
3. Separate the eggs, placing the yolks in a small saucepan and the whites in a medium mixing bowl. Place the egg whites in the refrigerator.
4. Add the condensed milk to the saucepan with the egg yolks. Stir over medium heat until the mixture begins to thicken—but don't allow to boil! (Note: The longer you heat the mixture, the firmer the pie filling.) Remove from heat when desired firmness is achieved.
5. For the pie meringue, beat the egg whites until stiff peaks form. While mixer is running, add the cream of tartar, then slowly add the sugar (about a tablespoon at a time). Beat until stiff peaks form again, then beat in the vanilla extract.
6. Fold approximately two-thirds of the crushed candy into the egg yolk mixture (while in the saucepan). Don't over stir, or the candy will dissolve… though it's okay if this happens.

But it's nice to have little bits of candy cane speckle the pie.

7. Pour the mixture into the baked pie crust, then pile the meringue on top, making sure to spread the meringue all the way to the edges of the crust. To finish, sprinkle remaining candy bits on top of the meringue.

8. Bake pie for 12 to 15 minutes, or until meringue is lightly browned. Let pie cool completely before serving. This pie tastes great with coffee or a glass of cold milk!

A NOTE FROM ALEXA

Thank you for taking the time to read *Snow Happens*. There are so many delightful holiday stories to choose from, and I am happy that you selected mine. If you enjoyed this book, please consider telling your friends, or you could even post a review. Word of mouth is a great way to give a compliment to a writer and is much appreciated.

Sincerely,
Alexa Darin

ABOUT THE AUTHOR

Alexa Darin makes her home in Washington State, where she spends most of her leisure time either hiking in the Alpine Wilderness or playing doorman to a couple of opinionated Labrador retrievers who think she should spend less time at her desk and more time outside throwing a ball. She believes every romance writer should keep a survival kit that contains plenty of dark chocolate, a supply of red wine, and a large selection of Barry White music.

You can learn more about Alexa and her upcoming books, or subscribe to her newsletter, at alexadarin.com. You can also join her at facebook.com/alexa.darin or twitter.com/AlexaDarin.

Or you might enjoy a peek at Alexa's *Snow Happens* Pinterest page at pinterest.com/alexa_darin/snow-happens.

www.ingramcontent.com/pod-product-compliance
Lightning Source LLC
Chambersburg PA
CBHW032006050726
47590CB00006B/2070